The

Line

Sarah,
Cole can't
wait to meet
you at The Line!
Amie

Amie Knight

The Line
Copyright © 2017 Amie Knight

ISBN-13: 978-1546611295
ISBN-10: 1546611290

The Line is a work of fiction. All names, characters, places, and occurrences are the product of the author's imagination. Any resemblance to any persons, living or dead, events, or locations is purely coincidental.

Editor: Mickey Reed
Cover: Jay Aheer of Simply Defined Art
Interior Design and Formatting: Stacey Blake of Champagne Formats

Dedication

Some heroes don't stomp into your life from the romanticized pages of novels. Some heroes don't wear cowboy boots or even call you babe. No, sometimes he eases into your life with his quiet thoughtfulness and captivating uniqueness. Some heroes are real, and sometimes, he even wears adorable, round Harry Potter–looking glasses and button-down shirts with khaki pants. And, sometimes, his shy smiles light you up, make you feel more than special, and send your young heart all a-damn-flutter.

I'm typing this up on our eleventh anniversary, so it's only fair that I dedicate this one to you, Tony. My favorite guy. My hero. And even though you've ditched the glasses and gotten grey with age and we have a constant gaggle of kids around us, you still make me swoon.

Prologue

Everly

It was eight p.m. when I boarded the train just like I did most nights—quietly, stealthily. I was a ghost. Hardly anyone ever saw me. What I was doing was wrong. I knew it, but even the best people did bad things when faced with unspeakable obstacles. And I wasn't the best. Not by a long shot.

A light sheen of sweat blanketed my body as equal parts adrenaline and dread filled me up. Dread and adrenaline, they were always there—heavy and cumbersome. I carried them around with me everywhere. It was a small miracle that nobody saw them. Only occasionally did they threaten to bubble to the surface of my skin, but I somehow always managed to push them back down. Down so far that only I knew they were still there—a living, breathing entity within me. I hated them, but I needed them. Dread was my tormentor. Adrenaline my savior.

When they weren't present, guilt was. And that was the worst of all, because I felt like I'd never be rid of it. I could feel it. See it. Smell it. Taste it. Always. The guilt. It plagued me, and it was never-ending.

It sat so thick and rich in my throat that, sometimes, I felt like I might choke on it.

I swallowed it down and walked up the aisle, my head bowed to the floor. I didn't need to look around. I knew this train like the back of my hand. I slumped my shoulders forward, curling in on myself—which made me invisible. The long strands of my brown hair fell around me, masking my blue eyes and the gaunt angles of my pale face. I pulled my old, black coat closer to my body, warding the chill off. Wiping my sweaty hands on my jeans, I finally lifted my head, darting my gaze around the familiar surroundings, checking for anything that might have been out of place.

An elderly couple was taking their seats on my left side. *Too old.* The mother with her two children two seats up and to the right? *Too complicated.* Two teenagers were chatting all the way in the back of the train car. *Too young.* I wasn't a good person, but I did have some standards—a conscience. Some morals—not many, but some. Hunger and cold had stolen most of them.

The train was filling up fast. I needed to get what I'd come for and get off. I scanned the crowd some more. Watching and waiting. Patience was my friend, and she almost always paid off.

"Do you need a place to sit?"

I vaguely heard the low pulse of someone speaking through the boisterous voices of the embarking crowd. It didn't register that anyone might have been speaking to me. People didn't speak to a ghost.

"Miss, do you a need a seat?"

When I felt a light touch, I flinched. Touch was something I was unaccustomed to. It was one of those unattainable things. Up there with love, trust, and all the other things most people took for granted.

I found a brown-eyed, brown-haired man in a black Stetson—a

beautiful cowboy. After a quick glance around, I realized everyone was getting settled. I was running out of time. Nausea rolled in my stomach. I was always trying to get off this train. I squeezed my eyes shut, willing the feeling of hopelessness away.

"You look tired," the cowboy whispered up at me. The pity in his eyes almost undid me.

He saw me. All of me. The sunken cheeks. The cold, weary, dead look in my eyes. My dirty hair. My old clothes. And I didn't like it.

I did the only thing I could to protect myself. I'd done it so many times that I'd lost count, but it didn't ever make it any easier to do.

"See something you like, Cowboy?" My hip popped out, and I threw my hand on it for good measure, giving him a provocative grin.

He stared at me solemnly. That gaze. That stare. I felt naked and not in the usual way that I did when a man glanced me over. I was just a sixteen-year-old girl, but I knew the difference between a lust-filled look and an all-knowing one. And this cowboy saw right through me with just one gaze.

"I do," he said, bringing me out of my thoughts and surprising me.

I quirked an eyebrow at him. "You do?" I asked. I had no idea what we were talking about anymore. His intense stare had completely thrown me off my game.

"I do see something I like," he said, smiling sweetly. It wasn't sexual. It was just kind.

I looked away in shame. It didn't matter how sweet he was. How he *saw* me. I still had to do what I needed to do to survive.

Glancing back at the beautiful cowboy, I took in his gentle smile and his kind, brown eyes. He had his hand placed on the seat next to him where he wanted me to take a seat, and self-condemnation and shame swelled in my heart. But I couldn't afford to feel guilty today. I couldn't afford anything, really. Not even for this sweet-looking man offering me a place to rest.

I was too cold.

Too hungry.

Too tired.

I couldn't afford to get off this line, no matter how much I wanted to.

Chapter 1

Everly

Four Years Later

Sunshine and fresh linens. It was probably my most favorite smell in the world. I breathed in deep, steeling myself for the same conversation I'd been having for a week. I was hanging clothes out to dry on the clothesline while simultaneously trying to talk Momma Lou out of sending me off for the summer. I hardly noticed the scattering of kids running around us—I was so used to them.

"I don't want to leave, Momma Lou. I'm happy here." I frowned, hanging a wet towel over the line and enjoying the sun shining on my face. And I was happy here. More than happy. From the outside looking in, one might think I was just content, but this life was a far cry from what my life had been before, and I was over the moon about it. I was damn near ecstatic here after the life I'd had. The past three

1

years had been the happiest of my life.

Momma Lou stood on the other side of the clothesline and helped clip the towel to the line with clothes hangers. Her big hips were swaying back and forth to some song she was humming not so quietly. When she was done, she pulled the line down between us and leaned forward so she could look me in the eye.

"Baby girl, you think for one second that I'm not gonna miss you when you're gone? If it was up to me, I'd keep you here with me forever, girl. It's not up to me though." She smiled her toothy grin that made me feel like the most loved girl in the world.

That same toothy grin had greeted me three years earlier and changed my life. And I was eternally grateful. Momma Lou had saved me that night. I'd shown up at the homeless shelter too late and it was full. So, I'd curled up into a ball under my coat and propped myself against the brick wall of the shelter, praying that they might at least send someone out with food. I was also kicking myself in the ass. I should have gotten there sooner. It was going to be a cold night. But I couldn't seem to muster the energy to care anymore. I'd been doing this too long. This homeless thing. This starving thing. This barely-living-life thing. It was wearing on me.

I'd seen Momma Lou working in the kitchen at the shelter from time to time, but I hadn't known her name. I hadn't cared to. She was just another face in a sea of faces that all had a place to live and food in their bellies.

She'd stopped on the sidewalk on her way into the building and stared at my seventeen-year-old-self hard. Studying me. She pursed her lips, and I knew what she saw. I was so starved that I was practically skeletal. I barely had the wherewithal to try to survive anymore. I could feel myself finally giving up. I'd been knocking on death's door. Too many years on the street had taken a terrible toll on my body. Not to mention what it had done to my soul.

And the running. You can only run so long, and I'd been doing it since the beginning. A slew of abusive foster homes always had me running back to the streets. A place where I, strangely, felt safest. The people on the streets ignored me, sure, but they didn't beat me, try to touch me, or starve me.

"I'm Louise," she'd stated frankly. "But everyone around here calls me Momma Lou." Her curvy body swayed as she made her way toward the door to the shelter, and I was confused as to why she'd taken the time to tell me her name until she barked out, "Well, come on, girl. Let's get you fed, and you can help me in the kitchen tonight." She smiled.

And she fed me. All the while telling me to slow down before I made myself sick. I got sick anyway. And I helped her in the kitchen that night—and every night since.

Momma Lou had taken me home and saved my life. I'd say that she had been an answer to my prayers, but I had long since given up praying. She was my miracle, though, and I'd been with her ever since. I helped her at the shelter in the kitchen and with the heaps of kids she brought home all the time. We'd have anywhere from ten to fifteen kids at a time, running all over our old three-bedroom ranch, but each had a place to lay their heads at night and a full belly when they went to sleep. The living and dining rooms were covered in framed photos of all of Momma Lou's children. Hundreds of small feet had pounded around this property, and all of their sweet, little faces graced the small house's walls. I loved it here. It was safe.

Before Momma Lou, I'd was like I was constantly drowning, like I was at the bottom of a pool, and every time I teetered to the top of the water, I'd be pushed back under once again, gasping for air. Now, I was free. I could finally breathe.

Momma Lou started coming around the clothesline, snapping me out of my thoughts. She took me by the shoulders. "Everly, you know how special you are to me." Her kind eyes shone in the sunlight.

Tears burned behind my own. My nose stung, but I blinked, sucking those tears back.

Everly Woods did not cry.

Her face was kind but so very serious. "We got you all healed up here, baby," she said, rubbing her chubby, wrinkled hands up and down my arms and over my shoulders, one lone tear burning a trail over her smooth, dark skin. "And here," she whispered, placing her palm over my heart. "Now, it's time for you to fly, Little Bird."

I placed my hand over hers, rubbing my fingers over her smooth and rough skin, trying to memorize the feel of her, of this moment, so I could replay it later—when I needed it.

My heart hammered behind the heaviness of her hand. The hand that loved me. The hand that fed me. The hand that had helped a young, starving homeless girl when no one else could. That hand meant everything to me.

I grinned at Little Bird.

Momma Lou had nicknames for all the children she took in, and I was her Little Bird. A name that I had to admit fit me a little too well. I was so tiny that I sometimes thought a small breeze might carry me away. It wasn't just my height, either. I was only five feet. My features were miniature, but my brown hair was big, wild, and untamable. Momma Lou jokingly said that my hair was bigger than my behind.

She might have called me Little Bird, but in no way did I want to fly. I was terrified of leaving this nest, the only place I'd truly ever been able to call home. So scared. I knew all too well what lurked beyond the sanctuary of this house and the shelter and didn't want to experience it ever again.

"You shouldn't be hanging out with an old black woman all the time, Everly. You should be out experiencing life. Meeting young men and making friends," she said, stepping back and wiping her face. "Besides, it's only for the summer, and it's good money. You wanted to make some money so you could go to school, right? If you don't like it there, you can always come back here. Momma Lou is always gonna be here for you, child."

I *did* want to go to school. I didn't want to always be dependent on someone else. Don't get me wrong. I pulled my weight around there, cooking and cleaning and caring for all the children that came through plus my work at the shelter, but I wanted to give back more. I wanted to help others the way Momma Lou had helped me. I needed an education to help people the way I wanted to though. She was right—I couldn't stay there forever. I was twenty years old now. It was only for the summer, but for some reason, it felt like so much more. I hadn't gone a day without Momma Lou in three years.

I glanced at the small, old, white house and took in the acre or so of property around us, thinking that, when people rode by, I bet they thought this place was nothing special. The house wasn't the best kept in the neighborhood. It definitely needed a paint job, and the lawn was so dry that huge patches of grass were missing, brown, dusty dirt there instead. We only had a washer. No dryer. And, with so many kids here, clothes were always hanging on the line. The kids. There were tons, and I was never guaranteed a minute alone. Pounding on the door almost always ensued when I was in the shower. There were only two bathrooms, after all. And I slept in the same room as a million children every night. But I was never lonely here. Not ever. I was safe and never alone. Yeah, this place may not seem like anything special to others, but to me—it was everything.

I launched myself across the space that separated us and right into Momma Lou's arms. She let out a big sigh and held me close, and I breathed in the smell of coconuts from the oil she put in her hair every day.

"I'm gonna miss you. You're my best friend," I whispered into her neck. "I love you." My small body shivered with unrestrained emotions. I didn't usually lay my feelings out so plainly, but in that moment, I had to. I didn't know what the future held for Momma Lou and her Little Bird. But I knew she meant everything to me right then.

"I'm gonna miss you too, Little Bird, but it's time. You can't stay here with me forever. I'm expecting big things from you, you hear?"

she choked out, her large, soft body shaking with emotion against my own.

This didn't feel like a goodbye for the summer. It seemed like so much more, and I pulled back on all the emotions that wanted to pour from me. I could be scared. I could be terrified, even. But I'd never let Momma Lou down. She'd never once let me down.

I spent the rest of the day going through my chores at home and the shelter in a daze, trying my hardest not to think about the bus ride the next day to my new job for the summer. It was only a few hours away, and I was lucky Momma Lou's friend had needed the help because I needed the money. But, when I lay in bed that night, I couldn't help the panic gathering in my chest. Would they be nice to me? Would they hurt me? Would they like me? The questions were endless.

I quietly and carefully climbed down from the top bunk of my bed so that I wouldn't wake the four children sleeping in the same room. I reached over to the small bedside table and removed the picture I'd been carrying around for four years. It was tattered, almost to the point of being trash, the corners bent in no matter how many times I'd tried to smooth them. The smell of smoke was still strong even four years later. But I could still make out the woman's sweet features. Her soft, blond hair and kind, chocolate-brown eyes. I could even see the small pearls hanging on her neck and the smile full of blindingly perfect teeth. That smile got me every time. It was so familiar, so sweet. I'd see it and the memories of one special day with one handsome cowboy would rush through me like wildfire, warming me to my core. That feeling had kept me cozy and snug on the coldest of nights. That feeling had pulled me through the most difficult of times.

The lady in the picture was wearing a pretty, blue sweater that made her brown eyes pop. She looked like someone I'd like to know. Someone I *had known* for one night. Someone I'd like to love me. Someone I'd like to protect me. She reminded me. That's why I'd kept her, after all.

"Looks like it's just me and you again," I whispered to my pretty lady in the photo.

She didn't say anything back. She never did. She just gazed at me with her loving smile, offering me the same comfort she had when I'd been all alone on the streets years ago.

Chapter 2

Everly

A few hours on a full bus and my muscles were stiff and sore, so as soon as my feet hit the asphalt, I stretched and took in my surroundings. It was a hot-as-sin day, as was usual in the summer in the South. The sign to my right read *Canton, Georgia,* and I picked up my bag with my few meager belongings in it and looked around for my ride. I was a nervous wreck. I patted the back pocket of my jeans, making sure my lady in the picture was still back there, like I sometimes did when I was nervous.

I'd hugged Momma Lou bye at the bus station that morning for what felt like the twentieth time, and each time, she'd made sure to tell me that someone would be waiting for me in Canton as soon as I arrived. I think she was more worried about someone being there for me than I was. I'd blown out a sigh and rolled my eyes at her, like I was annoyed about her protectiveness, but I secretly loved that she worried about me. It was nice to have someone fuss over me other than, well, me. That thought made me grin as I gazed around for whoever was supposed to be here to pick me up.

"Dang, I love a girl who can rock some shit kickers," a thick and rich voice that was as sweet as molasses said behind me.

I startled and glanced at my old, worn, brown cowgirl boots and skinny jeans before turning and taking in the man behind me. I guess he was talking to me? He was looking at me.

The first thing I noticed was a very large belt buckle at his waist that said *Save a horse. Ride a cowboy.* I almost laughed out loud.

I tilted my head to the side and blew my hair out of my eyes. "The better to kick the shit out of you with," I smarted, my voice thick with sarcasm. I didn't like men looking at me. I was almost always ready for them with hard smirks and snarky comments.

He didn't seem so bad though. I'd have been more concerned if the man in front of me didn't remind of a sweet puppy dog. With blond hair and bright-green, dancing eyes, he was adorable. He was wearing cowboy boots himself and a pair of jeans that nicely hugged his thighs. His blue-and-red-plaid shirt was only buttoned three quarters the way up his chest, which revealed a bit of nice, tan muscle. That unbuttoned shirt said a lot about him. Mostly that he was a cocky bastard. He looked about my age. He wasn't short, but he wasn't tall, either. He put his hands into his back pockets, and his lean frame swayed toward me a little.

"Feisty. That's how I like my women. I'm Cody," he said, holding his hand out.

I threw on a too-wide smile meant to intimidate. "I'm...busy," I said, dismissing his hand and his introduction.

I knew this type. Harmless flirts, but I also knew that looks could be deceiving and I'd been deceived too much in my short life. I turned away from him and scanned the parking lot again for my ride. I glanced at the old watch on my wrist and let out a sigh.

"Someone keeping you waiting, sugar?" Cody spoke again.

I could see his grin out of the corner of my eye and I knew. My ride was this shameless flirt. Of course.

"Busy," I sang back, hoping that Momma Lou was right and someone was coming. Someone other than Cody.

"Wha'cha busy doing?" he asked beside me now, scanning the parking lot too. He was being adorable and he damn well knew it.

"Looking for my ride," I growled out.

He was being too cute, and I was getting frustrated with our little game. It was hot, and I was tired from not sleeping last night. I was also nervous as hell about what lay ahead today.

Cody leaned over and picked my bag up, throwing it over his shoulder. "Well, it's your lucky day, Everly. *I'm* your ride," he said, wiggling his eyebrows and chuckling.

"Figures," I mumbled under my breath. Shoulders slumped, I followed him to a red Jeep he had waiting in the parking lot. It was huge and didn't have any doors on it. My immediate thought was, *Death trap.* My secondary thought was how in the hell I was going to get my tiny ass up into that thing.

Cody threw my bag into the trunk. If you could call the space behind the seats that. He came around to the passenger's side of the car and put his hands under my arms.

"Why does it figure, sugar?" he asked, his smile genuine, his eyes twinkling at me.

I rolled my eyes. "Because it's just my luck my new place of employment would send a ridiculous flirt to come pick me up." It was true. I had terrible luck. My bad luck had been in full effect since the day I'd been born.

"Aww, don't worry, baby girl," Cody said, hoisting me up and into my seat in the Jeep.

My eyes widened in surprise and the air whooshed out of me as he set me a bit too hard in the passenger's seat. He leaned over me and hooked my seat belt before looking my body up and down and stopping on my breasts. He leaned so close his lips were almost on mine.

"You ain't got the right parts for me."

He winked, and I snapped up my head, watching him walk around the Jeep and jump into the driver's seat. He buckled his own seat belt and peered over at me.

He placed his index finger under my chin and pushed up. "Close your mouth, Everly. You're gonna catch flies." He threw me a flirty grin, started the Jeep and we were off.

I was in shock for the first fifteen minutes of the drive. Did he mean he was gay or that he just didn't like *my* parts? I knew from experience that most men liked my parts. I might have been tiny, but I was curvy in all the right places.

The engine and the wind were loud between us, but I had questions, so I raised my voice over the noise. "So, you don't like *my* parts or…" I stopped, not really knowing how to phrase this particular question. I didn't really have any friends besides Momma Lou. I didn't want to offend Cody, and I wanted to start this summer off right.

Cody took his gaze off the road for a second and raised his eyebrows at me, still smiling.

I considered my next words carefully. "Or you just don't like girl parts in general?" I asked, holding my palms over my breast. I stared at my hands and felt my blush start at the roots of my hair. What the hell were my hands doing there? I quickly placed them my lap and clutched them together. Jesus. What in the hell was wrong me? I was terrible at this making-friends thing. I kept my gaze straight ahead and on the road. I couldn't bear to see Cody's face right then.

A boom of laughter made me jump in my seat, and I flailed my hands, looking for purchase, only to come up empty. I found myself hanging out the side of the Jeep where the damn door should have been, the seatbelt the only thing keeping me from falling to my death. A strong hand dragged me back and placed me upright in my seat, and I took a deep breath. I was beyond mortified. God, I was a hot mess.

Between hysterical fits of laughter, Cody asked, "You all right there, sugar?"

I nodded and clutched my hands in my lap again, afraid I would make another lewd gesture or reach for a door that wasn't there. I was usually a pretty put-together type of girl. But I could already tell that being thrown into this new situation was taking its toll on me. I was composed and poised in most scenarios. After all, I'd lived on the streets. I was cunning. I was smart. I was always ready. But today? Today, I was failing at life.

We pulled up to a four-way stop, and Cody peeped over at me. I could see him out of the corner of my eye, but I refused to look at him. I wasn't moving an inch until we arrived at our destination.

Leaning across our seats, he grabbed my chin and forced my gaze to his. His gaze swept up my body from the tips of my toes. He paused on my lips before he said, "You are gorgeous, Everly, but pussy just isn't my thing. I prefer cock. Big. Thick. Long. Cock."

My eyes widened in shock, and another boom of laughter almost sent me out the door again. Damn Cody. I eyeballed him. His head was thrown back in laughter as he pulled away from the four-way stop, and I couldn't help but join him. He was nuts and fun, and I needed a nutty friend. I'd never really had a friend besides Momma Lou, and Cody seemed just crazy enough to take on my own brand of insanity. My heart warmed at the thought of having a possible friend to confide in this summer.

"It's gonna be a fun summer, sugar," Cody said, patting my thigh with his big, tan hand.

And, in that moment, I believed him. Momma Lou would have been proud. I'd already made my first friend. He might have been a crazy-as-hell, gay cowboy, but beggars couldn't be choosers, and I'd been a beggar since the day I'd been born.

The wind whipped against my face, and Cody turned the radio up full blast. Country music pumped through the speakers, and I found myself singing along and giggling when Cody occasionally threw a glance my way. Periodically, he would turn the radio down and fill me in on little facts about the town of Canton. He showed me the local grocery store, a few large, family-owned farms, and a small restaurant that supposedly had the best fried chicken in Georgia. We rode past the town's small train station, and when Cody made a point to show it to me, my skin crawled. This girl did not ride the lines anymore. I was done with that. I pushed the train station out of my mind and enjoyed the rest of the ride.

The Jeep slowed and Cody turned the radio low as we approached a large cluster of what seemed like trees. Rows and rows of them sat before me. All of them were very green and heavy with some kind of fruit. Through the spaces between the trees, I could see a big, old, white house with a red roof off in the distance. The whole scene with the orchards in front of that house almost proved too beautiful. I couldn't look away and probably wouldn't have if Cody hadn't said something.

"Peaches," he said, looking at me pointedly.

"Huh?" I was too focused on the sights around me to pay much attention.

As we pulled near the orchard, I took a glimpse back at the sign again. Preston's Peach Orchard. I tried to find the beautiful, old house past the trees as we made our way around the orchard.

Unease unfurled low in my stomach. This wasn't the place for me. It was too grand. Too gorgeous.

"Peaches, baby girl," Cody said. "That's what we do here. We grow peaches and harvest them. I mean, we have livestock and other things we do, but peaches are our main business, and the summer is our busiest time." He looked proud.

He pulled the Jeep into a large, circular drive in front of the big, white house, and once again, my mouth fell open. It was huge. Even more so up close than it had been from on the other side of the orchard. It was also prettier than any place I'd ever seen in person. It reminded me of one of those graceful, old plantation houses straight out of old Southern movies.

Cody came around the Jeep and unbuckled me while I stared wide-eyed at the house some more. Once again, he gripped me under my arms and, this time, hauled me down out of the Jeep. He grabbed my bag out of the back and started walking towards the house.

I paused, still taking in the great, big house.

He glanced behind himself at me. "Well, come on, Everly. You gotta meet Joe. He's been waiting on you to get here all morning."

I hoped that Joe wasn't expecting a lot. Because me, my kind? We didn't belong in grand, gorgeous mansions on beautiful peach farms. I lowered my head, my body curling in on itself, all of my old insecurities coming back to me.

I heard a sigh and heavy footsteps, and then a big hand enveloped mine.

"Baby girl, you're gonna love Joe, and he's gonna love you. You ain't got nothing to be scared of. He don't bite."

I peeked up at Cody, and his face became playful.

"The only person who bites around here is me." He winked.

My shoulders uncurled, and I took a deep breath. I could do this. Cody was sweet and fun. It would be a blast to hang out with him over the summer. This was just a job, so I didn't need to be the kind of girl who lived in a place like this to work there.

"Thanks, Cody," I said, squeezing his hand, so very thankful for having a friend there already.

We passed through the large wraparound porch and went through two large, wooden doors. I stood in the foyer in shock. Gleaming hardwood floors and big, leather furniture filled the cavernous space to the left of us. The space to the right held a dining room table ten people could easily sit at. Off to the right was a long staircase that trailed up the wall of the foyer and spilled out onto a balcony that led to a hallway jutting off on either side. The house was positively stunning. And I'd never felt poorer or more out of place in my entire life.

Cody dragged me past the staircase and farther into the house. We passed a huge kitchen and finally came to a room that was obviously a living room, but it was more casual than the one at the entrance of the house. As much as I wanted to observe the room, nothing quite captured my attention like the man seated in a wheelchair, watching TV. His eyes came to mine, and I figured this must be Joe. Cody had told me that he didn't bite, so I bravely made my way over to him.

The closer I got to the man, the more I noticed how handsome he was. He appeared to be in his late forties or early fifties. His hair was salt and pepper, and his sweet eyes only beckoned me closer.

"Everly Woods," I said, putting out my hand to the man in the wheelchair.

When only his gaze moved to my palm, I stared at him in confusion until he quirked an eyebrow at my outstretched hand. My mind finally registered what was happening. My hand shot back to my side, and my eyes widened in horror. Holy fuck. This man could not move from the neck down. I figured when I saw the wheelchair that he couldn't walk, but it never, not for a second, occurred to me that he couldn't move at all.

"Oh my God," I breathed. "I'm so sorry. I had no idea. No one told me. I assumed you—"

"It's okay," he interrupted.

And thank God for that because I couldn't seem to stop myself from blabbering on. I did that when I was nervous sometimes. When I'd been on the streets, I didn't speak to anyone for months, but now, I couldn't stop the words from pouring out of me. Maybe that was my problem; I had kept them bottled up for too long.

The big man chuckled, and I was slightly less horrified. I couldn't stop myself from admiring his face when his smile reached his eyes. Gorgeous, blue eyes surrounded by plenty of wrinkles greeted me, and I thought that maybe this man had been very good looking in his younger years. Maybe this man had smiled and laughed a lot by all the lines around his eyes. I could tell, even though he was in his chair, that he was tall and big. I wondered how long he had been like this. Did he have a wife? Children?

"Everly Woods. That's a beautiful name." The man beamed at me. "For a beautiful girl."

For the first time in my life, my name from someone's lips didn't illicit a negative reaction, and it didn't make my skin crawl. It didn't make me feel less of a person. I didn't feel ashamed of it.

For that split second in time, I wasn't "The Everly Woods Baby." That was the name the firefighters had given me. After all, what did you call the five-month-old baby found in the trash at the Everly Woods Train Station?

The small town in Georgia, the train station, me—Everly Woods.

The name probably wouldn't have stuck if I'd been adopted. If I hadn't jumped from foster home to foster home. If maybe I hadn't run away and ended up back at that train station over and over throughout my short life. The Everly Woods Train Station and I were almost one and the same. It was the place I loathed the most. It was also the place I went back to time and time again when I had nowhere else to go. I hated it, but it was my safe haven.

But, for some reason, when Joe called me Everly Woods, I didn't feel like I wanted to hide. He made it sound beautiful, like maybe the Everly Woods he thought I was might be good and decent and special. He didn't know me at all, but it felt like he did. Not the old me and not the new me. Like he knew the me I wanted to be, the one I hid from the world.

He studied me far too intensely. "I'm Joe Preston."

His index finger moved on his right hand just a bit and his electric wheelchair came closer to me. He perused me up and down again before zeroing in on my eyes.

"You're gorgeous," he said sincerely, and my face heated at his compliment. Were all the cowboys around her so damn blunt and forward? "But you must be exhausted after your long ride. Why don't I get Cody to show you to your room, and you can take a rest before dinner?"

"Oh, no, sir. If you have some work for me to do, I'm happy to get started right away," I said firmly.

I was there to work, and after meeting Joe and Cody, I was actually excited about the prospect of being there for the summer. They seemed so nice, and I wanted Joe to know that I was a hard worker. I was ready to get to picking peaches or cooking meals in that fancy kitchen.

"How about we get you settled in today, and then, tomorrow, you can start helping around here." Joe's statement seemed final and brooked no argument, but I was stubborn. And I wasn't the slightest bit tired.

"Mr. Preston—" I started, but Joe cut me off.

"Joe. Please call me Joe, Everly. No one calls me Mr. Preston. Mr. Preston was my daddy." He smiled, and I couldn't help but return it. "And please, do me a favor, darling, and put your belongings away and take a rest. If you don't feel like resting, then have Cody show you around the property. But let's save the work for tomorrow. Okay?" He smiled again.

I pursed my lips and nodded, conceding. "Okay, Joe. But just for today. I'm anxious to work and like to be kept busy. I'm ready." I leaned forward, placing my hand on his shoulder and squeezing before I realized what I was doing. Christ. I was too damn nervous one moment and way too comfortable the next. I snatched my hand back to my side and mumbled a weak, "Sorry," under my breath.

Joe chuckled and turned his wheelchair towards Cody. "Go show Everly her room, Casanova. And, if she feels like a tour, show her around."

Cody winked and started out of the room. "Sure thing, Joe."

I rushed out of the room to keep up with Cody and threw a quick wave over my shoulder to Joe, who was still watching me intently.

I followed Cody back towards the front of the house and we made our way up the staircase I saw when I first entered the house. Beautiful paintings of the orchard and the house adorned the walls at the top of the steps, and I stayed a step behind Cody down a long, narrow hallway before he stopped at the second door on the left. He swung the door open and headed right in, throwing my bag on the floor and plopping his ass on the four-poster bed in the middle of a giant room.

"Holy shit," I breathed out. The room was incredible.

Lavender curtains hung around a large bay window complete with a beautiful window seat beneath it. Splashes of color dotted the walls from the gorgeous paintings of what I could only assume was this farm, and the corner of the room even held a small fireplace. I surveyed the king-sized four-poster bed Cody was currently reclining on and my chest pinched in panic.

This room. This house. It was built for a Southern princess. Not a piece of trash off the streets who didn't even know who she was or where she came from. Not a girl who'd picked through trash cans for her next meal.

"Are you sure this is my room?" I asked Cody quietly. It had to be the wrong room. This had to be a mistake. This could not be my room.

"Everly," Cody said from the bed in a singsong voice. "This is your room, sugar. Now, come get your sweet ass in this bed and give me a cuddle."

The pinch in my chest eased, and I smirked at Cody. "Not a chance in hell. I don't have the right parts, remember?" I said, making my way towards the en suite bathroom and groaning at the huge claw foot tub inside. Holy cow, my own damn bathroom. And that bathtub!

"I take it that groan is for the giant bathtub in that bathroom and, sadly, not for the hot stud in your bed."

I turned back to him in time to watch him clutch his chest and let out a long sigh while throwing himself even farther back into the bed.

I had a feeling my new cowboy friend would bring more drama into my life than any potential girlfriend I'd ever have. I giggled and threw myself beside him onto the big bed. I'd never in my life suffered anything as menial as girl drama, and I somehow found myself looking forward to it.

"Where is your room?" I asked, turning my head to face his on the pillow.

He seemed pretty far away, and I wondered how huge this bed really was. Did everyone's room here look like it was straight from the set of *Gone With the Wind*?

Cody turned to face me and propped his head in his hand. "Most of us don't live here, sugar. I rent a house a couple of miles from the property and drive in every day. We do have a small bed and breakfast on the front side of the farm that people stay in, and of course boss, Missy, and Joe live here.

"Boss?" I asked. Joe wasn't the boss?

Cody touched the tip of my nose with his pointer finger. "Yeah, Cole. He runs things here since Joe can't get around like he wants. Cole is his right-hand man and practically like family. His small cottage is right behind the house, and he keeps the farm and orchard running in tip-top shape."

I chewed on my lip and stared at Cody. I had no idea what I was doing here. Was I supposed to be helping on the farm? Helping care for Joe? I brought my hand to my mouth and chewed on my thumbnail. I hated the unknown—it almost always meant bad things for me. And the fact that my mood was fluctuating between giddy excitement and dread was making me sick.

Grabbing my hand and holding it in his, Cody said, "Everly. You're going to be fine here. You're going to love Joe. You're going to love Cole. Mostly because he is the most orgasmic peace of cowboy eye candy ever!" He chuckled quietly and then continued. "But mainly because everyone is going to love you, sugar! You're going to fit in just fine, so stop gnawing on those pretty fingers, yeah?"

I sure hoped Cody was right. I wanted to fit in there, but I'd never felt so out of place in my entire life. I glanced around, wondering how my poor, low-class, thieving self was going to make it a whole summer in this castle built for a Southern princess.

Chapter 3
Cole

Jesus fucking Christ. I didn't want to have this conversation with Joe again. We'd been having it for months now, and I was over it. Beyond over it. And no person should ever be as fast as Joe was in that Goddamn wheelchair. He'd been scooting behind me in that Godforsaken contraption for the past hour, hounding me to fucking death.

I was feeding the horses, and he had his ass parked right behind me. If he were any closer, he'd officially be up my ass.

"Cole, I know you're still hurting, but at some point, you have to think about the kid, ya know?"

He couldn't be serious. Of course I was thinking about the kid. I'd done nothing but think about that child for the past three months, and every time I did, my heart broke into a million pieces. I could barely breathe when thinking about him. Even now, as I shoveled shit and hay, an unbearable ache burned in my chest.

I threw my shovel down and turned to Joe. "Don't you fucking dare, Joe. Just don't. You have no idea what I am thinking about or how I feel. You're like family to me, but just back off. I'm done having this conversation." I wiped my sweaty hands on my jeans and pulled my black Stetson off my head. Then I used the end of my white T-shirt to wipe my forehead and let out a deep sigh.

"I had a child once, ya know?" Joe said so quietly that I thought I'd heard him wrong.

I placed my hat back on my head and stared at him. "What?"

"She passed, Cole. I didn't get the option to have her in my life. You understand what I'm saying? That choice was taken away from me. You still have the option. Go see that baby boy if you want to, son. Don't let your anger and hate keep you away from your son."

"Damn it, Joe. Don't you get it? That's just it! He isn't fucking mine! She lied. He lied. It was all a lie. He's not my son. He's Austin's, and there isn't a Goddamn thing I can do about it but accept it." I tagged the hat from my head and threw it across the barn.

And, God, it stung. The ache in my chest burned like fire, and my stomach churned. For six months, that baby boy had been mine, and to say it had been the most amazing time of my life would have been an understatement. I knew when I'd proposed to Marla that it hadn't been for love, but I had hopes that the accidental baby I'd put in her belly would bring us closer—until we'd grow to love each other.

All of my hopes had been dashed the moment I'd found her sleeping with my brother when I came home from work early one day. They'd grabbed my baby and hightailed it out of there like their asses were on fire. Not that I could blame them. I'd lost my mind. It hadn't even occurred to me until later that night that Greyson might not be mine. I'd lain there trying to figure out how long this had been going on right under my nose and the thought had hit me like a sledgehammer to the heart. What if those soft, chocolate-brown eyes and those dimples weren't mine after all? What if they belonged to Austin? And if I'd thought I had lost my mind when I had found

Marla with my brother, I'd been wrong, because nothing compared to the sheer torment and anger I'd experienced when the paternity test had confirmed that I was definitely not his father.

But, for six sweet months, I'd had it all. And, for the past three, I'd been in a living hell.

Joe's sad eyes on me were too much. I'd finally lost it, and he knew it. The pity in those eyes nearly undid me. I ran my hands through my hair, pulling on the strands, hoping the sting in my scalp would ease the ache in my chest or somehow eradicate the emptiness in my heart, which only six months ago had been full to overflowing.

"I know you're hurting, Cole, but it's only your stubbornness that's keeping you from being a part of that boy's life." Joe made his way around me with his chair and took off for the barn's exit. He was so damn fast that a trail of dust and dirt floated in the air in his wake.

Jesus. He was right. I was damn angry and I had every right. Marla had used me, all the while fucking my brother behind my back. When I thought back, it made perfect sense. I was the brother who had my shit together. I was nothing more than the safe bet, the better option. I had a vested interest in this farm. Meanwhile, Austin spent his days trying to get on the rodeo circuit and gambling, and he sure as hell wasn't reliable. I was steady like a rock, while Austin absolutely was not. It didn't take a genius to figure out why she'd pinned the pregnancy on me. I couldn't even really blame her. My brother has always been a fuck-up, and now, I could add my fiancée to the long list of shit he had put me through over the years.

I put the rest of the hay out and thought hard about Joe's words. Joe had been a father figure to me most of my life. I loved him like he was family. He'd been there for me and my family so much. Now that my momma was gone, he was pretty much all I had. I didn't feel cheated though. Having Joe was having an awful lot. I was beyond surprised that he'd had a daughter and she had passed. I didn't think Joe had any secrets from me, but still, my heart ached for him. I understood completely, because when I found out Grey wasn't mine,

I'd mourned just as surely as I would have had he passed away. He was no longer mine to hold in the middle of the night. I wouldn't be around to experience his first steps, his first tooth. He wasn't mine to teach to play catch or ride a horse. It wasn't just my child Marla and Austin had stolen from me. They'd taken my dreams, too.

I didn't know how I would ever get over this. It just didn't seem likely that I would ever be able to forgive Marla and Austin. I didn't know if I could ever see Grey's precious face and not wish he were mine. It just didn't seem possible.

Sweat trickled down my brow and into my eyes as I walked from the barn to the big house for dinner. My eyes burned, but I welcomed it. It was a good distraction from the desolate feeling that never seemed to go away anymore. I hated being angry and sad like this all the time, but I couldn't seem to help it, so I pushed the sadness away, embracing the anger. It made me feel stronger and more in control.

A female voice coming from the kitchen caught my attention as I entered the house. It didn't sound like Missy. She was here most of the time, cooking and cleaning and taking care of Joe when needed. She'd been with Preston's for years, and I could tell immediately that it wasn't her.

I came around the corner and found an extra person at the small eat-in kitchen table. She was female, but I couldn't see her face. Her head was lowered, her brown hair blocking my view of her features as she pushed the vegetables around on her plate.

Joe spoke as I pulled a chair out and plopped myself down in front of the new woman, who seemed to be studying her food a little too hard.

"Glad you are finally joining us, Cole. I thought I was going to have to come hunt your broody ass down for dinner," Joe said, pursing his lips.

Missy turned her chair sideways to feed Joe and pushed her grey hair off her forehead, giving me a scathing look. We didn't miss dinner together. It was one of Joe's rules, but after our fight today, I had been dreading this meal. I'd stayed out in the barn a little later than usual. I'd started working at this farm when I was just seventeen years old. My father had never been in the picture, and Joe had been all too happy to take my cocky teenage ass under his wing and teach me. Even though Joe was only fifteen years my senior, he was like a father to me. Fighting with him was the last thing I wanted to do.

"Sorry," I mumbled, placing my napkin on my lap and reaching for my sweet tea.

"Got that shit reined in now?" he asked, raising his eyebrows.

Missy spooned some chicken and potatoes into Joe's mouth while he waited on my answer.

"Yes, sir," I answered, digging into my own food. My jaw ticked in irritation and anger still, but Joe deserved my respect, and I'd always give it to him no matter how mad he made me.

"Good. I've been excited for you to meet Everly. She'll be here with us for the summer, helping out wherever we need her. Everly, this is Cole Briggs and he runs Preston's," Joe said, turning his wheel-chair towards the brown-haired girl.

Her head rose. Her eyes clashed with mine. I flinched in surprise, our gazes meeting like a head-on collision, and it was a wreck of epic proportions.

Recognition.

Shock.

Horror.

Resignation.

They all traveled across her face quickly, like the train we'd met on four years ago.

I clenched my silverware tight between my fingers, overcome with emotion. It couldn't possibly be. What in the hell was she doing here? What was going on?

Those blue eyes. They might have been brighter. That smooth, pink skin. It might have been healthier, fuller. But I'd never forget them. I'd recognize her anywhere. After all, I'd spent an entire day trying to save her. She'd been so thin. So young. So frail. And I'd wanted to help here so damn badly.

I was railroaded, bombarded with memories, submerged so deep in them that I immediately went back.

"I do see something I like," I said, smiling up at her.

I could tell she wasn't used to that reaction. She was trying to throw sex between us like a brick wall. She was using it to make me go away, and that wasn't happening. She looked starved and helpless. I'd once been helpless like that, and this small girl reminded me. I wanted to help her.

Tentatively, she took the seat next to me but made sure her body was in no way making contact with mine. She pressed her side all the way against the arm rest the farthest away from me and brought her knees up to her chest, wrapping her arms around them. Her hair fell all around her face, obscuring her features from me. I could feel her hiding behind all of her hair—behind her big, baggy clothes.

I reached into my black book bag on the floor and pulled a cereal bar out. "Hungry?" I asked, leaning over and holding the bar near her face so she could see it.

She quickly snatched it from my hand, opening the package just as fast and then taking a hungry bite. My stomach lodged itself firmly somewhere in my throat as I watched her. I knew when I'd seen her she was homeless. Her soiled clothes, her dirty hair, and her tiny frame had given that away. But seeing how hungry she was was heart wrenching. She was tiny, so I was having a hard time gauging her age, but she looked to be about fourteen-years-old. So young and helpless.

"I'm, Co—" I started, but she cut me off with a shake of her head as she shoved the rest of the bar into her mouth.

I raised an eyebrow at her. I wasn't allowed to tell her my name?

"Well, am I at least allowed to ask your name?" I asked, baffled.

She shook her again and chewed the rest of her food. I passed her a bottle of water out of my bag, and she tipped it back, nearly draining the entire thing.

"Thanks, Cowboy," she mumbled at me from behind her hair.

Ah, I was to be dubbed cowboy, then. I smirked. It was fucking cliché, but she was talking to me, so I'd take it.

She handed me the wrapper and the empty water bottle, staring straight ahead at the seat in front of us, and I placed them into my bag.

"And what am I to call you?" I asked, leaning my head forward so that I was in her line of sight.

She continued to stare straight ahead and deadpanned, "Nothing."

"Hmmph. Nothing?" I chuckled at the balls on her.

She'd just taken my food and drink and was sitting next to me in the seat I'd offered to her and she didn't even want to talk to me. I'd give it to her—the kid had plenty of spunk.

She tilted her head back to the headrest and blew out a big breath, and a low groan resonated from her throat. There was a hint of a smile on her lips, and I felt myself grinning along with her. I got the impression her belly hadn't been that full in a long time, and I was all too glad to be the one to feed her.

Studying her face, I noticed a bit of cereal bar stuck to her cheek. Leaning towards her, I slowly lifted my hand, careful not to frighten her. Her eyes widened, but she didn't shrink away, so I took that as the all clear. I gently wiped the crumb from her face. She immediately shot me a dirty look and growled.

"What? Were you saving that for later?" I asked, chuckling.

A small grin hit her lips, and the pale skin on the apples of her cheeks turned the prettiest shade of pink I'd ever seen. Those cheeks sporting that sweet, pink hue reminded me of the peaches that hung from the rows and rows of trees back home at Preston's.

"Peaches," I said into the air between us.

The smile slipped from her face, and a tiny wrinkle between her eyebrows appeared. "What?"

"Peaches," I said again. "That's what I'm going to call you."

Chapter 4

Everly

"Peaches."

The whispered name hit me like a bolt of lightning, and any hopes of him not recognizing me flew out the window—along with all of my plans for the summer. Because I immediately recognized him. He looked older, broader, and harder, but I'd know those eyes anywhere. My cowboy.

Yes. Mine. Somehow, over the last four years, he'd subconsciously become the star of every one of my hero-worship fantasies. I couldn't have stopped it if I'd wanted to. He'd seen me when no one else had, and he'd taken the time to try to help me when no one else did. He'd been handsome and kind, and he'd turned my sixteen-year-old self inside out—in just a single night, he'd stolen my young heart.

It had only been four years, but it could have been an eternity and I'd never forget *my cowboy.*

He seemed a little darker. His eyes didn't hold the gentle mischief and sweet understanding that they had four years ago. His hair was a little longer, and he'd lost his lanky build and was sporting muscles for days. He had a few more wrinkles on his face, but they only made him appear mature and more gorgeous. Cole'd been eating his Wheaties or drinking the hell out of some milk, because my cowboy had turned into…well, a cow-man. And I wasn't the least bit mad about it.

Still, my anxiety was through the roof, because while I considered Cole my cowboy, I could see that he didn't think much of me at all. Nothing good, anyway.

Unconsciously, I reached towards my back pocket, making sure the woman with the same eyes was still securely there. Feeling the frayed ends of the photo, I bit back my panic and eyed him, trying to gauge what he was going to do next.

Joe startled me, asking, "What about the peaches, Cole?"

I looked over to my cowboy, knowing that this was the moment of truth. A million tiny galloping horses took up residence in my chest and I wondered if anyone else could hear the thundering in my ears. I swallowed the dread that had crawled up my throat. I was good at that. I'd had plenty of practice. I was damn good at pretending.

In that moment, it seemed time had stopped—Cole and I were locked in a stare down so full of tension that my skin prickled. Sweat beaded on my forehead and my upper lip. My hands shook in my lap. My childhood had finally caught up with me. I had known that it was bound to happen eventually. I wasn't gullible enough to believe that the shit I'd done earlier in my life wasn't going to come back and bite me in the ass one day. That day was finally here, and the bite was brutal.

I had to admit, though, I couldn't stop the butterflies that took flight in my belly. He recognized me. He hadn't forgotten me, either. I was giddy, and that was just plain stupid, because at that moment, he held my fate in his hands. I bit my lip and gripped the napkin in my lap with both hands, holding my breath.

With a single blink, he broke the tension, rolled his shoulders, and turned his head towards Joe. "Just thinking, I gotta get up early. It's going to be a hot one, and we have a ton of peaches to harvest," he said, his face passive, like he hadn't been locked in a stare down with me seconds earlier.

Turned out Cole was pretty damn good at pretending, too.

He nonchalantly nodded in my direction, "Kid," he greeted me, digging into his dinner, basically ignoring the hell out of me.

Kid? I'd be a liar if I said it didn't sting how quickly he dismissed me, but I only nodded back at him and said, "Nice to meet you, Cole." I made sure to keep the waver out of my voice to hide the tremor in my hands. And the searing pain in my heart.

I blew out a breath I had been holding in and let my napkin go. I grabbed my fork and started moving the food around on my plate. He hadn't told. Why?

After all, he could have told Joe and Missy everything. He could have told them how I was a thief and a liar. I didn't know why he'd kept our night to himself, but in that moment, I was eternally grateful. I had fallen for this man years ago—and he still had me falling and falling.

Conversation about the farm buzzed around me. Meanwhile, I couldn't seem to keep my eyes off of Cole. Cole Briggs. I had a name now, and it didn't disappoint. That name fit my cowboy fantasies to a T. My gaze left his brown eyes so I could appreciate the scruff on his jaw, and I wondered how it would feel against my cheeks, my neck, my chest. I blushed and grinned to myself, pushing my food all over my plate. I'd wondered that same thing too many damn times over the years to count. Cole was even more beautiful than I remembered. Time had been damn good to him. I wondered if he thought time had been good to me too, but I had a feeling he wasn't all that happy about me being there, from the look he'd given me earlier. Who could blame him? He was clearly close to these people, and I wasn't the type of girl you brought into your family.

"Does that sound good to you, Everly?"

Joe broke me out of thoughts, and I glanced over at him. I didn't have a clue what he'd asked me, but he was the boss, so I just nodded and smiled.

"Great. Cole usually leaves at about five in the morning to start his day, so you'll have an early start, but he's been with me for over ten years, so I can't think of anyone better to show you around the farm. He loves this place almost as much as I do," Joe said, regarding Cole proudly.

My eyes bugged out of my head. Had I just agreed to spend the day with Cole? Crap. I needed to stay out of this man's way. Give him space, keep my head down and my nose clean. He'd called me kid. I needed to prove to him that I wasn't the same girl I'd been four years ago.

But, most of all, I needed to spend less time in hot cowboy lala land and pay the hell attention.

Cole's eyes narrowed on me, and my face flushed.

"Oh, Joe, I'm sure Cole has his hands full. I don't want to keep him from his work. I bet Cody would be happy to show me around." I wasn't ready for the confrontation that I knew was coming from Cole. And it was coming because, if looks could kill, I'd be dead as hell. Dead.

God, where the hell was Cody when a girl needed him? He'd have helped lighten the mood, but he'd told me earlier that he didn't always eat dinner here and he definitely wouldn't that night because he had a hot date. Damn him.

Missy leaned around Joe and winked at me. "Trust me, you want Cole showing you around."

If I thought my face had been hot before, it was on fire now. Good Lord. Was she trying to hook me up with Cole? That man who ironically hated my face. I would have laughed at this situation if I had been an outsider looking in. But I wasn't. I was deeply involved, and all I wanted to do was cry.

Joe had introduced me to Missy earlier as his caregiver and housekeeper. After meeting her, I had been even more confused about what my duties would be. She seemed really competent and super nice. And definitely not the busybody, hooking-people-up type I was seeing now. I was usually a pretty good judge of character. Maybe I was losing my touch.

"Yeah, Ev-er-ly," Cole said, sharply sounding out every syllable in my name like he was wielding a damn weapon. The man who had met me four years ago had just learned my name, and already, he was using it to hurt me. "I'm happy to show you around. Maybe we'll take the horses out," Cole said, his voice tight.

My hero worship of Cole Briggs started to fade with every smart remark, every ugly leer, and every fake smirk he threw my way. I wasn't the same person I'd been back then, and maybe Cole wasn't, either. Which was a damn shame because that Cole—the Cole from that night—had been every-damn-thing.

Horses? Damn him. I couldn't ride a fucking horse. And the bastard knew it. I'd never even touched a damn horse in my life, but I only nodded and smiled weakly at everyone. Regardless, I was riding a horse tomorrow. Fuck. Me.

"Maybe we'll take the horses for a swim while we have them out," he said through a smile that wasn't the least bit genuine.

Horses swim? Shit.

The rest of the meal was painful. The death glares from Cole's side of the table combined with the sweet smiles and glances from Joe and Missy were giving me emotional whiplash, and I just kept praying for everyone to hurry up and eat so we could wrap this the hell up.

When Missy stood to clear the dishes, I quickly jumped up to help her, eager to escape Cole and his scathing looks. We quietly cleared the table while Joe and Cole talked peaches, horses, and Cole's work for tomorrow. Through it all, Cole watched me like a damn hawk. And who could blame him? I'd done him wrong. So terribly wrong.

I decided right then and there that I'd make this right. I'd prove to Cole I wasn't that same girl. I'd work hard this summer. I'd earn his trust, just like he'd earned mine four years ago.

Chapter 5

Cole

I came in for lunch, prepared to face the inquisition from Joe and Everly, but I didn't really care. If she had wanted to go with me, then she should have been ready and awake at five this morning. I had peaches to harvest, animals to feed. Basically a list so long that it never got done. If Everly didn't know already, she would soon realize that there was always work here and it was never fucking done.

When I'd gone up to the big house to get her this morning and she hadn't been downstairs, I'd given her the benefit of the doubt and checked upstairs to see if she was getting ready. After knocking at her door, I'd received no answer, so I'd turned the knob and pushed the door open. The room had been still pitch-black, so I'd walked in and found her still snoozing. I'd stood there, frozen, watching a sleeping Everly. Only she hadn't looked like Everly lying there. She'd resembled the Peaches of years ago. Young, sweet, innocent, and alone, and for a moment, all the anger I'd felt last night at seeing her had taken a back seat to the need to protect her. Help her. Save her.

I'd been stupid then, and I was being an idiot now. She'd played me then, and she was probably playing us all now. I'd almost told Joe last night, but something in her face had stopped me. She'd seemed so sad and horrified at the prospect of being outed.

I was damn sick of cheating, lying, thieving women, but apparently, I was also still a sucker. I'd keep an eye on her. I wouldn't let her hurt Joe. I'd die before that happened. But, for some reason, I hadn't been able to rat her out. Maybe it was the fear that she'd end up back on the streets, or maybe it was the memories of our day together. Either way, I knew it wasn't smart.

I couldn't help but think about how Everly was going to make my already bad situation worse as I walked into the kitchen, expecting to get my ass grilled. What I hadn't been expecting was to see Everly perched on the kitchen table in front of Joe. Her head was thrown back in laughter, and she had tears running down her face.

"Oh God, Joe, I'm so sorry," Everly said, wiping the tears of laughter from her face. Her laughter wasn't soft or tinkling like a bell. It was big and boisterous—infectious. And I almost found myself smiling along with her. Almost.

Joe was laughing pretty hard along with her, and I noticed the spoon in Everly's hand and the chili all down the front of Joe's shirt. Was she feeding him?

"Where's Missy?" I demanded. Why was Everly feeding him? What was her motive for being here? What was she doing, buttering Joe up? I didn't trust her for a second.

"Well, hello to you too," Joe said through laughter, turning his chair towards me. "Missy ran out to the store to get a few things for the house, and Everly offered to help with lunch."

"Turns out I'm not that much help," Everly said, still laughing and peering at the front of Joe's shirt. She jumped off the table and landed on her cowgirl boots. She wiped Joe's mouth with a napkin and then cleaned the front of his shirt, her eyes still twinkling with laughter.

"I don't know," Joe said, still chuckling. "I haven't laughed this much fun at lunch in a long time, sweetheart. So I'd say it was a win."

Joe was giving her soft looks, and all I could think was that I couldn't let her hurt him. She was sucking him in. The same way she had me four years ago. She was no better than Marla, with her cheating, manipulations, and lies.

Everly grabbed the empty bowl of chili in one hand and lovingly squeezed Joe's shoulder with other before making her way over the kitchen sink to start dishes. "I'll help you change shirts after I finish washing up, Joe."

Joe zipped out of the room before either of us could blink.

"God, he's fast on that thing," Everly said, grinning into the sink of soapy dishes. "Sorry I didn't get up in time to go out with you this morning, Cole. I had a hard time getting to sleep last night. New place and all," she said, turning her smile my way.

I wouldn't be fooled with fake kindness. Not again. The steel around my heart reinforced itself.

I crossed my arms over my chest and leaned against the cabinets next to the sink. "What's your game here, Ev-er-ly?" Adrenaline pumped through my veins.

She let out a sigh and threw the sponge into the sink with a little more force than I thought was necessary for her pretend outrage. Then she wiped her hands on her jeans. She turned her body towards mine and the full force of her rage with it. "There's no damn game here, Cowboy," she said through her teeth. "And why the hell do you keep saying my name like that?" She took a step closer to me.

There was no way I was backing down. I took my own step forward, bringing us toe to toe. "Like what?" Ice ran through my veins.

"Like Ev-er-ly!" She sounded like a big, growly bear, her voice deep and gravelly in a way that I guess was meant to imitate mine.

"Is that even your real name?" I got straight to the point. I had a lot of fucking questions, but that was the first I wanted answered.

She looked taken aback and shocked, and I couldn't tell if it was genuine or some elaborate show she was putting on. "What?" she asked. "Of course it's my real name. Why the hell would you ask that?" She moved back.

I took a step forward to her retreating one. "You don't think I remember the name of the small town I met you in? You don't think I remember the name of the train station we were at when I offered you a seat? Come on, kid. I thought you were better than this." I shook my head and breathed in deep. I was short tempered on a good day, and I hadn't had a good day in three fucking months. I was going to lose it. What kind of game did she think she was playing?

Her head fell forward, and her shoulders hunched over. She stared at the ground, clutching her hands, seemingly broken. Broken like the girl on the train—Peaches.

Fire raced across my skin and my breath caught as I remembered.

The engineer stood over us, holding his hand out for our tickets. And Peaches—she looked panicked. Wrapped around herself tight, her hands clutched together in her lap.

"She's with me," I said, handing my ticket and some money to the train engineer.

Peaches's head turned quickly, and her narrowed eyes said it all. "I am not with you!" she whisper-yelled at me before turning back to the engineer. "I'm not with him," she said calmly, gazing up at the engineer.

The engineer glanced back and forth between us. "Ma'am, I couldn't care less who you are with, but either I need your ticket or you need to get off the train at the next stop." The man towered over her, intimidating.

Nervously drumming her fingers on the top of her thighs, she looked back at me and then to the engineer again, knowing she didn't have a choice in the matter. "Oh, then I guess I'm with him," she said, throwing her thumb in my general direction, that peaches blush hitting her cheeks again.

I chuckled.

The engineer shook his head, handing me my receipts back. "Have a good trip." He eyed Peaches. "And good luck. "

I laughed again, and Peaches rolled her eyes beside me. I was going to need more than luck. This girl was completely shut down and turned off. I was going to need a damn miracle.

It'd turned out I didn't get a miracle. I'd just gotten taken advantage of.

I took another step forward. I had her cornered, and our bodies were practically touching. I ignored the soft scent of honeysuckle and sunshine because everything about this girl was meant to deceive, and I was done with being duped. "I don't know what kind of game you think you're playing with Joe, but I have it on good authority that he doesn't carry a wallet."

She flinched like I'd slapped her in the face, her features crumbling. I was triumphant in that moment. Like maybe I'd protect myself and Joe from her. Like maybe she'd leave this place with our pocketbooks and our hearts still fully intact.

But then she surprised me. I watched her back straighten, her shoulders roll back, and her gaze meet mine head on, challenging me. She took two steps forward, pushing me back until the counter bit into my hips. Her gaze was piercing, her face a mask of determination. And all of a sudden, she wasn't the kid from the train four years ago. She was beautiful, like a phoenix rising from the ashes, transforming right before my eyes—from girl to woman.

"Pay attention, Cole Briggs, because I'm only gonna tell you this once. And the only reason I'm even telling you is because you were once kind to me at a time in my life when no one else was." She clenched her hands at her sides and the pulse in her jaw ticked. "My name *is* Everly Woods, just like the small town. Just like the train station my parents dumped me in when I was just a baby. And coincidentally the same train station you met me in sixteen years later. You'd think the rescue workers who found me there would have come up with something a little more original, but it seems that they didn't. So it seems like I'm stuck with it. Deal with it. I've learned to." She finished and backed away from me, heading back to do the dishes in the sink like the whole ordeal hadn't happened.

My heart dropped. I took a step, pressing my hand over it. I could feel the steel fortress around my heart starting to crumble, and I couldn't have that. I couldn't do this. Any of it.

And I wished none of it had happened. The baby abandoned in the train station. The rescue workers naming her after the place they'd found her. Us meeting years ago. Us meeting again now. I wished I could take it all back.

Fuck.

I walked out of the kitchen feeling properly chastised, but I still didn't trust her. Not by a mile. But my heart, my heavy fucking heart, got even heavier, and it broke a little for the girl on the train years ago.

Chapter 6

Everly

It had been a solid four hours since my confrontation with Cole at lunch and I was still spitting mad. I was making my way across the farm to the B&B located at the back of the property to deliver some papers to Jane from Joe, and with every step I took, I thought of Cole and his handsome bastard face. I looked around, wondering if the workers fixing the fence ten yards away from me could see the smoke pouring out of my ears, because surely it was.

He'd treated me like shit on his boots. He really hadn't even given me the benefit of the doubt and didn't seem like he had any plans to. He'd just automatically assumed I was a liar. Part of me understood that I'd wronged him years ago. But I hadn't ruined his life with my actions. I'd been a dumb, hungry kid, for sure, but nothing warranted this kind of reaction from him. What had happened to my sweet cowboy from the train? What had been so awful in these past four years that he'd turned not only hard and mean, but so unforgiving? I was angry as hell, but the younger me was hurt. She had worshipped that cowboy. She'd thought he'd hung the moon. When she'd been so cold that her toes had gone numb in her old, worn shoes, she'd thought of his smile and it had warmed her beyond measure.

I was mad, yes, but I was more angry and hurt for that girl. Because that cowboy was gone, and in his place was cold-as-steel Cole Briggs, asshole extraordinaire.

When we'd parted ways that night four years ago, I'd known a few things with complete certainty. One of them was that he would understand, and the other was that he would forgive me. There hadn't been a doubt in my mind. Only, now, I was thinking that maybe I'd been wrong. Maybe I hadn't known Cole at all back then. Or maybe he'd changed, just like I had. Only his change hadn't been for the better—that was for sure.

Good thing I was made of sterner stuff than Cole could ever give me credit for. I wasn't going to let him chase me away. I needed the money I'd be earning over the summer, and I couldn't disappoint Momma Lou. So Cole could take his huge ego and his temper and shove them where the sun didn't shine. I'd show him. I was different. I'd make him see the new me.

Almost to the B&B, I noticed a small cottage house off to the side of the property. I wondered if it was the house Cody had told me Cole lived in. It was a spur-of-the-moment decision and probably a bad one, but I stepped up onto the porch and rapped on the door with a little more force than I'd meant to. But I was still mad, and I had a bone to pick with him.

No one answered, so I turned the knob, thinking that surely it would be locked, but to my surprise, the door swung open. I stood there a little dumbfounded, surprised that Cole would leave his door unlocked when he seemed too damn untrusting.

I made a tentative step inside and shut the door behind me, taking in the rustic and very basic home. No curtains hung from the windows. No rugs on the floors. There wasn't a damn throw pillow or decorative blanket to be seen. My first thought was that maybe this wasn't Cole's place at all, because it looked like no one lived here. But then I spun in a circle and breathed deep, taking everything in. The smell of smoke and leather and man attacked my senses and shook me to my core. I knew without a doubt that this was Cole's place. For the rest of my life, I'd never forget that smell.

Smoke. He smelled like it. Like clean sweat, musk, and leather, with the undertones of earthy smoke. Not the filthy smell of cigarettes, but like a campfire—warm and deep and rich. I leaned a little closer, thinking that maybe it was his jacket or his hat but coming to the conclusion that it was just innately him. It was sexy, and it sent my young heart all aflutter. I knew he was too old for me and didn't see me in the way I saw him, but I couldn't help it. He'd fed me. Given me water. Called me Peaches. And he'd just kept talking even though I was doing my damnedest to pretend I wasn't hearing a word he was saying. He told me of his crazy brother. His sweet momma. How he loved farming and riding horses. On the outside, I was stoic and rigid, an impenetrable wall, but on the inside—God, I was open and laid bare. I was taking everything in.

I wanted to hold his hand.

I wanted to rub my hand over the stubble on his chin.

I wanted to brush my lips over his.

His voice. His stories. They were like listening to the deep timbre base of my favorite song. And I didn't want to miss a beat.

I was feeling as high as the fireworks I'd seen in the sky from the train station this past Fourth of July. It wouldn't take much more from this cowboy to send me soaring and flying and bursting wide open like them too.

He got quiet, and it took everything in me not to beg him to go on. Hearing his life was the best escape ever from my own. His stories took me far, far away. He glimpsed over at me, waiting for me to talk. I wasn't sure what he wanted from me because I didn't have grand stories of family and friends.

"*Play me a memory, Peaches,*" *he said, gazing at me.*

I turned my head his way, arching an eyebrow. "What?"

"*Play me a memory," he said again. "Tell me something. Anything. A memory."*

I frowned. I didn't want to tell him anything. It was all too bad.

Seeing my frown, he said, "Play. Me. A. Memory. A good one, Peaches."

I wracked my brain, trying to remember if I had any good memories.

I couldn't tell him about the nights I'd thought I would freeze to death outside the train station while I'd tried to sleep, but somehow, I didn't. I couldn't tell him about the days I'd managed to get a wallet or money off someone and hadn't been caught. The days I'd managed to have enough food, despite not having the money for groceries. I couldn't tell him that those were my good memories. Days where I'd just survived.

"*My mom used to say that," he said. "Any time I was sad or having a bad day, she'd just look at me and say, 'Play me a memory, baby,' and I'd think of the last good thing that happened to me. Something that made me feel good. I'd pick the last thing and I'd tell her and she'd smile and then my day didn't seem so bad anymore, ya know?".*

I nodded, thinking of my last good memory. It didn't take too long.

"*One night on the train, a stranger offered me a seat, his food, his water. My belly was full and I was warm." I didn't add that he made me feel higher than the tree tops. I didn't tell him that I hadn't smiled so much in years. Because that was what I really wanted to say. I wanted to tell him that he had done more than just given me food. He'd fed my soul when it had been so very starved.*

His smile fell, and sadness settled in my heart, but that was my last good memory. The only one I'd had in a really long time.

I sighed because thinking back on that night only made me more emotionally conflicted. I took another gander around Cole's place, the younger version of me swooning at the memories of long ago and the me of today feeling all the anger drain out of me. No one had ever made me feel like Cole had. Not in all of my twenty years.

I'd given men my body. I'd given a lot of things away in order to survive, but never my heart. Only one man had ever held that.

But this empty house said way too much about my cowboy. The lack of family photos. The absence of personal effects. This bare house said it all, and I hated what it communicated.

It physically pained me to see how alone Cole was. I couldn't bear to be in this house for another second, so I swung on my heel and quickly walked back out of the door before slamming it behind me. I noticed the guys who were fixing the fence walking nearby and hoped like hell they hadn't seen me in Cole's home. That was the last thing I needed. The man was already out to get me.

My emotions were all over the place. Sixteen-year-old me adored Cole. And me now—well, I wanted to hate him for the way he had treated me. Only, now, after seeing his sad house, I just pitied Cole. Because I still remembered our tender talks on the train so long ago. Now, I remembered his deep love and devotion to his family and friends. My cowboy would have photos scattered all over this house, blankets his momma had made him thrown over the back of his sofa—he'd have memories everywhere. But Cole didn't. Where were they?

I reached the B&B with so many questions that I felt like my head might explode. I opened the back door and stepped inside, the screen door slamming behind me. I heard two arguing voices, and one of them was Cole's. I made my way through the big, white kitchen and down the hall to the front desk. When I rounded the corner, Cole was leaning over the desk and grinning at an old, grey-haired lady.

"Come on, Jane," he said softly, laying his Southern charm on thick before lowering his voice. "Pretty please," he begged in a whisper, a small smirk on his lips.

Jane rolled her eyes and shook her head. "I told you, Cole. No more quarters. I have to have change too, you know? Just go grab a soda out of the fridge in the kitchen like everyone else does." She nodded towards where I'd just come from.

"I thought I was your favorite?" Cole batted his thick, brown eyelashes and frowned for effect. He lifted his hand and rubbed his thumb across the paper thin skin on her cheek. "Besides, you know I only like my cola from the glass bottle out of the old machine out front."

I leaned against the wall, watching. A giggle almost escaped my mouth, so I clamped my hand over my smile and continued to enjoy his theatrics from my secluded spot in the corner.

"The answer is still no, Cole. Now, quit batting your pretty lashes at me, you flirt. My old lady heart can't take it." She placed her hand on her chest. "Just get a drink from the kitchen. That machine out there is old as dirt. I don't even know why they keep putting sodas in that old relic."

Cole leaned farther over the desk so he was closer to Jane. "Aw, Ms. Jane. You know better than anyone that *everything* gets better with age." He quickly pulled his hat off, kissed her on the cheek, and winked before leaning back just as fast and turning to make his way out the front door.

I could hear his deep chuckle, and it would be a lie if I said that it didn't make my skin prickle. I remembered that laugh—or, better yet, my younger self did. My face flushed. I guess the younger me still thought Cole was all that. It seemed childhood crushes could endure a hell of a lot.

Even though he was well on his way, Jane shouted, "You get on out of here, Cole Briggs, before I tell Joe on you!" She shook her head and giggled like a damn schoolgirl, and I smiled along with her. Because *this*? It was freaking adorable.

Cole didn't turn around, but he raised one hand and said, "I'm leaving, Ms. Jane," through his laughter.

Jane started studying the book in front of her, but I didn't miss the small grin and the, "Shameless flirt," she whispered under her breath.

Well, at least I knew that Cole wasn't a bastard to everyone he encountered. Seemed he saved that special brand of assholery just for little old me. Super.

I didn't want to take the brunt of all of Cole's anger. I wanted my cowboy back. I wanted his smiles, his jokes, his deep laughter. I wanted his hushed conversations, his stories that transported me to another place. A place where homeless girls didn't live in train stations. A place where there wasn't hunger or cold. A place only my cowboy had taken me. I needed to figure out how to get there, and I needed more info on Cole to do that. But what I didn't need was for nosy-girl-drama Cody to know I needed information on Cole. So I did the only thing I could think to do.

I abandoned my place in the corner, let out a long sigh, and threw in a fake chuckle to seal the deal. "That Cole is something else." I grinned, extending my hand with the papers for Jane.

"He is!" Ms. Jane exclaimed, fanning her face. "He's a mess, but I'm just glad to see him getting back to normal."

I smiled because, *ding ding ding,* we had a talker on our hands and I needed all the freaking words. So I just nodded and kept grinning, trying to telepathically communicate that I needed all the Cole dirt.

"That fiancée sure did a number on him," she said, taking the papers from me and staring at them.

My stomach plummeted, and an odd buzzing filled my head. *Fiancée?*

She looked back up at me. "You must be Everly! It's so nice to meet you. Joe has been telling me good things." She came around the desk to pull me in for a hug like she hadn't just rocked my entire world. Like she hadn't just wrecked a part of me.

She squeezed me hard, but all I could manage was a small pat on her back in return. I just stood there, shocked. Cole had a fiancée.

Why hadn't that ever occurred to me? *You know why, Everly,* I told myself. *Because he was always yours and the thought never occurred to you, not in a million years, that he could be someone else's.* But still, a fiancée. Where was she? His house was so empty. Was that because he had just moved in? Were they separated? God, it seemed like the questions just kept coming when it came to Cole.

"A fiancée," I uttered—more to myself than to anyone else.

But Ms. Jane took that as a cue to go on. "Yep, that Marla bitch," she spat, her eyes narrowed.

I didn't know if it was the shock of the entire situation or Ms. Jane's blatant use of the word *bitch*, but I giggled a little uncontrollably. I sucked my top lip into my mouth to stall the laughter because I had a feeling I was coming off a bit manic. Ms. Jane didn't seem to notice. She just kept right on chatting while organizing papers on her desk.

"That Marla really messed Cole up. It's taken him months, and he still ain't right. Cheating, lying, no-good bitch."

Again, a laugh almost escaped, but I sucked my lip back in, and before I could think about it, "Who would cheat on Cole Briggs?" flew out of his mouth. I immediately wanted to suck the words back in, but Ms. Jane was already grinning at me and nodding.

But seriously, Cole was gorgeous and rugged, and if he was anything like my cowboy from years ago, his kindness—his giving nature—knew no bounds. What woman could have all of that—all of the sheer perfection that was him—and throw it away? Who in the ever-loving hell would cheat on Cole Briggs? It made absolutely no sense, and I had to agree with Ms. Jane—she was a bitch, although that might have been too kind a word.

"Amen to that, sister," she said, slowly sitting in the chair at the desk, a small pinch forming between her eyebrows.

I came around the desk and grabbed her arm, helping her sit.

"Thanks, baby," she said, patting my hand that rested on her arm. "These old knees don't work like they used to anymore."

"No problem," I said, smiling down at her, and it wasn't. I could tell that Ms. Jane was good people, and I knew without a shadow of a doubt that she would give me what I was about to ask her. I just knew it.

I reached into my back pocket and took out a small wad of cash. Then I held a ten-dollar bill out to Ms. Jane. "Can I, by chance, buy a roll of quarters off of you?" I asked, smiling sweetly, just like Cole had moments ago.

Ms. Jane studied the ten-dollar bill in my hand and then peered up at my face. She smirked knowingly at me and turned her head to the front door, where Cole had exited minutes ago. Then she gave a big sigh.

"All right, Miss Everly," she said, reaching into her bottom drawer on her desk. She placed a roll of quarters on the desk.

I extended my hand with the ten-dollar bill dangling from my fingers. She snatched the bill and placed it in the drawer where the quarters had come from.

"Go on," she said, motioning with her hand towards the quarters in front of her. "Take them, but don't you dare tell that man I gave them to you, you hear?" She rolled her eyes. "I don't need everyone around here thinking I've gone soft."

I grabbed the quarters and leaned over, pressing a kiss to her cheek. "Never." I squeezed her hand once more before darting for the door. "Thanks, Ms. Jane," I threw over my shoulder as I ran down the front steps, a plan starting to formulate on how to win Cole Briggs over.

Chapter 7

Everly

Sweet baby Jesus, it was still hot as all get out even at ten at night. I pulled my sticky, white tank top away from my chest a couple of times, trying to cool myself as I walked from the big house to Cole's small cottage. Yep, I was hardheaded. I was determined to go ahead with my plans even though Cole hadn't shown up at dinner. Joe had spent the entire time brooding quietly, so I could only assume that it had pissed him off that Cole hadn't been there. But I knew why Cole hadn't come to dinner. He was avoiding me.

But you know what? It's pretty hard to avoid someone banging on your door, so I stepped up onto Cole's porch and let my small fist fly against the wooden door, my other hand gripping the roll of quarters.

What? I wasn't a damn fool. Of course I came with a peace offering.

My fist was raised to bang again when the door flew open. I had a speech fully planned out. It was all there on the tip of my tongue. I was going to tell him I was sorry. That I hoped he'd forgive me. That I wasn't that girl anymore and I just wanted a chance to prove it. Only none of those words came out of my mouth because Cole was looking like every dirty fantasy I'd ever had. And I'd had plenty.

His hair was messy, like he'd run his fingers through it over and over. His eyes were piercing and assessing. That five-o'clock shadow—God, it was gorgeous And I contemplated reaching out to rub the soft pads of my fingers along those whiskers. But nothing—nothing—distracted me from my cause more than Cole's shirtless torso. He had a huge barrel of a chest with just a small smattering of brown hair down the middle, and I followed that trail of hair to his rock-hard abs and all the way past them to the waistband of his jeans—which were, holy hell, unbuttoned.

I wanted to climb him like a damn tree, and I'd never actually climbed a tree in my life, but I was willing to try for Cole. The things I would do to this man. And thinking about that only made me hotter than the Sahara Desert.

I raked my gaze down the rest of his body, past the legs of his well-worn jeans to his bare feet. Never in my life had I thought a pair of bare feet could be sexy, but Cole's were. And that's where I was still staring when Cole let loose on me.

"What the fuck do you want?" he snapped.

My gaze shot from his feet to his face, which was a mask of rage. Stunned at his angry outburst, I stood there, speechless. Cole's gaze raked me up and down before stopping at my white tank and then my cut-off jean shorts. It came back to my face. His nose wrinkled, and his lips pursed like he smelled something bad. And the whole thing just pissed me the hell off.

"You know what?" I turned and started down the porch steps. "Not a Goddamn thing, Cole. I don't want anything from you!" I yelled, determined to get the hell away from him.

It was clear there was nothing left of my cowboy here. Whoever this man was, he was a complete stranger to me, and I wanted nothing to do with him.

All of a sudden, I was dragged by my arm back up the steps and forcibly turned to face Cole, my head level with his barrel of a chest and way too close to it for comfort. The wooden porch creaked under his weight as he leaned so close to me that our lips were almost touching.

"What. Do. You. Want?" Cole gritted out between his teeth.

I could smell him everywhere. The smoke. The man. Sunshine and whiskey. It was heavenly. It was clear he'd been drinking, and I should have been scared. I should have hightailed my ass back to the big house. I should have stepped off that damn porch and never looked back, but just like four years ago, his presence held me captive. I was rooted to the spot, swaying on my feet. His body so close to mine. His smell surrounding me. His bare chest and feet. It was all too much, and I was dizzy—drunk on him.

I did the only thing I could think to do. I extended my trembling palm between us, trying to raise the roll of quarters. Only he was too close and the back of my hand brushed the smooth, taut skin of his stomach. My breath caught and my nipples tightened at the contact. My trembling turned into a full-body quiver. God, I wanted to touch this mean man again. Only Cole hissed and stepped back like it had pained him to feel my hand against him. And, just like that, the spell was broken and I remembered that this beautiful beast of a man hated me. That he didn't trust me, and he definitely didn't want my touches. It felt like a bucket of cold water had been dumped on my heated body.

I opened my palm between us, showing him the quarters. "I just wanted to bring you some quarters for the cola machine," I said quietly. I stared at the porch. I didn't dare look at him. I was embarrassed by my reaction to him, but more, I was horrified by his.

God. He really couldn't stand me.

"Why?"

I'd heard the question, but I couldn't quite answer it because there were a million reasons why. Because my younger self had given him her heart years ago. Because I wanted him to like the me I was now. Because I was sorry. Because he'd fed me. Because I was his Peaches and he was my Cowboy.

"Just take it." I extended the roll of quarters. "Just take it," I begged. And it reminded me, sending me back to a time when the roles had been reversed. The goodness of those memories settled on my chest like a heavy weight, and it hurt so good.

"Just take it. Do it for me. Peaches, it's just a meal. Take it. It'll make me feel better to know you got a hot meal today. Okay?" he pleaded. He was really working me with those sweet puppy-dog eyes. Damn him.

It was weird to take something from someone they were willingly giving me. The craziness of this wasn't lost on me. I wasn't used to taking handouts. I was used to stealing. At least, when I stole, I'd earned my meal through being smart and working hard. This? Well, it just seemed wrong. Yep, I was fucked up. Through the years, I'd somehow justified my thievery in my head. But I'd had to. It was the only way I could deal with the guilt of it all.

I stared at the cheeseburger and fries, and they smelled so damn good. It didn't matter that he had fed me his snacks on the train hours ago; I was still ravenous now. The train had made a stop for an hour and my cowboy had begged me to make a trip to the small diner a couple of blocks over from the station. He didn't have to beg long. I couldn't say no to him.

Cole started going on and on about horses. He did this often, and I could tell by the light shining in his eyes and the grin on his face when he talked about them that he loved them.

The waitress placed his cheeseburger and fries in front of him, and he sweetened the deal.

"A chocolate shake for Peaches over here, too," he said, nodding at me.

"I've never ridden a horse. I've never even seen one in person," I said, studying my food.

His eyebrows rose in surprise. "Seriously? We gotta do something about that." He smiled kindly. "Eat up."

I forced myself to eat one fry at a time. One bite of that delicious burger at a time. And it was pure torture because I was starving and the food tasted amazing. I moaned low after a juicy bite of burger and he laughed. I grinned at him.

"We're making another memory you can play, Peaches," he said as the milkshakes arrived.

I frowned, sad because we had to be back to the train in less than an hour and I didn't need to get back on. I needed to get on the train back to my station. Time was almost up with my cowboy, and soon, all I'd have left were these memories.

"I've never had a milkshake before," I said, staring at the chocolat-ey iciness in the cup before me.

He stared at me, surprised. "Seriously?"

"As a heart attack," I said, glancing around the diner. It was cute in the '50s kind of way, with red, spinning stools lining a white counter and red-and-black booths thrown in the corners. He and I were sitting across from each other in one of them.

Excitedly, he said, "Well, then. Go on. I can't wait to see if you like it." He nodded towards the shake.

But I just kept staring at him until he stopped eating and stared at me too. "Why are you doing this?" I asked. I didn't understand why this man had paid for my train ticket. Bought me food. Wanted to watch me try my first milkshake. If he didn't want to fuck me, if he didn't want to hurt me, then why the hell was he helping me? It just didn't add up.

"Doing what?" he asked. He frowned, and a tiny wrinkle formed between his eyebrows.

"Helping me. Why are you helping me? I don't get it. What's in it for you?" I demanded. I was feeling overwhelmed by his kindness—completely bombarded by all of these emotions.

"There's not a damn thing in it for me. Does everything have to come with strings attached?" he asked. He seemed upset at my questions, but I still didn't hold back.

"In my experience, yes, Cowboy. Nothing in this life is free, so what gives?" I leaned over and took a sip of my shake. And good God, it was probably the best thing I'd ever tasted in my life.

I couldn't stop the look of euphoria that crossed my face, and my cowboy couldn't stop the chuckle that passed his lips at my expression.

Eventually, he stopped laughing. His face got serious, and he leaned back in the booth, sighing. "When I was a kid, we had a really bad house fire. Pretty much lost all of our belongings. We didn't have anywhere to go. A lot of people helped us, Peaches. And, without those people, I don't know what my family would have done. So, while hanging out with you tonight is no hardship and I'm having fun doing it, it's also a way for me to pay it forward and help someone the way people helped my family."

"I'm sorry," I said, looking at my empty plate. And I was sorry because never in a million years had the kind man across from me deserved any bad in his life. He was one of the funniest, sweetest, most generous people I had ever had the pleasure to meet in my life, and I knew I'd never forget our night together. Never.

And, in one night, I'd opened up to him more than I had to anyone ever in my life. My cowboy was something special.

He leaned over, chucking me on the chin with his finger. "Hey, Peaches. It was a long time ago, and there are worse things, right?" he asked, his face kind.

He was right. There were definitely worse things. I knew better than anyone what those worse things were.

The quarters fell to the porch from my palm, snapping me out of my memories and back to the present. I leaned down to pick them up. I faced Cole again head on. He seemed furious.

"I heard you with Ms. Jane," I said, averting my gaze to the porch again. "You wanted them and—"

"And what, Everly? You thought a roll of fucking quarters was gonna convince me you aren't a thieving, lying bitch?" he thundered.

I flinched, finally taking him in.

He leaned towards me more, intimidating me with his height and his size. "I know you were in my house today. Leo told me he saw you here. Were you trying to steal from me?" He sneered. "Well, good fucking luck! 'Cause guess what, Everly?" He threw his hand up into the air around him. "There's nothing left here! Not a Goddamn thing!" Spittle flew from his mouth.

God, my heart broke. My cowboy was so lonely, and he was screaming on the porch because I saw it. I saw his loneliness, his sadness—just like he'd seen mine once—and he hated it.

"I have no one. And nothing, *Peaches!*" He stepped forward and screamed in my face.

And that name. Peaches. For so many years, I had longed to hear that name from him again. Only now, disgust and hate dripped from it. It pierced like a dagger to the heart. It hurt. So much.

My body jerked, which sent me a step backwards, only my cowboy boot found air instead of the porch. My body swayed back, which almost caused me to tumble down the porch steps. A startled scream built in my chest, nearly ready to release. But, instead, a strong arm grasped my waist and dragged me into a firm, solid chest.

Our breaths came fast and steadily, either from the fight or the header I almost took off the front porch. Cole wrapped his other arm around my waist. I settled in closer to his chest, and he brought his forehead to mine, resting it there.

Seconds turned to minutes as we quietly held each other. Eventually, I couldn't stand the quiet anymore.

"I'm not that girl anymore, Cole. I know you don't want to believe it. But I'm just not," I said, feeling dizzy again at this big man's close proximity, his huge body all around me, dwarfing mine. His whiskey breath mixed with mine, and my mouth watered with the need to taste it.

He sighed heavily. "Then who are you, Everly Woods?"

His breath ghosted across my lips, and I wanted to freeze time. I wanted to stay right there in that moment with Cole's muscled arms wrapped around me. His whiskey breath in my hair. His smoke-and-leather smell surrounding me. It felt safe, which was ridiculous, because moments before, he'd been screaming at me.

But I knew he'd never hurt me. No matter his anger. Not matter his drunken state. I knew in my bones he'd never lay a hand on me in anger. I also knew I didn't have a fucking clue who Everly Woods was. I only knew who she wanted to be.

"I don't know."

Chapter 8
Cole

Fuck. I was a bastard. A mean, *drunk* bastard. I'd almost knocked Everly off the damn porch in a fit of rage. God. I didn't even recognize myself anymore. I was turning into a monster. Every day, it seemed I lost a little more of myself, and I didn't know how to stop it. I didn't know how to get me back. I'd lost him right along with my son.

Everly's small, meekly mumbled, "I don't know," only made me feel a hundred times worse. This poor, lost girl. I'd been practically torturing her since she'd arrived. It wasn't even really about her. What was happening was about Marla and her awful games. I knew why I'd been blaming Everly. She'd been another big regret in my life. I hadn't been able to save her, just like I hadn't been able to save myself.

I pulled Everly closer to me, cradling her tiny body in my arms and pressing my forehead harder against hers. "I'm sorry," I said into her honeysuckle-smelling hair. "I'm so sorry," I whispered across her pink lips.

Everly pulled her forehead from mine and gave me a small grin before burying her head in my neck. Clutching me tightly around the waist, she whispered, "It's okay, Cowboy."

And, in an instant, I was transported back to the only other time she had ever hugged me—to the last time she'd called me cowboy.

"Peaches, hop on," I said, holding my hand out to her from the top of the train steps.

Only she just stood on the sidewalk, her hands firmly in her big coat's pockets, a small smile on her lips. We'd run back to the train after dinner at the diner with little time to spare. Any minute now, we were going to pull away, and she just stood there, refusing to take my hand.

"Hop the fuck on, Peaches," I repeated in a growl. I was starting to panic. She wasn't moving, and soon, the train would be.

Her eyes were bright on mine, and I knew this was goodbye, but I rejected that idea. It couldn't be. I wanted to help her, to take her back to Joe's with me. He'd help her just like he'd helped me. He would adore her just like I did. She'd be tough and hard to break, but he would because he was tougher and loved harder. I knew from experience.

"This isn't my line, Cowboy. It's time to part ways," she said, shrugging her shoulders like she didn't have a care in the world. But it was all a lie. The tears shining in her eyes, the small tremble in her voice—they gave her away.

The train hummed to life, and I had seconds to get her on it. "Give me your hand," I said, extending my hand farther.

She shook her head from side to side, her hands still planted in that old coat. I dropped my hand, growling low in my throat.

An engineer motioned for me to get on and take a seat, and I gazed at Peaches, pleading to her with my eyes. My panic was at an all-time high.

Take my hand. Get on the train. Let me help.

She jumped up onto the step, and relief flooded my body. She was coming with me. I'd take her home, Missy would cook for her, and before we would know it, she wouldn't be so skinny anymore. I'd teach her to ride horses, and Joe would teach her everything about peaches. She'd be taken care of.

She wrapped her arms tight around my waist and stood on tiptoe. "Thank you so much, Cowboy. For everything," she whispered into my ear.

Leaning back, she stared into my eyes and rubbed the tips of her fingers across the hair on my jaw like she'd been dying to do it all day. I smiled at her, thinking I'd finally won her over. It'd taken all day, but she was finally giving in. She studied every angle of my face, memorizing it, while she continued to stroke my jaw. A frown formed on her chapped lips.

And then it hit me like a sucker-punch to the gut. She wasn't coming with me; she was saying goodbye. No.

"No," I said, gripping her waist, holding her to me. "No, let me help you." I pleaded.

Oh God. She had made her mind up. I saw it in the firm set of her face. In the desolation in her young but wise eyes. Panic and sheer terror for this tiny girl squeezed my heart. I couldn't let her go.

Her tiny hands cradled my face, and her eyes shined with tears. "You have," she said. Then she leaned in, placed a long, sweet kiss on my cheek, and hugged me once more, whispering in my ear, "You just did."

She moved back off the step of the train with a practiced ease that said she had done it a thousand times before. I reached out for her, but it was too late. The train was moving and all I could see was her tiny frame becoming smaller and smaller. With every yard that separated us, my gut churned.

I took my seat in a daze, stunned. I hadn't expected her to leave. That small girl had done nothing but shock me all damn day, and now, here I sat, baffled and feeling like a failure. I hadn't helped her, really. I'd given her a hot meal and warmth for a few hours, but what was that in the grand scheme of things? She was out there in the cold now, and tomorrow, she'd be starving again.

It wasn't until later, when I tried to order a coffee at the food cart on the train, that I noticed I was missing my wallet. At first, it didn't even occur to me that she'd taken it when she'd hugged me goodbye. I'd trusted her so implicitly. I checked all over for it before recalling her whispered, "You just did," before stepping off the train.

I smiled at the memory, just like I had when I'd found out she had taken it. My small Peaches, with all the guts of a prize fighter. Her stealing my wallet after the day we had spent together had only proved one thing. My girl was a fighter. I'd taken solace in that. That she could take care of herself on the streets, that she'd live to see another day. And there she was, hugging me tightly again four years later. Fate was a crazy bitch.

I knew I'd been blowing Everly's betrayal out of proportion, but I was working through my demons. Demons that had nothing to do with Everly and everything to do with Marla.

Fuck, but it was good to hold my Peaches. To know that she was there and safe. That she was healthy and warm and right where she should be. But I couldn't be her cowboy anymore.

I wasn't that guy anymore. My head pounded as the effects of the alcohol wore off, but nothing was as bad as the defeat that soured deep in my gut.

"Well, aren't we a pair?" I said quietly to Everly. "Because I don't really know who I am anymore, either." I pulled back and set her away from me.

I couldn't do this. I couldn't save her again. I couldn't even save myself anymore. Everly would have to figure out who she was all on her own.

"Go back to the big house, Everly," I said. I couldn't be trusted. I'd almost knocked her off the damn porch. I'd screamed at her. I was a maniac, and I didn't need to be around her anymore until I got my shit together.

Her eyebrows pinched together, and she crossed her arms over her chest. "God, Cole. Don't send me away. Just talk to me. Let me help." Her eyes pleaded.

I grunted a sarcastic laugh. There was nothing she could do for me. Not a damn thing. I needed to take my ass back into my empty house and sober up so that I could continue to live my empty life.

"You can't help me," I muttered under my breath before turning towards my front door and heading inside. I closed the door on a wide-eyed Everly, who was still standing on my front porch.

It reminded me of the night I'd left her on the platform at the train station, only it was worse because it wasn't just her who was lost anymore. It was me, too.

I slid my drunk ass down the door and sat on the floor, waiting to hear the click clack of her boots making their way off my porch steps. Only I didn't hear them retreating. They came closer until I knew she was standing right on the other side of the door. She knocked tentatively at first, barely loud enough to hear. I ignored her because I'd had all I could take for one night, and eventually, her light knocks became pounds.

"Goddamn it. I wasn't done talking to you, Cole," she said, still hammering at my door like a maniac.

The knocking stopped, and I heard her soft voice through the door.

"I just wanted to say I'm sorry, Cole. Okay? I'm sorry for stealing from you. It wasn't right after all you did for me." She got quiet for a minute. "God, just open up, so I can do this to your face." Her voice was slightly louder, and then I heard a quiet, "Jesus Christ," which I didn't think was meant for my ears.

I grinned at her tenacious antics. Maybe Everly didn't need me anymore, after all. She seemed pretty damn strong all on her own.

"Well, I'm sorry, but I don't owe you anything, Cole Briggs. Because you stole something from me that night, too. You don't know it, but you did. So we're Goddamn even. You hear that? We're even!" She finished on a huff and I think a cowboy boot to my door. Her footsteps thundered across my porch and down my steps.

I let out a relieved sigh and slumped over, laying my head in my hands. I shook my head back and forth in my palms, surprised at Everly's actions, but also in awe. The kid still had spunk. It'd been a fucked-up night, but now, it could finally end.

I crawled my ass to my bed and fell asleep before my head even hit the pillow. For once, I didn't dream of Grey's tiny face. Instead, I dreamt of tiny fairy-like girls who wore cowboy boots and cussed like sailors.

I woke up feeling like hell, but I'd never missed a day of work in my life and damn well wasn't starting today because I had a hangover. I opened my door and immediately noticed the roll of quarters sitting right in front of my door. I put them in my jeans pocket and remembered Everly yelling last night. Then I wondered what in the ever-loving hell I'd stolen from her four years ago that made us even.

Chapter 9
Everly

It was four thirty in the morning, and I hadn't been up this early in years. But I had plans today. I'd meant what I'd told Cole last night. We were even. Only, on my way home, I'd thought about how ravaged my cowboy had been—his dismal face when he'd told me to leave. His lonely, sad, empty house. Him drinking all by himself. He needed a friend. Someone to fill all the empty nooks and crannies in his life.

I'd once needed a friend. And, for one day, I'd had one. It had made all the difference. That day of friendship had kept me going for years. The memories had been there for me to play whenever I'd needed them. I could give Cole a whole summer. I'd be his friend when he needed me, whether he liked it or not. Even if it meant getting my behind up before the ass crack of dawn.

I dragged my feet to the coffee maker in the kitchen, relieved to find that the coffee was already going. I popped some toast into the toaster and grabbed a cup out of the cabinet, prepared to make quick work of my breakfast before Cole got here. He was taking me out today. He didn't have to like it, but it was happening. I would make him. And I'd make him like me too. I was in that kinda mood to-day—determined as hell. And a determined Everly was a dangerous thing.

I had a piece of toast hanging out of my mouth and a fresh coffee in my hand when I felt someone press up behind me, crowding me into the counter.

"Morning, Gorgeous," Cody said into my ear, the grin evident in his voice.

I turned towards him, grinning. Then I set my coffee cup down and used my hands to boost myself up onto the counter to sit. I nudged him away with my cowboy boot, but not before he snatched the toast from my mouth.

"You got something against personal space, Cody?" I arched an eyebrow and tried to grab my toast back, but he shoved the entire piece in his mouth. "And you did not just eat my breakfast!" I whis-per-yelled because it was early as hell in the morning and I didn't want to wake the entire town.

Clearly, Cody didn't realize how seriously I took my food.

"Personal space is, well…boring," Cody said through a grin full of chewed-up toast.

I rolled my eyes and pursed my lips. "Keep your mouth closed when you're eating. It's disgusting." I tried not to smile and nudged him with my swinging boot, but he backed up and raised his hands in a gesture of surrender.

"Whoa there, baby girl. You're feisty this morning," he said, sit-ting beside me on the counter.

I huffed out a breath. "You invaded my personal space and took my food. All before daybreak, Cody," I mumbled before taking a sip of my coffee.

Nudging my shoulder with his, he said, "We already discussed this, Everly." He waggled his eyebrows. "Your personal space has never been safer from invasion." He laughed.

I giggled and laid my head against his shoulder, thinking it was too damn early in the morning for Cody's antics but loving them anyway.

"What are you doing up so early, anyhow? I figured you'd still be sleeping in that big-ass bed or maybe lounging in your orgasmic bathtub," he said, winking.

I sat up and looked him in the face seriously. "Are you crazy? I'm here to work, Cody. Not to be lazy and take bubble baths." I smacked my teeth. "Besides, Cole is supposed to be here shortly and I wanted to make sure I was up in time for him to show me around the farm."

"Is 'show me around the farm' code for something sex related?" Cody deadpanned, his face serious. "Please, God, tell me it is, because I need *all* the details."

This time, I nudged him so hard that he fell off the counter and onto his feet. "It's not like that. He's just showing me around because Joe asked him to." I jumped to the floor holding my coffee. "In fact, I'm gonna head outside so I don't miss him," I finished, heading towards the front door.

"Have fun." Cody poured himself a cup of coffee, smirking at me. "I hope, after he shows you around the farm, he invades the hell outta your personal space."

He laughed at my eye roll as I exited the house. I plopped myself in one of the old rockers on the front porch, beaming behind my coffee cup. One good thing had already come out of this summer and I'd only been there a few days: Cody.

I finished my coffee and drummed my fingers on my jean-clad thighs. Maybe Cole wasn't going to show this morning. I was ready to head back inside when I saw a flash of white in the distance. It was still dark out, but I could vaguely make out a large man sporting a white Stetson and heading my way.

I sat in my secluded spot on the porch, not moving, watching as Cole got closer. I tried to tamp it down. I really did, but I couldn't seem to stop the galloping horses in my chest. Excitement. If Cole was in my presence, it seemed that those horses were too. It didn't help that he looked good enough to eat. I couldn't yet make out his face, but a black, tight T-shirt covered his broad chest and an unbuttoned, grey flannel shirt hung over it. Worn blue jeans hung low on his waist, only held up by a thick, brown belt with a big, shiny buckle in the middle.

He thundered up the porch steps in black boots, purpose in his stride, exhaustion and irritation evident on his face.

"You're late," I said quietly from my spot on the porch, startling Cole.

He jumped and whispered, "Shit." Taking a deep breath, he turned my way. "Everly." His shoulders slumped.

My name was full of resignation. He appeared so tired. I wanted to hug him. But I didn't want to push my luck.

"You scared the shit out of me," he accused, adjusting his hat. His voice was apprehensive. He didn't want me tagging along today, but I'd win him over.

I laughed. "I thought cowboys were supposed to be constantly aware of their surroundings. Ya know, stealthy, sneaky—ready for absolutely anything." I arched an eyebrow, smiling.

Cole grinned. And my heart did that damn fluttering thing it had done when I'd been just a young girl. So I placed my hand over it, silently willing it to stop.

"You know a lot about cowboys, huh?" Cole asked, raising his own eyebrow, his eyes twinkling.

Stupid twinkling eyes. Friends. I want to be friends.

"Not a damn thing," I laughed, getting up off my rocker and walking over to him. "But I'm hoping to learn a few things today."

"So, you got big plans today, huh?" he asked, still with those twinkling eyes.

"Big?" I shook my head. "Cowboy, you don't get up at four in the morning unless you have *epic* plans," I deadpanned.

He chuckled quietly. The sun was finally starting to rise, so I walked to the edge of the porch, startled by the beauty of the sun— the color of a ripe, cut peach coming up behind the orchard. It was breathtaking.

"All right, Ms. Everly. I'll bite. What do your epic plans today involve, exactly?" He'd taken a spot beside me, also enjoying the view, and I hadn't even realized it.

"You," I said, glancing his way before looking back to the sunrise, feeling like I was in a dream—standing next to the only man who'd ever held my heart, witnessing one of the most beautiful things I'd ever seen.

He was quiet, so I glimpsed over at him. And it was no easy feat, pulling my gaze away from the beauty in front of me. His brow was pinched and he was frowning when he asked, "Me, huh?"

He was going to tell me no. I could feel it.

"Yep," I replied. "You owe me a tour of this amazing place, so I hope you're ready for all. Of. This." I gestured towards myself, grinning. I was full of all kinds of false bravado.

He looked me over, from the tips of my boots, up my jeans, to my pink tank, his eyebrows raised in question.

"Ya know," I sang, widening my eyes for effect. "All of this cow-girl badassery right here."

Cole's head flew back, and a big boom of laughter hit my ears. It was gorgeous, and my insides immediately warmed at it, which made me feel all melty, languid, and hot.

I blushed and turned my gaze back to the sun, pretending to take in its beauty but really trying to tamp down the heat low in my belly.

Still laughing, Cole said, "All right, badass cowgirl, but if you want to hang with big boys, you gotta follow a few rules."

I glanced over at him and nodded for him to go on, thankful that he wasn't fighting me on this. Cole needed me, even if he didn't realize it yet.

"Sunscreen. Lots of it. We don't need you getting burnt. You need a hat to keep the sun off your face. I don't need any badasses fainting on my watch. You gotta hat, cowgirl?" he asked, his expression playful.

Gah. He was being cute. So adorable. I shook my head. Friends. Just friends. If I let myself, I could imagine having more with this man, but I couldn't jump on that bandwagon. I was just there for the summer and Cole had a boatload of issues I couldn't even begin to touch on.

He got closer to me, and his voice dropped low near my ear. "Are you telling me that you, a cowgirl, don't have a hat?" His pretend look of horror almost made me roll my eyes and giggle.

"Nope," I answered, peering up at him, trying not to smile at his playfulness.

He raised his hand and pushed my hair behind my ear. "Well, we'll just have to do something about that, huh?"

"All right," he sighed, and then he stepped back before grabbing my shoulders and physically turning me towards the front door. "Go on. Get your sunscreen on and maybe a shirt for over your tank top to keep the sun off your shoulders and arms and get back down here in five minutes. We have a full day ahead of us." He clapped his hands. "Chop chop."

I sucked my bottom lip into my mouth, trying to hide my wide smirk. Because Cole didn't stand a chance against me. I was already charming his damn pants off. We'd be the best of friends before he could say giddy up.

Winning.

Chapter 10

Cole

Losing.

I was fucking losing my mind. I shouldn't have been taking Everly out today and spending time with her. My life was a disaster right now. I didn't need to drag anyone else into it. And she wanted in. I could see it. Her eyes shone too damn brightly. Her gorgeous smile held just a bit more than friendship. And I sure couldn't give her more than that. Bigger than any of that, she was just a kid. Hell, I was almost ten years older than she was. I hadn't a clue what her experience with men was, but I knew she was nowhere near as experienced as I was. Not that I got around. I was discerning about who I slept with, but I also had enjoyed my share of women.

I walked into the kitchen to grab a quick breakfast before I took Everly out to show her the farm. Missy was at the stove, cooking, and Joe was already at the table. Cody was next to him, already digging into biscuits and eggs.

I sat down across from Joe.

Missy placed a cup of coffee in front me. "Morning, Cole."

"Mornin'," I mumbled behind my coffee cup, helping myself to a biscuit.

Joe's brow furrowed in thought. "You taking Everly out today?"

Before I could reply, Cody chimed in under his breath. "Oh, yeah, he's taking her out, all right." He winked and smirked.

I gave Cody a hard stare. Usually, I found Cody's ridiculousness pretty damn funny, but not today. She was a kid. I was a man. A fucked-up man. Everly was off-limits.

Joe turned his wheelchair to face Cody. "That's enough from you, Cody. Everly is here for the summer and we will treat her with the respect she deserves. You knuckleheads got me?" He turned his wheelchair towards me, raising his eyebrows.

I didn't know what Joe thought was going to happen while showing her around the farm, or maybe Everly had told him what had happened last night, but his protectiveness surprised me. Joe knew me better than anyone. He should have known that Everly was safe with me, but I still reassured him.

"Of course, Joe. I'll take good care of the kid," I said, grabbing another biscuit.

The concern on Joe's face eased. God, I hoped I was right. I could barely take care of myself right now.

Cody chuckled. "That fireball upstairs is not a kid, y'all. She's all fiery, wonderful woman, and the sooner you guys accept it, the better."

And, just as fast as Joe's face had eased, it filled with thought again. His mouth flattened into a hard line. He was opening his mouth to respond when Everly breezed into the room, looking so farm-girl hot that she halted all conversation. Fuck. My. Life.

"I'm ready," she sang in that way she did sometimes when she was happy or excited—like life was too good just to *say* words simply. Like she just had to sing them. It was too damn cute.

And it made me want to make her sing every word she said.

She had on skintight jeans and the same pink tank as earlier. Only, now, she had a blue-and-white flannel shirt over it—unbuttoned, the ends tied together under her chest, which accentuated her breasts. I choked a little on my biscuit, so I took a big gulp of coffee, trying to gain some kind of composure. Cody sat across from me, smirking and giving me I-told-you-so eyes. Asshole. I grinded my teeth and stood up.

"Time to go, Everly," I said, nodding her way but not giving her my eyes. I couldn't. Not with her shirt like that. Not with Joe and Cody watching me so intently.

"Y'all have fun," Joe said, smiling through gritted teeth. "And behave." He looked at me hard.

Christ almighty, make this breakfast end. Please.

"Bye, y'all," Everly called out behind me.

I made my way down the porch steps and to the back of the house to the little, blue shed outside. I opened the door, stepped inside, and proceeded to uncover the four-wheeler. It would be the easiest and fastest way to show Everly around. And I needed this to go fast.

Everly came in a few moments behind me and took in the four-wheeler. "What's that?" she asked, chewing on her bottom lip.

"Our transportation," I responded, trying to keep my eyes off her breasts, which were tied up tight in that shirt like she was trying to accentuate them.

"We're riding that thing around? Both of us?" She was gawking at the seat of the four-wheeler, her eyes wide.

"Yep. I'll drive and you can sit behind me and hold on," I said, walking over to her.

"Oh." A knot in her throat bobbed as she swallowed. I wondered if she was nervous about riding with me or just riding in general.

I nodded towards her. "Surely a badass country girl like yourself ain't scared to ride a four-wheeler?" I raised my eyebrows in a dare.

She swallowed again, and I grinned. Fuck. This was actually fun. Teasing her. Forgetting all of my worries and problems for a bit. I hadn't enjoyed myself like this in quite a while. Maybe today wouldn't be so bad, but before we got on with our day, I had to take care of something.

"I'm not scared of any—" she started, but she stopped dead when I leaned forward and untied the knot in her flannel shirt.

My hands grazed the underside of her breast through her tank top, and I bit a groan back.

"What—" she said as I used my hands to grab the end of her shirt and pull it straight with a snap.

I started at the collar of her shirt, buttoning one button at a time. I needed every inch of this creamy, white skin covered, and not just because of the sun. I needed it for my own sanity.

"What is happening here?" Everly screeched, looking up at me, clearly baffled. She tried using her hands to swat mine away, but I couldn't be stopped.

I was a man on a damn mission. And that mission consisted mostly of making sure I wasn't staring at Everly's tits all day.

I didn't stop until I got to the last button, pulling her shirt straight again. "There. That's better," I said, letting out a pent-up breath.

"What the hell?" Everly said under her breath, already unbuttoning the top two buttons on her shirt. "He's trying to kill me."

I sat astride the four-wheeler and turned to the side, facing Everly. I patted the empty space behind me on the seat and said, "Hop on."

She swallowed again but didn't hesitate to get on.

I leaned back, grabbed both of her arms, and wrapped them around my waist. "Hold on tight," I said, smiling before cranking her up and gunning it.

We were off. I stuck to the trails through the grass that I normally took, speeding through the property—the wind in our hair as we took it all in. At first, Everly's back was rigid and straight, her arms awkwardly cradling my waist in her attempt to keep her body from being too close to mine. But, it wasn't long before her entire front was pressed against my back, her arms tight around my waist, her head resting on my shoulder.

I wanted to groan at the physical contact. It had been months since a woman had touched me, and even though my head knew Everly was young, my body was totally on board.

"She's not that young. She's legal. At least nineteen, twenty," my cock whispered. I ignored the horny bastard.

We rode through the orchards first. I took my time cruising through so that she could take in the peach trees first thing in the morning. I stopped periodically, turning off the four-wheeler so that I could tell her something important without yelling over the loud engine. The bed and breakfast, the watering hole, a long stream that ran along the property—I showed her it all, my arms motioning and pointing to every little thing I knew she'd want to see. I didn't think I'd have so much fun showing her around, but it was pretty damn awesome showing off the place I loved most in this world. We drove all over the entire property for hours while I showed her all our live-stock—chickens, goats, a few cows—before we ended our trip at my favorite place.

I pulled up to the barn and turned the engine off. We'd only been at it a couple of hours, but it was already hot as hell. That's why it was early mornings here. We liked to be done by the time the full heat of the day happened.

I hopped to my feet and stretched before offering Everly my hand and helping her off the four-wheeler.

She looked at the red barn. "What are we doing here?"

"I've got some friends I want to introduce you to." I smiled, grabbing her hand and dragging her to the front of the barn.

The shade the barn offered was a welcome reprieve from the blistering sun outside. I took my hat off and ran my hand through my sweaty hair as we approached the horse stalls. I placed my hat back on my head and pointed towards one of my babies.

"That's Beauty," I said, motioning to one of the horse stalls. The large, white horse was in the far corner from us, so I clicked my tongue a couple of times.

Beauty's eyes met mine, and she slowly sauntered over our way, hanging her head over the stall door so I could give her a rub.

"Wow," Everly breathed. "She's huge. And gorgeous." Her eyes were big with wonder. I could tell the horse intimidated her. She was nervous.

"Yeah, she's big, but she's timid, too," I said, rubbing behind Beauty's ear how I knew she liked.

Everly was watching me. Then her gaze darted behind me and got big again. Two seconds later, I felt my hat lift from my head and hit the ground beside me. I turned around, grinning.

"And this here trickster is Beast," I said, stepping back to pet the black horse in the stall next to Beauty, his head hanging over the door. "He's a troublemaker." I smiled when Beast pushed his face harder into my hand.

Everly laughed. "Beauty and the Beast?" She grinned, her eyebrows raised.

I held my hands up. "Hey, don't look at me! That was all Joe. He's a romantic at heart." I picked my hat up off the ground.

"I'm not surprised," Everly said, her eyes on Beast.

I chuckled. "Yeah? Why?"

She shook her head. "Joe's just… Well, he's sweet. He's just a really nice man. A good man."

She wasn't wrong. He was the best. He'd helped me when my family had lost everything. Back then, he hadn't had much to offer besides this farm, but at the time, that had been more than enough. It still was.

I gave Beast one final pat and opened the door to Beauty's stall. I grabbed a brush and stepped inside. Everly stood apprehensively outside of the stall, so I motioned her in.

"Don't worry. She won't bite."

Everly seemed terrified, and I couldn't help but chuckle at her being scared of the shy horse. I grabbed her hand, pulling her in. Beauty went back to her corner, far from us. I placed Everly in front me, her back to my front.

I dug into my pocket and pulled a baby carrot out. I always made sure to keep treats for the horses on me when I knew I was coming out here. I pressed my front close to Everly's back and leaned in towards her ear.

"Stretch out your arm." I placed my hand on her shoulder and ran it down her arm all the way to her hand. I lifted her arm straight out in front of her. "Now, open your hand. Keep your palm and fingers flat." I turned her hand palm up. I placed the carrot in it.

It trembled slightly. My gaze moved up to her neck, and I noticed the goosebumps that pebbled her skin. I didn't know if it was fear or if I had caused the reaction, but I couldn't think about that right now.

"It's okay," I cooed into her ear, soothing her.

Her breath whooshed out and her hand trembled again, her fingers curled slightly around the carrot.

"Uh uh," I mumbled into her ear, placing my hand back under hers, pulling her fingers straight with mine, and stretching her arm out towards Beauty.

"That's it," I said. "She'll come. You'll feed her." I used my other hand to rub Everly's back. "She's timid. Scared, even, but not dumb."

Everly turned her head, meeting my eyes dead on.

"You'll talk to her, coax her, brush her, win her over. You'll dazzle her. Eventually, she'll fall in love with you. And, one day, you'll ride her. But you have to earn that," I said quietly. I looked at her lush lips, the creamy pink on her cheeks.

Her eyes shone with tears, and I knew she was remembering our time on the train, just like I was. How I'd fed her. How I'd talked until my throat had hurt. Had I dazzled her?

A ball of emotion swelled in my chest at her tears. I didn't want to feel these things for her. I didn't want to feel anything at all for anyone, but I couldn't seem to help myself with her.

"Oh God," Everly whispered, whipping her head back to Beauty, who was grabbing the carrot from her outstretched hand.

"It's okay," I said, smiling, holding her hand steady. "I got you." I scooted even closer to Everly, encircling her, grabbing her other hand, and placing it on Beauty's neck. "That's it," I quietly coaxed her. "Give her a rub. She likes it. I promise, and I got you."

She trembled between me and the horse, but she never backed down. She was as brave now as she had been back then. I placed the brush in her hand, showing her the proper way to groom Beauty, all the while staying close to her so that I could reassure both of these timid girls.

"I know," she whispered, using both hands to pet Beauty now. "I know you've got me."

Fuck. That whisper. It did things to me. It made me remember that night long ago too clearly.

I laid my forehead on the back of Everly's head, breathing in her sweet-smelling hair. "Why didn't you come with me? Why didn't you let me help you?" I murmured into her hair.

Her languid body grew rigid at my question, but I didn't back down or back up. I leaned even closer to her, moving her hair to the side so I could see her face. Only, now, I could really smell her.

And fuck, it was heavenly—her honeysuckle smell, sunshine, this farm, and me. It was right, that smell, so I ran my nose from the spot where her neck met her shoulder to just under her ear, where it was stronger.

"You did help me, Cole. More than you know," she said, breaking whatever spell her fragrance had me under.

"I wanted to do more for you," I said, watching her face. I smiled. "I wanted to bring you back here, to Joe, so he could take care of you. I wanted to show you the peaches. My horses." I let out a baffled laugh. "God, but you're here anyway. Isn't that crazy?"

And I wondered what would have been different had Everly come back with me then instead of showing up now. I wondered if maybe I wouldn't have been so broken, so angry. I didn't want to think about that now though. Not when I had Everly opening up to me. I wanted to know more about her.

"How did you end up there? At the train station?" I asked, reaching into my pocket and pulling another carrot out to hand to Everly.

She took the carrot in her palm and made sure her hand was flat before offering the food to Beauty.

"Good job. You'll be riding her before you know it," I said, smiling. And she would. She seemed to be a natural.

Her voice was small when she spoke and she wasn't facing me, but I could still make out her words. She shrugged and I saw her body slump forward. "I was dumped there. The Everly Woods Train Station." She let out a sarcastic laugh. "God, I hate my name. It's just a constant reminder that no one loved me. No one cared. Of how lonely I was." She got quiet. "Anyway, I was placed in several foster homes. Bounced around plenty. Some all right, some bad. The all right was just all right because they ignored me and collected their check from the state every month, but the bad was real bad sometimes, Cole. I'd run away, always back to the train station for some reason. Always. It just seemed to call to me. Maybe because it was the only home I'd ever had. A lot of the homeless hang there. That and it was easy to steal or find food."

I gritted my teeth at the onslaught of emotions barreling through me. I couldn't stand to hear everything she went through. It burned me to my soul how she'd had no one to love her. I couldn't imagine waking up as a child every day without the love of a mother and father.

Her cheeks were red, and she frowned at the brush in her hand. I could tell she didn't want to talk about this anymore, and I couldn't stand to see her sad, so I grabbed her hand with the brush in it and brought it to Beauty's side, helping her groom the horse.

My stomach sank. What the fuck did I think I was doing? I couldn't do this. I couldn't be there for her. I couldn't help her. We were different people now; she was healing and moving forward with her life, and I was in pain and stuck.

I pulled away from Everly and the horse. "I'm gonna go and check on the boys and get a few things done. You stay here, hang with Beauty. I'll come back and get you in a bit."

I bolted out of there, not even giving Everly a parting glance. I had to get my emotions in check. I was feeling all over the damn place. On my way out of the barn, I ran into Leo. He was newer to the farm and young, but he was great with the horses and seemed like a nice enough guy. He'd also proven he could be trusted when he'd let me know that Everly had been in my house.

I didn't stop walking when I said, "Hey, man. Keep an eye on Everly. She's in there with Beauty and I have some things to check up on."

He nodded. "No problem, boss."

The sunshine almost blinded me as I made my way to the four-wheeler. I got on before cranking her up and gunning it. I headed for the north field, where a fence needed to be mended. I had a few other things to check on, but I needed the time to myself. I fixed the gate, but not before my flannel shirt caught on the side of it and I ripped a giant hole in it. I cursed the fence and gave it a firm kick, wanting to scream. Even the smallest things seemed to send me over the edge lately.

I stopped by the big house to grab some water for Everly and me before heading back to the barn to pick her up. Joe was hanging out in the kitchen.

"Where's Everly?" he asked, but it sounded accusatory.

"Jesus, Joe, she's fine. I told you I wouldn't let anything happen to her on my watch. She's down at the barn with Beauty. Totally damn smitten." I grabbed a jug of cold water out of the fridge.

Joe smiled. "Yeah? Think she'll ride her eventually?"

I shrugged. "I don't see why not. She was a little scared at first, but she warmed up right quick. Seemed like Beauty liked her too." I set the jug on the counter and took my flannel shirt with the hole in it off before chucking it into the trash.

"You know, Cole, in my day—" Joe started.

But I cut him off. "I know, Joe. In your day, people walked uphill to school both ways in the snow." I laughed. "And, when a shirt got a hole in it, you'd just patch it up with fabric from an old pair of jeans." I laughed some more. I'd heard this story too many times to count.

"Yeah, laugh it up, Cole," Joe said, chuckling a little. "But it's true. When I was younger, we didn't have a lot of anything." His face got serious. "Not a lot of money. Not a lot of material things. But we took care of what we had. We knew that nothing was *really* broken or irreparable. Not really. Anything could be fixed, even with something as small as a hug or friendship." He smiled again. "Or a simple jean patch."

I pictured Everly out in the barn, her tentative hand petting a skittish Beauty, both of them so afraid. Already, my protective instincts were back in full force when it came to her. Like four years ago, I couldn't help but want to take care of her, no matter the drama happening in my own life. I was truly fucked.

I didn't know if Joe was talking about me or that damn shirt. I didn't need a patch. But Everly's friendship? I'd take that, but only because I knew I wouldn't be able to resist it.

Chapter 11

Cole

One week. One week, and Everly had me under her spell. I'd drink too much at night, and then I'd wake my cranky ass up in the morning and head for the big house, determined to have a miserable fucking day. And there she'd sit in that damn rocker like she owned the place, all careless grace and unrestrained smiles. I couldn't help but smile back, and when she threw her snark my way, I was gone. She made me laugh. I knew she did it intentionally. Whenever I was in a mood, she'd get this determined look on her face, and she never let my sour moods get her down. If I got surly, Everly only had to shake her head at me and call me cowboy while throwing some smartass comment my way. Then I was instantly better. She worked hard all damn day, helping Joe and Missy in the house but also visiting and grooming the horses most days. I couldn't help but respect her work ethic. She was amazing like that. She was doing something I hadn't managed to do in the months since Marla and Grey had left. She was making me happy whether I liked it or not.

Everly was fireflies and freedom. I couldn't resist her.

I didn't know how she was going to snap me out of it today though. Beast had managed to get loose, so I'd spent the better part of the day trying to find him, which put me greatly behind on the rest of my chores. To make matters worse, Marla had called. I don't know why I'd picked up the phone, but I had. She'd immediately started crying, claiming that Austin had disappeared and taken all of her savings with him. I couldn't say I was surprised, and I'd wanted to tell her that she'd made her bed, so she could lie the fuck down in it, but I hadn't. I couldn't stand for Grey to go without because of my fuck-up of a brother, so I'd transferred some cash from my account to Marla's. Needless to say, I was in a mood, and not a good one.

So I wasn't the least bit surprised to find Everly sitting outside the big house on a large blanket with some of Missy's fried chicken, coleslaw, and rolls laid out in front of her. She was pouring something I could only assume was sweet tea from a thermos into a red, plastic cup. It was like she knew. The woman could sense my bad mood from a mile away.

She wasn't doing this. Not today. I didn't want her damn sympathy picnic. I would just walk right past her big, pretty quilt and dinner.

"Don't act like you don't see me right here, Cole," she smarted from her spot on the ground.

And, even though I already felt the left side of my lip twitch with the need to smile, that's exactly what I did. I continued on to the front porch.

"There's no dinner in there, Cowboy. Missy ran Joe to town, so they're eating out, but she left me and you quite the spread." She grabbed a chicken leg and took a big bite, moaning.

God, I loved Missy's fried chicken. Damn Everly and all of her meddling. I stomped down the front steps.

"Fine!" I yelled. "But I'm not talking about it."

She shoved almost an entire roll into her mouth, chewed, and swallowed. "Fine by me. I didn't want to talk anyway."

I growled low in my throat as I eased myself onto the blanket. I'd give her two minutes and she'd be talking my ear off.

But I was wrong. Ten minutes later, most of the food was gone. Everly was lying on her back, staring at the pink sky, the sun almost gone. She had her hands over her stomach like she was full to the gills. And she was too quiet. I didn't think I'd ever heard her this silent since our time together long ago, and I didn't like it. It reminded me of the small, broken, young girl on the train. The one who wouldn't talk to me until I'd practically begged.

So I lay back next to her, placing my hands behind my head. "It's pretty out this time of day." I squinted over at her.

Her mouth lifted into a lopsided grin before she turned her head to look at me, "Thought we weren't talking tonight, Cowboy?" She batted her pretty eyelashes at me and smirked.

I gazed at the sky and laughed. I couldn't help it. She was a damn nut. "Well, turns out I don't like you quiet. And I have a feeling you could outwait me any day."

She looked back over at me, pulling my attention in. Her eyes got soft before she said, "For you, Cole, I'll wait however long it takes." She turned her head back to the pink sky, breathing deep.

We lay side by side there, watching the sun go down together, the full length of her arm pressed to the full length of mine.

Before I knew it, it was dark. I could hear the crickets chirping in the background. I didn't want to go in. I didn't want to be alone. I didn't want to think about Marla and Grey. I didn't want to be pissed off about Austin anymore today.

"Play me a memory, Cole," Everly whispered into the night.

I didn't think I'd heard her right. "What?" I asked, rolling up onto my side so I could look down at Everly, my head in my palm.

"You heard me." She grinned. "Play me a memory," she said, her eyes dancing.

My smile was so wide that my cheeks hurt as I stared at her. She'd remembered. She had remembered our conversation about my momma on the train. I'd almost forgotten, but she hadn't.

Play me a memory. I thought of Grey's tiny face first.

Fuck.

I swallowed the emotion down in my throat. I closed my eyes at the ache in my gut.

I rolled back onto my back. I couldn't look at Everly when I played this memory. It would be too much.

Placing my palm over my aching heart, I said, "It was the first time I'd heard him cry. I was there the day he was born."

Everly gasped beside me, and I knew her eyes were on my face, but still, I couldn't look at her.

"It took nearly all day for him to get here. We were all so excited. I don't think I've ever been as happy as I was the moment he took his first breath." I stalled at the emotion. "As soon as he did, the nurse handed him to me."

I smiled and ignored the burn behind my eyes. "I was the first one to hold him. He cried for just a moment, and then he stopped and just stared up at me. He had these big, wise eyes, and I knew he was going to change my life forever." I let out a shuddered sigh, so overcome with emotion.

It was devastating—how one of my happiest memories had become one of my saddest.

I wanted to get up off that blanket and go hide. I'd never talked to anyone about Grey like this. Not even Joe. It hurt too much, but in the darkness, with Everly's arm pressed to mine, I had wanted to tell her.

Everly's small hand wrapped around mine on the blanket, our arms still pressed together. "Who is *he*, Cole?" she asked.

"Greyson. He was my son. I call him Grey. Named after my great-grandaddy," I said so quietly that I almost didn't hear myself. I didn't know if Everly had heard me or not, but I hadn't needed her to hear it. I'd just needed to say it.

She squeezed my hand tighter with her tiny one. "What happened?"

I let out a hard chuckle. "He wasn't mine. Turns out Marla liked to sleep around. She especially liked it if your last name was Briggs. Grey's not mine. He's my brother's—Austin's," I finished. God, my chest was heavy, like every bit of the night's darkness was resting on it.

Everly rolled to her side and covered the top of my hand with her free one. She cradled my big, rough hand in her small, soft one. "I'm sorry, Cowboy," she said quietly, laying her head on my shoulder. "For what it's worth, I think she's a damn fool."

I smiled. Marla was that and more.

We lay there in the hot, humid night for who knows how long before Everly eased off my shoulder and rolled onto her back again, bringing our hands with her and resting them together on her stomach.

She took a deep breath, like she was readying herself for an important conversation. "But tell me something in all seriousness, Cole?"

"Yeah?" I asked, studying her while she gazed at the stars.

"Do you want me to kick her ass?" she asked, not even cracking a grin. "Because I can totally do that," she deadpanned, finally giving me her eyes.

Throwing my head back, I laughed deep and hard like I hadn't in months, and all the weight on my chest lifted away. With Eve there, it was like I could breathe for the first time in a long time. It was pretty stellar to have someone at my back.

"You cuss like a damn sailor, you know that, right?" I said, still laughing.

"Meh." She shrugged, gazing back up at the stars, and smiled. "You like it."

She was not wrong.

Chapter 12

Everly

"**M**omma Lou," I said, grinning into the phone.

I was lying in my giant bed with the prepaid phone Momma Lou had given me before I'd left pressed to my ear. I'd spent all day helping Missy clean the big house, and I was exhausted. The good kind though. The accomplished kind of tired that made me feel all blissed out and lazy. This kind of tired was my new addiction. I lived for it.

"It's been three weeks, Little Bird," she returned in that matter-of-fact way she did, but I could tell she was still happy to hear from me.

But it *had* been three weeks. Time had flown by, and I'd meant to call sooner, but days passed like minutes in this place. We were all busy from sunup to sundown, and by the time I hit the sack in the night, I was so exhausted that I tuckered off almost immediately.

I frowned. "I know. I'm sorry. It's just so busy here that I barely have a moment to myself. I've been meaning to call—"

"Stop. Just tell me how things are there. Do you like it? Are they good to you?"

I grinned. "It's amazing here, Momma Lou. This farm. It's beautiful. You would love it. I get up real early almost every morning just to watch the sun rise from my rocker on the front porch. And Joe—he's so awesome. He and Cole show me new things every day. I've been taking care of the horses, and eventually, I'll get to ride. They make me feel like family. This place…" I paused, swallowing hard to gather my emotions. "It's just special. I don't know what I'll do when the summer is over." I got quiet. It only hit me then that the summer would end and I'd have to leave.

I didn't want to think about leaving Joe, Cody, or especially Cole—who I could tell I was helping more and more every day. He was happy. My cowboy was coming back to me. It was a slow process, but I saw him. His smiles over dinner. Our rides around the property, his head thrown back in laugher.

Sometimes, anger or resentment or sadness would cloud his eyes, but I could almost always snap him out of it with a joke or sass. That man loved my sass, and I adored making him happy.

I was beyond shocked to learn that Marla had lied to Cole about her and Austin's baby. And to hear Cole talk about it, well, it broke my heart because Cole clearly loved that baby. My fix-it personality wanted to help Cole, but I quickly realized there wasn't a thing I could do to help him get back a son who wasn't his. This wasn't the type of situation one could make better. Only time could fix this. He'd have to heal from the loss before he could move past the bitterness of her betrayal.

Our night under the stars, with his hand in mine, was my best memory yet, even better than our day on the train or our day spent exploring the farm with my arms wrapped around his waist. I was making plenty of memories with Cole.

"I'm so happy you love it there, baby girl." She sniffed, and her voice wobbled with tears as she continued. "You deserve every bit of happiness. You know that, right, Little Bird? That place. Those people. They're lucky to have *you*. Just as lucky as you are to be there."

Smiling, I held the phone a bit too tightly in my hand. I missed her. So much. And maybe Joe and Cole were thankful for me, but nothing compared to how thankful I was for them—and this place. Nothing had ever been as good as my mornings on the big house's front porch, watching the sunrise, or dinners crowded around the table with Cole, Cody, Missy, and Joe. These people had quickly wormed their way into my heart.

Joe, with his big, kind, open heart, had made me feel so safe and at home. Long chats with Missy at night had eased some of my fears about being in a new place, and Cody, with his hilarious antics, always kept me laughing, and his selflessness was so endearing.

Even Beauty had somehow managed to steal a little of my heart. When I'd first seen her, she'd been so big—so intimidating. But, now, I literally had her eating out of my hands, and I'd grown to love her over the last couple of weeks. Every day, I went out to the barn, fed her, and brushed her. Just like Cole had told me to. Sometimes, it was just me, Beauty, and Beast, but most days, Leo was out there, putting out hay and cleaning stalls. He usually talked to me while I brushed Beauty. I liked Leo, and he seemed to be about my age, but I could tell he might be interested in more than friendship. And, even though I knew that Cole wasn't interested in me like that, I couldn't help but only have eyes for him.

"So, tell me what's going on there? Any new kids?" I asked, quickly changing the subject. I didn't want to share any more with Momma Lou. These people. This place. I wanted them as mine alone, especially if I only had them for one summer.

She went on and on about the shelter and the kids at home, letting me know who had left and who had come while I'd been gone the past three weeks.

After a heartfelt, "I love you," I hung up and lay back on my bed, wishing someone would come undress me because I could hardly move.

I was still lying there, thinking I might just have to sleep in my clothes, when there was a small knock on my door. I grinned, hoping that Cody was bringing me ice cream or a movie.

"There better be ice cream or a crane behind that door!" I yelled from my prone spot on the bed. I couldn't even be bothered to lift my head.

"A crane?" Cole smiled, peeking his head in between the door and doorjamb.

I blushed. "Sorry. I thought you were Cody."

"That still doesn't answer my question," he said, coming into the room. "A crane?"

I laughed, lifting my head a little to glance at him. "Ice cream and a crane are pretty much the only two things that are gonna get me out of this bed right now. I'm wiped."

"Ahh. Missy had you cleaning all day?" He took a seat at the end of my bed.

"Yep. She's like a damn drill sergeant, that woman."

We both laughed.

He scooted over closer to me on the bed, surprising me. Positioning himself behind me, he grabbed me under my shoulders and pulled me up until I was leaning back against his chest and sitting snugly between his legs. His hands made their way to my shoulders and rubbed hard.

"Oh, God," I groaned. My body melted into his. I had been sore everywhere all the time since I'd arrived here. I didn't mind though. I loved the hard work and the fact that there was always something to do.

Cole and I had fallen into an easy friendship, but still, his touches lit me up. I bit a moan back as his fingers skimmed my spine. My nipples pebbled beneath my bra, and I fought the urge to turn towards him so I could run my hands down his chest, towards the abs that I knew hid under his shirt.

Cole motioned with his hand to the phone that was now in my lap and went back to rubbing my back and my shoulders. "Did I interrupt?" he asked.

"You are never, *ever*, interrupting if you are coming to give me a massage," I said loudly, and Cole laughed. "And, no, I was just talking to Momma Lou."

"Momma Lou?" he asked, and it occurred to me that, in all of our days spent together there on the farm, I'd never told him about her.

"Yeah. She's the one who found me this job. Said Joe was an old friend of hers who needed the help," I answered.

Cole's eyebrows furrowed, and his lips got flat.

"Something wrong?" I asked, turning around to get a good look at his face.

His face eased. "Nah." He showed me his pearly whites and went back to massaging my back. "How'd you meet Momma Lou?"

I frowned, thinking about that night. How desperate I was. How close to just giving up I'd been. I'd been right on the cusp. "She worked at one of the shelters, cooking. She found me outside one night in the cold and took me in. I've been with her for the last three years. She saved me. She saves a lot of kids," I finished quietly.

I still couldn't quite believe I had Momma Lou in my life. She made me one of the lucky ones. It might have taken a while for her to find me, but she had, and I felt like the luckiest girl in the world for it.

"She sounds amazing," Cole said quietly behind me.

I turned towards him again. "She's more than amazing. She's my very best friend in the whole world. That woman means everything to me."

"Oh, you wound me, baby girl!" Cody said loudly, standing in the doorway to my room, a carton of ice cream in one hand and using his other to dramatically clutch at his chest.

His shiny, rhinestone-studded belt buckle caught my attention.

This time, it read *Cocky* and had a picture of a shiny rooster on it. He noticed me staring at it and winked.

"I think me and my ice cream are gonna have to find a new best friend to hang out with," he said, mock sadness all over his face.

Every bone in my body protested, but I sat up off Cole and pointed a finger at Cody. "Do not even think about leaving this room with that ice cream. Bad things will happen, mister."

Cole laughed behind me. "Sounds like she means business, man."

Cody's face lit up like he hadn't seen Cole behind me. I rolled my eyes.

"Oh, I didn't see you there, Cole. I think we'll stay," Cody said, hopping onto the bed with us.

I smirked.

He produced two spoons from his pocket and opened the carton of ice cream. "I only have two spoons though." He pursed his lips at Cole. "Looks like Cole and I will have to share." He waggled his eyebrows at me.

I giggled.

Cole stood up next to the bed. "I think it's time for me to head out," he said, chuckling.

With his gaze on Cole, Cody licked his lips and bit his bottom one before saying, "Don't leave on my account. There's plenty of ice cream, and Everly and I *love* to share."

A panicked laugh-gasp bubbled out of me, and I ended up choking on my own spit. Cole did the gentlemanly thing and patted and rubbed my back until I stopped coughing, but his eyes stayed on the door to my room like he couldn't get out fast enough.

"I'm fine. You can go." I waved him away. Embarrassing much?

Cole nodded. "Okay. Well, I just came by to tell you I'm taking you out to harvest peaches in the morning and tomorrow is a big picking day. So make sure you guys don't stay up too late. Yeah?"

"Sure thing," I croaked out, still half choking.

Cole left the room, quickly closing the door behind him like a slew of gay cowboys were after him, and he wasn't too far off the mark.

I threw a pillow at Cody. "What is wrong with you?!"

How could it be so damn hot at seven in the morning? I wasn't sure, but it was. Even in a thin tank, cut-off shorts, and my boots, I was melting. I stood at the top of a ladder Cole had placed against a tree so that we could reach the peaches up top. I used the rubber band on my wrist and tied my hair into a knot at the top of my head, hoping that it helped.

Cole climbed up behind me on the ladder and stood a couple of rungs below, but still, he towered over my small frame.

"Okay?" he asked.

"Yep," I answered, even though I wasn't okay. He was so close, and that familiar earthy, smoke smell I loved almost as much as rocky road invaded my senses.

"Good." He looked at the peaches. "Alrighty. You see the ones that have that pink color?" He motioned to a cluster of fruit in front of us.

I nodded, trying not to breathe in too much. Because Jesus, he smelled delicious.

"Those look ripe and done. The paler ones behind them don't look ready yet."

I nodded again, and Cole grabbed my hand. He pressed his fingers in, wrapping both of our hands around a peach. He pushed the tips of his fingers into mine at the top of the fruit, near the stem.

"Feel the give, how it feels soft there?"

I squeezed my fingers around the stem again without his help and said, "Yep. Feels softer there."

He smiled down at me. "Good. That's also a sign it's ripe for picking. But be gentle. They bruise easily."

Cole's front pressed closer to my back, and I shivered. The way Cole taught me to do things here was pure torture. It was also outright ecstasy. I lived for these moments as much as I loathed them. Because the man was a damn tease. He'd sent me back to the big house a sweaty, panting mess more times than I could count, my panties drenched.

He gently squeezed our hands around the peach and twisted and pulled. The peach came free, my tiny hand gripped it and his big, rough hand wrapped around mine. He brought our hands to my face and pressed the peach closer to my nose.

"How does it smell?" he asked in my ear.

I wanted to say, "I don't know. I can't smell a damn thing but your smoke and leather, and I don't want to."

Instead, I closed my eyes. I pressed my nose right up against the peach and concentrated on the smell.

"Sweet," I said, my eyes still closed.

Our hands moved, and I felt the peach at my lips. My heart hammered and fire raced across my skin, and it had absolutely nothing to do with the weather.

Cole positioned himself even closer, and it seemed, in that moment, that every breath he took sucked up every bit of air in the atmosphere.

My own breath quickened, and a growl rumbled low in Cole's chest.

"Taste it," he whispered in my ear, his lips so close that I was sure he could taste *me* on them.

I opened my mouth and wrapped my lips around the fruit, the fuzzy skin tickling my lips. I bit down, and that rumble I heard from Cole made an appearance again. I moaned as I pressed my teeth to the fruit, the juicy sweetness of the peach sliding over my tongue.

"So good," I groaned as Cole pulled our hands and the peach back. A little juice rolled down my chin and I attempted to lift my free hand to wipe it.

"I got it," Cole said, brushing his hand over my chin, slowly picking the juice up with his finger, and ever-so-Goddamn-enticingly placing his finger in his mouth before sucking it clean like it was the best thing he'd ever put in his mouth.

"Delicious," he said, his hooded eyes on mine as he popped his finger out of his mouth.

And fuck me. I swayed on that ladder, my own eyes closing as I willed my cowboy to kiss me with every breath I took. I made myself only will this about once a day, so I thought I was doing pretty good.

He brought our hands holding the peach to his mouth. He wrapped his mouth around it, his lips brushing my fingers, and I felt it deep in my core. I pressed my thighs together and swallowed a moan.

"Perfect," he said, staring into my eyes. He held my gaze for a moment more before shaking his head and letting my hand, which was still clasped around the peach, go. Then he stepped off the ladder like he hadn't just made sweet, sweet love to that peach with his mouth right here in front of me.

I watched him walk off to another tree, place a ladder against it, and climb up like nothing in the world had happened. I kicked the rung of the ladder and turned back to the tree. Damn peach molester.

I reminded myself that Cole needed a friend, not a fuck buddy. Besides, I was pretty sure, if he'd wanted to take things further with me, he would have already. He didn't strike me as the type of guy to hold back.

I gazed up at the pink peaches all around me and let out a sigh. I'd pick every peach in that orchard until my insides didn't ache—until I forgot about Cole's lips pressed to my ear and his mouth sucking that finger clean. Until my panties were dry. I started feeling the tops of the peaches with my fingers before pulling them off the tree and smelling them. I was tender with them the way Cole had taught me and placed them in a big bucket in the back of the four-wheeler.

I grabbed a water bottle from the floorboard and took a quick drink, thinking there wasn't very much water in it and I wanted Cole to have enough. He was triple my size and working twice as hard. Besides, I'd gone without water for a lot longer than a day.

For the next few hours, I stayed busy picking peaches. It seemed everyone was in the orchards today. Cody and Leo were busy picking a couple of rows over from me, and I was pretty sure I'd seen a trail of dust where Joe had sped by earlier.

Leo came over after a bit to chat, but Cole chased him off with low growls and get-back-to-work looks. Cody made a few lewd gestures with his fingers and his tongue at me from the top of a nearby tree, and I giggled. I occasionally glanced around for Cole, and whenever I found him among the trees, he was almost always there—watching me. It made me smile, and he'd always smile back.

We'd been out most of the day, and I was putting the last of my peaches in the back of the Jeep when I felt a little lightheaded. White spots clouded my vision and I closed my eyes a couple of times hoping to blink them away. I grabbed the door to the four-wheeler to keep myself steady because I felt like I was going down any second.

"Cole," I tried to say, only it came out a strangled whisper. I tried again, but I couldn't seem to manage more. And then—blackness.

"Come on, sweetheart. Open those eyes," I heard from somewhere above me. "Open those eyes, Eve. Come on. Wake up."

I didn't know who Eve was, but I wished she would wake the fuck up so I could go back to sleep.

"Open your eyes, Eve," Cole pleaded, his lips pressed to my ear.

His anguished pleas roused me from sleep. My eyes fluttered open, but I snapped them back closed. The sun shining in them made my head feel like it might explode. I groaned and tried to sit up, realizing I was lying in the orchard. Jesus. I must have passed out.

"Stay still, baby. I got you."

Cole always had me.

I cracked my eyes open again and found Cole's face right above mine, blocking out the harsh rays of the sun.

"My Cowboy," I whispered, raising my hand to caress the stubble on his chin. And I knew in that moment. God, I knew. My back on the hard ground. Cole's ruggedly handsome face over mine. The sun shining behind his head like a warm, delicate halo. His brown eyes full of love and concern for me.

Cole Briggs had stolen a piece of my heart when I was sixteen years old, and over the past few weeks, he'd somehow managed to strip me of the rest of it. Because, even at his worst, Cole was the very damn best. I couldn't have hidden the rest of my heart if I'd wanted to.

I pictured him carrying my heart around in his big, rough hands the way I carried his momma's picture in my back pocket: with the utmost care. He'd handle it the way he picked peaches from these beautiful trees--tenderly.

One lone tear trailed down my cheek. And I felt overwhelmed in the most awesomely beautiful way ever.

People started crowding around, and I saw Cody and Leo among the faces.

"Back up," Cole demanded. He crowded in around me and lifted me off the ground and into his arms. He kissed the top of my head. "Fuck, you're burning up. It's too hot out here for you." He kissed the top of my head again. "Have you been drinking enough water?" he asked, concern shining in those big, brown eyes.

I shook my head. "I had some earlier, but I didn't bring any and I didn't want to drink all your water. You need it. You're bigger than me." My throat felt scratchy and raw like my heart.

He became furious. He set me across his lap on the four-wheeler, pushing his water cooler into my lap. "Drink. Now," he demanded as he rushed us back to the house, not saying a word. He looked positively murderous, and if I hadn't thought it was so sexy—if my heart hadn't been so full—I might have been terrified.

I guzzled the cool water, feeling the iciness hit my belly, and sighed.

I'd heard him. He'd called me Eve. I smiled at the nickname, glad to be something other than Everly. Another tear trailed down my cheek.

He slammed into a spot in front the big house and quickly marched us inside. He sat us on the couch. I was still draped across him, so I lolled my head across his chest and closed my eyes, the cold air from the air conditioning feeling like a Godsend.

He glared down at my smiling face and sneered. "Christ almighty. Why in the ever-loving hell are you smiling right now?" he asked, irate.

I opened my mouth to answer.

"Never mind. What in God's name were you thinking? You have to have water out there. It's the heat of fucking summer." He held me tighter to him, rubbing his jaw on my head. "It was stupid. You stupid, stupid, caring girl. I could have come back here for more water." He placed a million kisses on the top of my head again and held me so tight that I could barely breathe.

"You scared me," he whispered, but I barely heard him. "Promise me you won't ever do that again," he rasped on a plea to the top of my head. His warm breath was in my hair—his smell all around me. "Promise me, Eve."

I wanted to be mad that he'd called me stupid, but I couldn't. His tight grip, his concern, and his whispered Eve's wouldn't let me.

I smiled again. "I promise."

Chapter 13

Cole

I sat on the couch, a sleeping Eve in my lap. I ran my callused hand over the silky tresses of her brown hair, thankful she was asleep so I could enjoy the sight of her unobserved.

Clutching her to me, I couldn't help but press my lips to the top of her head again. I wanted to spank her ass as much as I wanted to kiss her. I gazed at her sleeping face and tried to imagine this self-less woman being my stealing Peaches from the train. How could it be? But it was, and she'd sacrificed her own health for me. I'd seen her when she fainted, and I didn't know how I'd made it to her so fast. One moment, I'd been at the top of the ladder, and the next second, I'd been cradling her in my arms. And I'd prayed. I'd prayed that nothing was wrong with her, because in that moment, I knew.

Yes, I'd wanted to kiss at her at the top of the tree, my front pressed to her back. She was beautiful; there was no doubt. And my attraction to her was almost always constant, but when she'd gone down, I hadn't expected to feel the way I had. Like I couldn't live without her. Like I couldn't wake up in this place if she wasn't here. Like I couldn't bear if something ever happened to her. It hurt, and then she'd told me about the water and I'd become so angry at her.

Somehow, the anger felt good. Because, for once, I wasn't angry about Marla and Grey like always. It was nice to care about something other than myself and my problems. The realization hit me like a brick to the stomach. I didn't just want to fuck Everly. No, I wanted her. I wanted her to be mine. I wanted her kindness, her selflessness. I wanted all of her sweet, tender looks. I wanted her smartass mouth. It scared the shit out of me, this feeling. I'd never felt like this about anyone.

I rubbed my hand up and down her back, thinking I was too damn content with her in my lap. Contemplating how I could keep her here forever with me. Going over in my head about what it would be like to have a woman like this forever. The kind of woman who'd do anything for you. The kind of woman Eve was.

Chapter 14

Everly

I sang in the shower. But I wasn't good at it, so really, I didn't sing as much as I did howl like a banshee. So imagine my surprise—okay, and embarrassment—when Missy banged on the door like the daggum police.

"Everly, my aunt fell and I need to run over to her house and check on her. I'm gonna need you and Cole to help put Joe to bed, but I should be back tonight as long as everything is okay." Her voice was muffled through the door, but I'd heard every word she'd said, which probably meant she'd heard my terrible rendition of a Carrie Underwood song about cheating.

"Coming!" I yelled back, rinsing the soap from my body. I hopped out of the shower and hustled into some clothes as fast as possible. I didn't even run a brush though my wet hair. I was exhausted from the day's work, but if Joe needed me, I'd be there. By the time I got downstairs to his room, Cole was already moving around the room like he had obviously done so before.

I'd never been in there before. Joe's bedroom was on the ground floor of the big house, and I didn't think I'd ever seen him upstairs. There didn't even seem to be a way for him to get up there if he'd wanted to.

I observed the space, taking in the tans and hues of blue splashed all over the room. It was huge and open, with gleaming, dark hardwood floors. A large bed took up the middle of the room, and other than that, there wasn't much furniture besides an old dresser pushed up against the wall across from the foot of the bed. I guess it made it easy for Joe to get around in his wheelchair. At the foot of the bed, there was a door to a huge bathroom open. It was rugged and manly in a tame kind of way. It smelled like the cologne Joe always wore and was spotless. It was homey. It was simple. It was Joe.

Cole was already helping Joe get into bed when I walked over to stand behind him. He raised the seat on the electric wheelchair until it was level with the bed. He then squatted low until he was level with Joe. Leaning forward, he pulled Joe into him, laying Joe's head on his shoulder. He wrapped his arms under Joe's and scooted him little by little until Joe was perched on the end of the seat. The whole process was so painstakingly slow, and Joe seemed so helpless in that moment, so childlike. My heart broke for him.

Cole leaned even farther forward towards Joe, and with one big heave, he transferred him from the chair and had Joe on the bed, his feet to the floor. I let out a whoosh of air, glad that it was finally over. Joe looked over at me and smiled, giving me a wink. He was trying to make me feel better, but up until that moment, I hadn't realized how helpless Joe was. And the enormity of the situation caught me off guard, unaware. I was dizzy with it. God, all the things Missy must do for him that we didn't see. Joe's personality was so large that it had never occurred to me how little he could do for himself. My heart wrenched.

Cole piled pillows high and turned Joe's TV on before pulling him up on the bed, laying him back, and moving his feet in. He covered him up to his waist and made sure to place his hands on his stomach. And then it occurred to me. Cole was good at this. He'd obviously done this many times, and again, I felt my heart clench. My sweet Cole—he'd probably learned to do this long ago.

"Alrighty, Joe. I think you're good to go, and Missy said she'd be back by later tonight, so she could check in on you," Cole said.

"Thanks, Cole. Get a good night's rest, yeah?" Joe said.

Cole nodded before making his way out of the room.

I was just about to tell Joe goodnight and head out too when he said, "Everly, you think you could hang out awhile until I get tired?"

"Sure." I smiled at him from the bedside. I really enjoyed spending time with Joe. He was funny and smart, and we always had the best talks.

He motioned with his eyes to the remote next to him on the bedside table. "Good. Turn that TV off and make yourself comfortable."

I grabbed the remote, turned the TV off, and rounded the bed. I sat down, propping myself up on the pillows on the other side of the king-size bed.

Joe rolled his head until he was facing me. "Are you liking it here, Everly?" he asked so genuinely that it squeezed my heart. He wanted to make sure I was okay. He cared.

Being there was plum filling up my heart. Seemed everyone around there was always checking up on me.

I could only answer with the absolute truth. "I don't just like it here, Joe. I love it. This place—it's magical."

He grinned. "Yeah, I've always thought so, too. Even when it wasn't much. I bought this place over twenty years ago. It was old and run down. God." He sighed. "It needed so much work, but I didn't mind because I knew what it would be one day. I didn't really have the money to buy this farm, but I did anyway because I loved it from the moment I saw it. Love at first sight." He chuckled quietly.

He got quiet, but I wanted to know more.

"Joe?" I asked. "How'd you get like this?" I nodded towards his body.

"Like what?" he asked, knowing damn well what I was talking about. "This dashing? This handsome and charming?" He laughed.

I gave him a smile, but it was sad. But I tried. For both of us.

"It's okay, Everly. I've been like this a long time. I had a lot of trouble accepting it at first, but I've made my peace with it. Everything happens for a reason, even the terrible things, ya know?"

I didn't know. I didn't understand how a baby got left on the street outside a train station. I couldn't for the life of me fathom why a woman who had a man as good as Cole would cheat on him. And there was no way in hell I'd ever understand why sweet, amazing, bigger-than-the-sun Joe was stuck in that wheelchair. Life was fucking unfair, and there was just no damn rhyme or reason to it.

Joe studied my face like he knew what I was thinking. "If I hadn't been like this, I'd have never taken in Cole and his family after the fire that burned their home to the ground. I needed the help, and they needed a place to stay. There are a lot of people in my life now that I wouldn't have had it not been for that accident, and I wouldn't trade a single one of them for a pair of working legs."

I nodded, understanding. I wouldn't have traded my Momma Lou for a pair of working legs, either. Still, it didn't change the fact that it sucked.

"What happened?" I asked, rolling to my side and placing my hand over his.

He couldn't feel it, but I could.

He sighed, clearly resigned to telling the story. "It wasn't too long after I bought this farm. I was young and stupid and not at all prepared for the life of a farmer. I was newly married. Anna was her name. She was skittish on a good day and downright manic on others. She had a lot of mental issues, but back then, people didn't get diagnosed with those things like they do now. Thinking back, I realize she was probably bipolar. But it didn't matter, because just like this farm, it was love at first sight." He sighed and smiled longingly.

I saw his love for her pass over his face in a wave of emotion.

"We'd only been here a couple of months and the farm wasn't making any money, so we were struggling, like most young couples do. I was a cocky shit back then, thinking I could do everything myself. I knew peaches. My daddy grew them my whole life, but I didn't know horses. Short story is, I was riding and I shouldn't have been. Fell right on my neck. And here we are," he finished.

I gave his hand a squeeze. "And what about Anna? Where is she?"

The longing on his face sent a pang right to my heart.

"She couldn't handle it." Tears shone in his eyes. "It wasn't her fault. She could barely handle regular life, and I knew that. A failing farm and a husband who couldn't do anything for himself were too much for her. She left."

God, my heart broke into a million pieces. Clearly, he had loved this woman and still did. It was the most tragic love story I'd ever heard.

"I'm so sorry, Joe." It didn't seem like my words were enough, so I leaned over, wrapped my free arm around him, and laid my head on his chest, hugging him as best I could.

"Oh, Everly. Don't be sad for me. Like I said, I've made my peace with it, and besides, I have a big family here. Lots of people to love." He gazed at me, smiling, his eyes watery. "And, now, I have you, too."

Damn him. My heart split right open then. A tear slid down my cheek. Damn these cowboys and their innate goodness and kindness. Being here was changing me and I didn't know what to think of it. I never cried. Not even when I'd been on the streets and so hungry that I was doubled over in pain. Not even when I'd left my beloved Momma Lou. I was a pillar of emotional strength.

Being here, with these people, in this gorgeous, surreal place, was breaking me wide open, and it hurt as much as it felt good.

This feeling made me feel like I could fly, but it also made me feel weak. Helpless, even.

I trembled against Joe's chest. He'd just confessed so much to me and I hadn't told him the entire truth. I knew what I had to do. I leaned up and looked down at Joe.

"Hey, what's wrong, sweetheart?" he asked, studying my face.

Before the words were even completely out of his mouth, I said, "I knew Cole."

Confusion colored his features. "What—"

"I mean, I know him now, but I also knew him. From before. When I was sixteen, I met him. Just for a day." I bit at my quivering lips.

A confused smile covered Joe's face. His gaze implored me to explain.

"I was homeless." I swallowed hard. I didn't want to tell Joe about that part of my life. I wanted to be the woman he considered family. The woman who had lain next to him and held his hand while he'd talked about his Anna.

I didn't want to taint that woman with the girl from the train.

The girl who stole.

The girl who had nothing and no one.

I beat back the urge to get up, leave the room, and never mention that girl again.

"I slept in the train station sometimes, on the streets outside, or, if I was lucky enough, in a shelter nearby some nights." I paused, studying Joe's face.

His nostrils flared. His lips flattened into a firm line. He seemed angry and upset but said, "Go on."

I wondered if he would ask me to leave in fear I'd steal from him, but still, I continued. I'd said too much to stop at this point. "I stole from people on the train. They were easy marks, being travelers, and I'd never have to see them again." I laughed harshly, the irony of the situation striking me.

"Anyway, most people didn't see me. I was good at hiding. But

Cole? He saw me that day. My guess is he was on his way back here. The train was headed this way. He offered me a seat. He gave me food, and I was so, so hungry. He talked and talked, and I listened."

Joe smiled sadly. "That sounds like my Cole." His voice was so full of pride, and for the second time that night, I cried—only it came like a flood this time, big hiccupping sobs I couldn't make stop.

"Shhh, sweetheart. Don't cry. Come here," he urged.

I laid my head back on his chest and wrapped my arms around his torso again, so thankful that he wasn't about to throw me out, but I should have known better. Joe was good down to his bones.

I cried into the shirt. "You don't understand," I choked out between sobs. "After all he did for me that day, I still stole from him." I keened into his chest.

Joe pressed his head to the top of mine, offering me comfort, and it only spurred on another bout of hiccupping sobs.

"I needed it," I defended through my tears. And I had. Without that money, I wouldn't have eaten. Without that picture, I couldn't have made it until Momma Lou found me.

"Shhh," Joe soothed, and I didn't know how long I cried into his chest, but it seemed to me like it went on and on forever.

When I finally quieted, I was horribly embarrassed to have let such a torrential outpouring of emotion out on a man I'd only met a month ago. God. What in the hell was happening to me? Turned out Everly Woods did cry, and I didn't like it one bit.

I sat up next to Joe, scrubbing my face with my hands. "I'm sorry, Joe," I said, beyond embarrassed.

"Don't ever be sorry for talking to me, Everly." He looked at me kindly. "Thank you for telling me that. It must have been so hard for you."

I wondered if he meant telling him my story or living on the streets my entire life. I had a feeling it was both. His sweet understanding almost sent me into another crying jag. But he kept going.

"But I want you to know something. You did what you had to do to survive. It wasn't a good thing, but sometimes in life, good people do bad things because they feel they have to. It doesn't make those people bad. And you're good, Everly, down to your very core. I know it." Tears shone in his eyes. "I see how you've taken care of my Cole. I see *you*." He paused. "And I wouldn't change a thing."

Chapter 15

Cole

Something was different. I could feel it. The winds were changing. Everly would call this feeling my cowboy intuition, but that wasn't really a thing. How little she knew about farm life made me smile, and I admit I'd been doing that a lot more lately. So had Joe. At breakfast this morning, he kept giving Everly soft looks, smiling her way. She'd just grin back and shake her head at him like he'd lost his mind. She was at home here, and it seemed Joe liked it like that. I wondered if he would offer her a place to live here full time—for more than just a summer. The winds were changing, yes—because of her.

Everyone loved her. Any time I saw Ms. Jane, she'd go on and on about what a good girl that Everly was. It was no surprise that Cody and Everly had become the best of friends. Their big personalities suited each other. On more than one occasion, I'd caught them cutting up together. Even shy Leo made an effort to always be in the barn when Everly was there with the horses. I'd overheard them more than once talking and chatting. Sometimes, I'd feel a slight ache in my chest when I heard them laughing together. I'd just ignore it, though. I couldn't afford to have those feelings. It would ruin the good thing I had going.

Because, while everyone else got Everly, I got *Eve*. And, while Everly was pretty damn amazing, she didn't hold a candle to Eve. Eve had a lot of Everly's traits. She was crazy, loud, hilarious, genuine, and sweet. It wasn't surprising how everyone loved her. But Eve was more. And she was all mine. She was fiercely protective, so tender, so kind, and so caring sometimes that it hurt. It was a good kind of hurt, like when my Momma would drive Austin and me down the big hill near our house real fast. We'd yell, "Faster, Momma!" and she'd put the gas to the floor of our tiny pickup. We'd fly down the hill, our stomachs would flip up and into our throats, and the backs of our teeth would ache. We'd laugh and laugh, half elated, half terrified.

I got that feeling every day with Eve. Every day was a new adventure where I felt equal parts electrified and scared to fucking death.

She just fit here like some kind of puzzle piece we hadn't even known we were missing. She'd bulldozed in, surprising us, snapping her piece into place, and all of a sudden, here we sat, so damn complete that none of us knew what to think about it.

There was a lot I still didn't know about her. Like this Momma Lou person, who she'd spent the last few years with. I'd never heard of her. I knew most of Joe's friends. It was strange that I'd never heard of her. I didn't really understand how she had gotten here from Momma Lou's. Joe had only told me that someone would be joining us to help Missy with things around the house. There was still quite a bit more I needed to know about Everly and her life.

I did know one thing though. I wanted her to stay. I couldn't imagine a day without her here. I was thinking about all the things I wanted to still show her around the farm as I was saddling up Beauty and Beast because today was a big day for my Eve, and I couldn't wait.

"You're gonna be good to our girl today," I told Beauty, rubbing her behind her ear when I heard Everly's and Joe's laughter.

I came out of the horse stall just in time to see Joe speed around the corner and into the barn with Everly perched on his lap, her arms draped over his neck in a death grip. Her head was thrown back in laugher, her eyes closed, her hair a riot of toffee strands surrounding her head. They were practically up on two wheels when they sped into the barn, and I found myself laughing right along with them.

Joe was watching Everly, his eyes dancing, his smile wide, his laugh loud like Everly's. No wonder they got along so well. They were so similar—so daring, carefree. They were wearing identical grins.

They came to a sudden stop about two feet in front of me and a cloud of dust surrounded us, which sent Everly into another fit of laughter. She let go of Joe's neck and wiped the corners of her eyes with her fingertips. Then she fanned the air around us.

"You're gonna kill us one day on this thing," she said, grinning up at Joe.

"Never," he said, gazing at her. "I'd never hurt a hair on your pretty head and you know it. Besides, I had this wheelchair specifically designed to race all over the farm and I've been doing it for years. I'm a professional." His eyes twinkled.

She climbed off his lap. "A professional race car driver," she mumbled under her breath, smiling. She looked up at me. "What you doing out here, Cole?"

"I have a surprise for you today. You're gonna have to skip grooming the horses, though." I winked at Joe behind Everly. He knew that today was a big day, too.

Everly looked towards Beauty's stall and pursed her lips. "Can't we do whatever you want to do after I visit with Beauty? She'll miss me."

"Alrighty," Joe interrupted. "I gotta head out and check on a few things. Y'all kids have fun today." He sped off, leaving a trail of dust in his wake.

I put my arm around Everly's shoulder, dragging her to Beauty's stall. "Come on," I urged.

After we came around the corner, Everly stopped dead in her tracks. She stared Beauty up and down and then at the saddle on her back.

"Seriously?" Her eyes shone with hope and fear.

I could tell that she was scared. I wondered if she knew Joe's story.

"Yep. You think you're ready?" I gave a strand of her hair a gentle tug, grinning. I was so proud of her. She'd earned this moment.

"Yes!" she practically shouted. "Do *you* think I'm ready?" Her face was serious.

I hugged her into my side. "Of course I think you're ready, or I'd never let you get up on that horse. You've put in the time. Now, it's time to ride."

I let Everly go and grabbed her hand, bringing her over to Beauty. "Grab her reins and let's walk her out to the paddock. We'll get you used to riding out there first."

She looked nervous, but my girl was brave too, so she grabbed the reins, and I helped her walk Beauty outside.

"So, how do I get on?" Everly was so excited that she was practically jumping in place. "I'm a little nervous and I want to be as safe as possible."

I shook my head and smirked. "I don't know." I glanced her over. "I think you need one more thing before you ride."

Her face fell. "Are you for real?" She pinched my arm. "You're messing with me right?" She pursed her lips.

"Nope." I slowly took her in, from her cowboy boots, past her jeans and old worn flannel, straight to her hair hanging loose around her shoulders. "I think you're missing something."

Her brow scrunched. "Well, spit it out so I can get on this horse, Cole Briggs. You're making me crazy," she huffed.

"Wait a second. I think I have something in the Jeep you could use." I walked out of the paddock and to the Jeep before reaching into the trunk. I jogged back to Everly as fast as I could, hiding my surprise behind my back. I hadn't been this excited in a long damn time. I couldn't wait.

Everly watched me approach, her face full of questions and annoyance. I huffed out a laugh.

I brought the small, white Stetson from behind my back and held it out between us. "If you're gonna ride, you need a hat, right?" I smirked.

Surprise painted every feature of her face. "Oh my God," she breathed.

"Unless you don't want it?" I frowned, feigning sadness, and lowered the hat. Still, I worried that maybe she didn't care about a stupid hat. My heart thundered in my chest. I wanted her to love it.

"Oh my God," she said again. "That's mine?"

I held the hat out once more. "Had it made just for you, Eve."

The hat was weighty in my hand. I looked down at it. It didn't feel like I was handing over a simple hat. The banging in my heart said I was giving her something more.

The softness—the kind that only she gave me—sat heavy in her eyes. "Cole," she said sweetly.

And that *Cole* was loaded. It said nothing, but it said everything. And, all of a sudden, I was riding down that hill in my momma's car again. My stomach flipping up into my chest. The rush and the excitement thrummed beneath my skin.

I wanted to devour her.

Make her mine.

I wanted to kiss her.

I wanted to feast on her lips until my taste was permanently on them.

I didn't want her to ever be rid of me.

My cock thickened behind the tight fabric of my blue jeans. It wasn't the first time I'd been hard for Everly. Nearly every moment in her presence, I'd craved her.

My body had wanted Everly's for a while now. Only, now, my heart wanted her too.

The realization was staggering, and I took a step back and cleared my throat, fighting the emotion. I wanted this. I wanted it right now. I just couldn't have it. I needed to get things right in my life first. She deserved something more than I could give her at the moment. And I wanted everything for Eve. I wanted it all.

"Well, I'll just take this and put it back in the Jeep," I joked, trying to break the emotional tension.

She smiled sadly, like she knew what I was doing. "You better give me my damn hat, Cole."

I laughed. "Are you sure?" I walked over to her, holding the hat over her head.

She jumped up and down in excitement, clapping her hands a bit. "Hat me, baby!" she yelled.

I threw my head back, laughing loud before placing the Stetson on her head.

She gazed up at me, her eyes shining. "How do I look, Cowboy? Do I look badass?" She arched an eyebrow and smirked.

She didn't look badass.

I didn't smile because this wasn't a damn bit funny. "You're beautiful, Eve."

Fuck. She was. She looked like the most beautiful woman I'd ever seen wearing that hat.

That softness traversed her features again, but I didn't want that gut-fluttering thing again, so I glanced away.

But Eve knew. She knew me better than I knew myself, so she spun in a circle, her arms out towards the sky, her head tilted that way too. "A beautiful badass," she sang to the clouds, laughing.

I couldn't *not* look at her. "My Eve. A beautiful badass," I agreed, laughing with her.

Chapter 16

Everly

Cole showed me how to ride Beauty with the same painstaking slowness he always did. He pressed himself against me. He smelled my hair when he thought I wouldn't notice. His body was always too close to mine, but somehow still too far. I didn't know if he did it to torture himself or torture me, but I didn't care.

I was in love, and not just with my cowboy.

I was in love with Joe, these people, this farm. I was in love with sunrises from my front porch rocker. I was in love with long family dinners after a hard day's work. I was in love with dessert in my bed while cuddled up with Cody and a movie. And, now, I was in love with riding. I'd been out on the horse for a bit now and Cole had finally let me out of the paddock. I had Beauty going at a gentle trot. It was terrifying but exhilarating.

"Sit up straight, Eve," Cole said beside me, always there, taking care of me—looking out for me.

I straightened my back, grinning over at him astride Beast. He looked delectable, his big, muscular thighs tight around Beast's torso. His black T-shirt snug against the bulge of his biceps. His skin was tan and taut, and those hands that held those reins were rough and large.

I'd dreamt of those hands touching me since I'd arrived and first seen him. When, on occasion, Cole did innocently press those callused hands to my skin, I'd burn up. Once, this man's touch had just warmed me. Now, it was all fire and heat. A wild inferno blazed inside me. I couldn't think of that man's hands without igniting. So I averted my eyes and did what I did best—hid my feelings with hilarity and sass.

"How badass-cowgirl am I right now, Cole?" I said, raising my eyebrows.

He chuckled. "Extremely badass-cowgirl. The baddest badass I know."

I giggled. I was damn giddy. I reached one hand up and touched the Stetson on my head. Cole had given me a hat. I bit my bottom lip to keep from smiling too hard. He cared for me. I could tell. It was a sweet feeling to have someone besides Momma Lou care so much for me. And, when Cole had handed me that Stetson, his face had said it all. He wasn't just giving me a hat. I didn't know what else he was giving me, but I knew that it was something big.

We rode in silence, and the goodness of the moment settled over me. Until I noticed the wrinkle in Cole's brow as he stared off into the distance. He seemed distracted. His lips turned down in a frown, and I could feel him thinking beside me. I knew what troubled Cole. That look had become as familiar to me as Cole himself.

I'd promised myself I'd above all else be a good friend and help Cole, even if it pissed him the hell off. So I spoke up.

"Why don't you just go see him?" I asked.

He snapped his head my way, surprised by my question. "See who?"

I pushed my lips. "You know who. If you want to see Grey, go see him. He may not be your son, but he's still your nephew, right?" I said, slowing Beauty a bit so I could talk to Cole.

He shook his head. "You can't just leave shit alone, can you, Everly?"

No, I couldn't just leave shit alone. I wanted him happy, but I'd really pissed him off. He never called me Everly anymore. I was Eve, and I loved it. Everly felt like a slap in the face.

That slap hurt like hell, but I was tough and I'd survived a lot worse, so I kept on. "I'm sure your brother wants you to see him, be a part of his life—"

"Just stop right there. You don't know anything about Austin. He's a selfish shit, and last I heard, he'd taken all of the money and run off on Marla. I don't give a flying fuck what he wants."

I stopped Beauty next to Cole and Beast. I let out a deep breath. "All the more reason to go check on Grey, then, right?" I asked gently—quietly.

I wasn't trying to get Cole riled up, but he was still torn up about Grey. And the kid clearly needed him. A selfish part of me didn't want Cole within five feet of Marla, but another part of me knew he had to make peace with this situation, and he couldn't do that without seeing her and Grey.

"Maybe," Cole acquiesced. He stared off into the distance, deep in thought again, and I gave Beauty a nudge to get her going again.

The rest of our ride was silent. I wondered if I'd made a mistake by sticking my nose where it didn't belong, but what did it matter now? I'd been doing that since I'd arrived, and Cole seemed to be dealing with it okay. Besides, I cared, and I wasn't the type of girl to care and not do anything.

I walked Beauty back into her stall, and I was taking her saddle off and rubbing her down when Leo came in to help.

"Have a good ride?" He grinned at me.

Excitement was still coursing through me. "God, it was amazing,

Leo. I was scared, but Beauty was great, and Cole was so patient."

I heard Cole in the stall next to us putting Beast away. He'd likely stew on what I'd said for a bit, but he would come around. He was, at times, quick tempered, but he was also one of the smartest, most caring people I knew. He would do the right thing.

Leo snapped me out of my thoughts. "So, a few of the guys are going to Jack's tonight to have some drinks and I was wondering if you wanted to go with us?" He was bouncing from foot to foot and sporting a nervous smile to boot.

The slamming of Beast's stall door made me jump, and I wondered if Cole was really in that bad a mood from our talk.

I sighed and continued rubbing Beauty down. "I don't know, Leo. Isn't Jack's a bar? That's not really my scene. I don't drink." That was a lie, but only a small one.

I'd only drunk one time. I'd been fourteen and freezing and hungry. An old bum that hung around the train station—everyone called him Percy—had given me some of his gin. He hadn't resembled a Percy to me. More like a Ralph or a Bart, but I'd been starving and so cold that, when he'd offered me a few sips, I'd taken them gratefully. The liquor had burned my throat going down, and I'd almost coughed up a lung, but it had warmed me up enough to sleep soundly that night. The way I'd felt the next day had kept me from indulging again. I'd felt bad enough on a regular day without adding a hangover to the mix.

"It's a bar, yeah, but it's totally low-key, and Cody said he was going to go. You could ride with him." Leo seemed hopeful.

I wanted us to be friends, and it wasn't like he was asking me on a date. He was just trying to be friendly, and if Cody was going, I could tag along with him. Suddenly, it occurred to me that I hadn't left the farm in the weeks since I'd been here. I hadn't even wanted to, but I guessed some time away would do me good.

"All right." I nodded at Leo. "Sure. Sounds like it'll be fun. I'll hitch a ride with Cody."

I flinched when I heard another slam. This time, it sounded like it was right outside Beauty's stall.

Leo looked towards the sound, confusion furrowing his brow, before glancing back at me. "Awesome. I'm excited. See you tonight, Everly," he said, giving me that same nervous smile, leaving me and Beauty alone.

I had to admit I was excited to get out tonight and hang with Cody. I thought about what I was going to wear and how I was going to do my hair. I wondered if Cole would be there. I wondered if he would be alone.

Chapter 17

Everly

Low-key, my ass. I stopped dead in my tracks when I entered Jack's. It was most definitely a bar and there wasn't a damn low-key thing about it. And I was underage. Good thing Cody knew the bartender. It was loud and beyond packed. It was a Friday night, so I'd expected it to be crowded, but I honestly hadn't thought that this many people lived in the small town of Canton.

Everyone was wearing cowboy hats and boots. Voices were loud, and the alcohol was flowing. Dark paneled wood covered the walls and the floor. A few people milled around the old jukebox in the far corner and by the bar, but for the most part, people were doing some very fancy-looking line dances on the dance floor. I had never danced in my entire life. I hadn't planned on drinking, but alcohol was looking better and better at the moment.

"Sugar, you gotta keep moving your feet to actually get into the bar," Cody said behind me.

I glanced at him and rolled my eyes before looking back at the crowd. "I think I'm gonna need a drink." I wasn't old enough to drink, but Cody was.

He wrapped his arm around me and pulled me to him. "Come on. I gotta show off my sexy-as-hell date. How else am I gonna get the attention of every hot man here?"

I laughed, hoping that Cody was right and I did look sexy. I'd pulled out an old, white second-hand sundress Momma Lou had found me at Goodwill. It had spaghetti straps and a high waist, and it fanned out into an A-line skirt. It stopped right at my knees, and I'd paired it with my trusted brown boots. Very little makeup and silver hoop earrings had completed my look. I'd left my hair down because Cole liked it like that, and I was hoping I'd run into him. On the way out, Cody had grabbed the hat Cole had given me and placed it on my head. "Perfect," he'd said, dragging me out the door.

Cody slowly walked me over to the bar, his arm resting languidly around my rigid shoulders. "Relax, baby girl," he muttered under his breath so only I could hear. He ordered two shots of some kind of whiskey and placed one in front of me. "This should take the edge off." He brought the glass to his lips.

I picked the glass up and studied it. It didn't seem like too much, so I tossed it back, mimicking Cody. It burned like the damn dickens. I coughed a bit, and Cody rubbed my back.

"All right there?" he asked, chuckling.

"Yeah," I croaked out, already feeling warm from the liquor.

I gazed around the bar with pretend nonchalance, but Cody wasn't the least bit fooled.

"Looking for your Cowboy?" he questioned, a knowing smirk on his lips.

"No," I lied and shrugged. "Just checking out the atmosphere."

"Bullshit, baby girl, but I don't blame you. I'd be looking for his hot ass, too, if I didn't already have my eye on that one over there."

The bar was a big square in the middle of the room, and Cody motioned his head to a bartender serving the other side. As if he knew Cody was staring a hole through him, the bartender turned our way and…

"Wow," I breathed.

Emerald-green eyes set in a tan face danced as he shot Cody a wide smile. Gorgeous, deep dimples bracketed his pearly whites, and a bit of his thick, brown hair hung over one eye. He was wearing a tight, white T-shirt that showcased his very impressive muscles, and I spotted what looked like the outline of a nipple ring beneath his practically see-through shirt. He winked at Cody and turned back to his customer on the other side of the bar.

"Goodness." I fanned myself as I admired the bartender's ass in his tight Wranglers, because while I was in love and totally devoted to my cowboy, I was not dead.

Cody cleared his throat with an embarrassed cough and stared down into his drink.

"Oh my God. Are you embarrassed?" I shoved my shoulder into his.

He glimpsed up at me, his cheeks pink.

"You are," I said in awe. "You're totally embarrassed. Well, now, I gotta know. Who is this man who can embarrass the unembarrassable?"

Cody smirked. "I'm not embarrassed." He pulled at his collar awkwardly and peered at the bartender through hooded eyes. "And that gorgeous man across the bar is the one and only Beau Williams, star quarterback in high school, firefighter by day, bartender by night, and my best friend since I was six years old."

I placed my palm to my chest. "You're cheating on me?" I gasped in mock horror. I was shocked, but not because Cody had another best friend. The fact that he so obviously had a crush on him was shocking. I couldn't blame him though; the man was beautiful. "So is he—"

"Nope. Straight as an arrow our whole lives," Cody finished.

I frowned and poked my bottom lip out. "Well, that blows."

"And not in the good way," Cody said, frowning.

I scooted closer to Cody and rubbed his back. "So, nothing's ever happened with you two?" I asked genuinely concerned. It seemed like he had deeper feelings than friendship for Beau.

Cody spotted Leo across the bar and gave him a nod. "Something happened a couple of weeks ago when we were drunk and I've been avoiding him ever since. It's weird now, and I'm not ready to talk to him about it yet."

"What the what? And you didn't tell me? What the hell happened?" I needed all the damn information now.

The time for information had passed though, because Leo and a few guys who helped around the farm crowded us, shaking hands, bumping fists, and all the other general macho shit that guys did when they saw each other.

Leo claimed the stool to my right because Cody was on my left. "What do ya think of Jack's?"

I raised my eyebrows and gave him a pointed look. "It looks like a bar, and not a low-key one."

He looked a little sheepish, and I felt bad for giving him a hard time.

"Yeah," he said. "I may have bent the truth a little, but I wanted you to come out with us."

I smiled and nudged him with my shoulder. "It's cool."

"Can I get you guys something else to drink?" Beau asked, standing there in all of his movie-star-looking glory. He was still sporting that dimpled grin.

I examined Cody, who was staring into his drink again.

"Ryder," Beau said, at Cody. "Haven't seen you around lately." He'd said it casually, but I'd heard the undertones of accusation.

Cody finally looked at Beau before staring at the bar again. "Yeah, man. Sorry. Been busy at the farm." He fidgeted with his empty glass. "We'll take a couple more shots of whiskey."

Beau turned around to make our drinks.

Under the bar, I pinched Cody's leg. "Ryder?" I mouthed, my eyes large and round, because I wanted the story behind that nickname.

Cody rolled his eyes at me just as Beau sat our drinks in front of us. I thought Beau missed our interaction, but turned out I was dead wrong.

"Cody's always liked to ride. Ain't that right?" he asked, scowling over at Cody. Once again, his statement was loaded with accusation.

I made big eyes at Cody again because, now, I was more than intrigued. I wanted all the details.

Beau leaned over the bar and flashed me his show-stopping smile, and I couldn't help but grin back at those dimples and dancing eyes.

"I'm Beau, by the way. You must be Everly." He took my hand and brought it to his lips before pressing a slow kiss to the top.

He placed my hand back on the bar and bit his lip giving me those dimples, and I was pretty sure I heard every pair of panties in the bar hit the floor. I blew a breath out, picked my shot up, and downed it. Holy moly. Beau was a smooth operator. Cody didn't stand a chance.

"Ryder's never had good manners, but I'd say it's gotten worse lately, not returning my calls or introducing me to his pretty lady friends and all," Beau said, casually wiping the bar, but there was not a damn thing casual about his comment.

Cody's eyes were narrowed on Beau.

I gave Beau a friendly smile. "Nice to meet you, Beau, but I think we're gonna need a couple more shots."

"No problemo," Beau said, giving the top of Cody's head one more glance before going to get our drinks.

I rubbed Cody's back and pulled him in for a side hug. "You okay?"

"I don't know," he grumbled, pulling his hat off and running his hands through his hair.

My heart went out to my boy. I'd never seen him so stressed, so serious. We needed more alcohol STAT.

Two shots later, I was surprisingly only feeling slightly buzzed. Beau came over every now and then and threw a few comments Cody's way, which only served to make my friend want to pull his hair out. Cody brooded on his stool, hardly saying a word most of the night, and I spent the next couple of hours fending off advances from Leo.

I should have stayed home. My shoulders slumped when I thought about how I hadn't seen Cole all night, and trust me, I'd been looking for him—nonstop. *Home.* I didn't know when I'd come to think of the big house as home, but somehow, over the past few weeks, that is exactly what I'd thought of Preston's and the people who inhabited it. Home.

Leo made one final attempt to get me on the dance floor, to which I responded with a polite, "No, thank you. I have to use the restroom." And I did, so I didn't feel bad about blowing him off.

When I stepped off my stool for the first time that night, I realized one important thing: I was completely drunk. Like, fall-on-my-face drunk. One step off my seat and my body registered every bit of alcohol I'd poured into it.

My vision swam, and I teetered on my boots all the way to the bathroom, praying that I made it there without making a spectacle of myself. I peed for what felt like ten minutes and then checked myself in the bathroom mirror. Red eyes and smudged mascara stared back at me, and I spent the next five minutes trying to scrub the black from beneath my eyes. I wasn't very good at it because…drunk. Fuck. I splashed cold water on my face a couple of times. I was going to feel like absolute hell tomorrow. And I really only had my socially awkward self to blame. And Cody. And Leo. Bastards.

I stumbled out of the bathroom and back into the noise of Jack's. Cody was gone from his station at the bar, and Beau was gone too. That left Leo sitting there, nursing his beer. I'd hit my limit with him and his flirting for the night and thought some fresh air might do my alcohol-riddled brain good, so I stepped outside and leaned against the building for a minute. I closed my eyes and breathed deeply, hoping that I didn't get sick.

The air smelled like pine trees and something else familiar, so I took another deep breath.

Smoke.

Leather.

Galloping horses in my chest.

I cracked one eye open and smiled. "Cole."

Chapter 18

Cole

"You shouldn't be out here alone," I said, feeling like a stalking fool.

This town was safe, but I couldn't help my protectiveness when it came to Eve. I'd been watching her most of the night, her sexy ass perched between Leo and Cody in that dress. God, that dress. I'd never seen Everly in anything other than jeans and tanks, and that dress had almost sent me stomping across the room and throwing her over my shoulder. I wanted to take her home so only I could see how gorgeous she was. I wanted to strip her to her panties and taste every inch of her peaches-and-cream skin.

And, now, she was being fucking cute. She was leaning against the wall, one eye cracked open, an adorable Goddamn grin on her lips. One I wanted to kiss right the fuck off.

Popping her other eye open, she ran one finger down the middle of my chest. "I've been looking for you, Cowboy."

"You have, huh?" I arched a brow. I was calling bullshit.

She'd spent the entire evening chatting with Leo. She hadn't been flirting though. I was paying special attention. I sat in the corner, making sure that fucker didn't put his hands on my girl. I'd have killed him. I'd heard him in the barn today, asking my Eve out. Reining my temper in had always been hard for me, but hearing him practically beg her to come out tonight and then her saying yes? Well, I'd lost it. I'd slammed a few things around but managed to keep enough control not to stomp in there and demand that he never speak to Everly again. That's what I'd wanted to do, but I'd still been angry from my talk with Everly while riding. It hadn't been the time for more confrontation.

"Mmmhmmm," Everly hummed. Then she stepped forward and buried her face in my shirt. "Fuck. You smell good," she mumbled into the fabric of my shirt.

Her hot breath was warm through my T-shirt. She kept her face planted between my pecs and breathed in deep, and I chuckled.

I couldn't resist wrapping my arms around her and pulling the rest of her body into mine. I shook my head. "Still cussin' like a sailor, huh?" I asked, laying my chin on the top of her hat and taking her in too. Eve smelled damn good, too.

She laughed. "Still loving it," she accused in her singsong voice, gazing up at me.

I did love it. I fucking loved everything about her.

Her eyes were on mine, her lips mere inches from my own. I pushed the brim of her hat up so I could really see her baby blues. She ran her soft hand down the side of my face.

"You, Cole. You are the most gorgeous man I've ever seen." She slurred a bit, and I tried not to laugh because she meant it.

Fire burned in her blue orbs. I didn't want to diminish that fire, but this couldn't happen right now. Not yet.

"Alrighty, baby. I think it's time to get you home." When I stepped back out of her grasp, she fell forward a little, so I grabbed her arms and righted her. "I better find Cody and let him know that I'm taking you back to the farm."

She giggled and blushed. "Noo. You can't bother Cody right now. I think he's somewhere talking with Beau," she whispered.

Placing her away from me against the wall again, I said, "It's fine, baby. He won't mind. He'll be worried if I don't let him know."

"No!" she yelled. "You don't get it. They're talking." She started whispering again. "You know?" She winked real slow. "Talking." Her eyes got big.

I was looking at her like she was crazy. "Beau and Cody are"—I made air quotes with my hands—"talking?" I asked, making sure I was understanding what she was telling me.

She nodded, her eyes still big, her face serious.

"Wow. I didn't see that one coming." I was stunned. Those two had been best friends for as far back as I could remember. Was something going on with them?

"Me either," she whispered, shaking her head. "But I wish I could." She blushed again, and I shook my head, smiling at her antics.

"Well, come on." I grabbed her hand, pulling her towards my truck. "I wouldn't want to interrupt their talk."

"I would," Everly said, giving me a wink and waggling her eyebrows. Fucking adorable, this girl.

"Enough outta you. Behave," I warned, narrowing my eyes playfully.

She pouted while I practically dragged her to the truck. "I'm sick of behaving, Cole. I wanna have fun."

I opened the door to the truck and lifted her in, ignoring her comment. Because I was sick of behaving too. In fact, I couldn't stop thinking about all the bad things I wanted to do to her. She scooted back in the seat and her dress rode up, revealing the tops of her tan thighs. I groaned as I closed her door. I didn't think my dick had ever been this hard in my life.

I got in the truck and cranked it up. Everly's eyes were closed, her head resting back against the seat. I moved closer to her on the bench seat and reached across her to grab the seat belt behind her head.

"God, it smells like you in here," she breathed across my face.

I swallowed hard. I wanted her. I wanted her so damn badly that I felt like I'd die if I didn't have her pussy around my cock right that moment. But now wasn't the time. She was drunk. And Eve was right—I had shit to get straight with Marla and Grey. I couldn't put it off anymore, and I couldn't be mad at Eve for having called me out on my bullshit.

I snapped her in, moved back to my side of the truck, and willed myself to calm the fuck down.

I was backing the truck out of the parking lot, but I didn't miss the way Everly's hands grabbed the bottom of her dress and eased the hem a little up her thighs.

"I'm so hot," she groaned. "It's hot in here, and it smells so good."

The woman was going to fucking kill me. I adjusted my cock and cracked the window on her side. "That should cool you down." I cracked my own as well, hoping it would cool my ass down, too. After grabbing her hands with one of mine, I stilled them in her lap. If that skirt rode up one more inch, I couldn't be held responsible for my actions.

Her eyes on me, she smirked. "Aww. Don't be a fuddy-duddy, Cowboy." She pretend pouted.

I laughed. "A fuddy-duddy? What the hell is that?" I focused on the road.

"That's you." She pointed her drunk finger at me. "You're a fuddy-duddy, but that's okay. I don't mind."

"You don't mind? Why's that?" I was grinning because she was cute and crazy.

She leaned her head back and closed her eyes again before saying, "You can put up with a lot if a man is sexy, and you, Cole Briggs, are smoking."

I tried to watch the road and not gawk at her gorgeous ass as she told me how sexy I was. It was damn hard. I wanted to hear more.

"Yeah?" I asked as I pulled into the drive for the farm.

"Yep." She took her hat off, placed it on the dashboard, and ran her fingers through her hair. "You're so hot..." She stopped, pursing her lips in thought and tapping her pointer finger against her bottom lip. "You're so hot that I wouldn't kick you out of bed for eating crackers." She undid her belt and moved across the bench to me as I pulled up in front of the big house. "And, Cowboy, I hate crumbs in my bed," she said right next to me, her lips a mere breath from my ear.

I sucked in a quick breath. Chuckling, I cut the truck off. "Noted," I said, trying to lighten the mood because it was thick with sexual tension. "You hate crumbs in bed, but not my crumbs. My crumbs are all good."

She climbed across my lap to straddle me and stared me in the eyes. "I don't hate anything about you, Cole." She lowered her ass to my lap, and I fought a groan back. "And everything about you is all good."

With the windows opened the air drifted in around us and I could smell rain in the air. And Eve. I could smell her. The sweet, pungent smell of her wetness floated around me, and I knew that more than a simple storm was headed my way.

Still, I just sat there, and it was like watching a tornado approach, only I didn't try to flee. I wanted it.

I stared at her legs on either side of mine, her white dress up around her hips. Her smooth, bare thighs were snuggled tight around my jean-clad ones. I leaned my head back against the headrest and closed my eyes. Eve could try the patience of a saint. And I wasn't even close to being saintly.

Fuck.

She rocked against my cock, and my head snapped forward, our eyes meeting dead on.

"Everly, this is not a good—"

"Uh uhh. Not Everly, only Eve," she purred close to my ear as she rocked her core against my throbbing cock again. "Yes," she hissed when my cock rested in the cleft of her pussy.

It was the kind of ecstasy I'd never experienced. The kind of deep connection and intimacy that only came with really knowing someone—best friends, family. Heat blazed across my skin.

I placed my hands behind her on the steering wheel to keep from touching what wasn't mine yet. She was drunk, but I was powerless to stop her. She felt too good, the only thing separating us, her thin panties and my jeans.

I was too caught up. I couldn't stop. I could only feel. I gripped the steering wheel and pressed myself up, meeting her every thrust. "Fuck," I growled out.

I could feel her wetness and her warmth through my jeans, and it wasn't long before I was meeting her every thrust. I was crazy with lust and want. I kept my hands locked on the steering wheel, but I never took my gaze from hers.

"Yes. You feel good. So good. Just like I thought you would," she said, rocking rhythmically against me. Her skin was slick with sweat, and her cheeks were flushed with the most brilliant shade of pink I'd ever seen.

Our faces were only an inch apart, her hot breath coming in pants and mingling with mine.

I couldn't help but encourage her. I was too gone. Too in the moment. Powerless against her wet heat and want.

"That's it, baby. Ride me." I gazed into her eyes and whispered, "God, you're beautiful and so wet for me. Come on my cock."

I barely recognized my own voice. The gravel and rasp in it only seemed to send her higher.

"Yes, yes, yes," she chanted, grinding on me. She placed her hands on my shoulders, gaining leverage to press into me harder. She rode me hard, her gorgeous breasts rubbing my chest, her pussy soaking the front of my jeans, our gazes locked in an intense, sexually charged stare down.

I was going to come in my jeans any minute like a fucking teen-ager, but I didn't care. I had Eve in my lap in the throes of ecstasy. I'd imagined this moment more than once, but it'd never been this good. I fiercely clenched the steering wheel between both hands, begging, "Come for me, baby. Come, Eve. I need you."

She threw her head back. "Fuck!" she yelled into the quiet cabin of the truck.

Her hair cascaded over the top of my hands, and I longed to reach out and grab the strands so that I could pull her to my lips and taste her. But I wouldn't taste her when she was drunk like this.

I wanted her to remember our first kiss because she wouldn't have any more firsts. Just me. But I took what I could, and I wanted her eyes. I wanted her to see me while she fell apart. I wanted her to know who made her feel this way.

"Look at me, baby. Look at me when you come for me," I ordered.

Her head fell forward, her hooded eyes once again on mine, her pink lips parted in desire. Her breath came in small pants.

"That's my Eve. That's a good girl. Keep those eyes on me," I whispered.

She groaned. "I'm coming," she said, gripping my shoulders. "I'm coming, Cole."

Fuck yes. She needed to hurry. I was so close.

"That's it, Eve. Come on my cock," I urged. I wanted to see her fall apart for me. Only me. Always me.

Her breath stuttered. "Fuck, fuck, fuck," she said over and over, her voice ricocheting around the cabin of my truck and hitting me square in the cock.

She quivered against me on one final thrust and moan. I groaned low and long in my throat as I emptied myself into my jeans, pressing up against her, wishing that I were inside her—apart of her. Our bodies shook and jerked against each other, and I pulled

131

her towards me, holding her tightly as we both came down.

"Mmmm," she moaned and collapsed against me, her face buried in my chest.

"Eve?" I said quietly.

Nothing.

"Baby?" I asked again, only getting a snore in return.

Chapter 19

Everly

I cracked an eyelid open. Sun. Oh God, it hurt. I closed my eye and sighed. Much better. I'd just stay in bed all day. Mmmm. Bed.

I shot up into a sitting position and groaned at the banging in my head. How had I ended up in bed? Fuck. I rubbed my fingers hard into my closed eye sockets, praying for some relief. I peeked my eyes open and peered down at my bra. I pulled the covers back and looked at my panties.

Oh. My. God.

Cole must have put me to bed. And undressed me. I groaned and threw myself back on my pillow and pulled the covers over my head. *Ya know? He just put me to bed after I'd molested him on the bench seat in the front of his truck. Like a two-bit whore.*

Oh Lord. He hadn't even touched me. He'd just let me ride him until I'd come all over the place. Okay, maybe that was a bit dramatic, but still. And had I ever come. It had been so good. I felt my face heat.

I slapped my forehead. Jesus. I must have passed out right after that. What in the hell was wrong with me? It was like I had no control when he was around. It was the damn alcohol. Even if it weren't, I was still blaming it on the alcohol. I'd stupidly drunk too much, and clearly, drunk Everly had zero fucking inhibitions. *Someone kill me now.* But he'd smelled so good. He was being so sweet and taking care of me. And I'd wanted him for so long. *Well, you had him Everly. Only he didn't even touch you. He didn't even kiss you. Stupid girl.*

What was I going to do now? I couldn't hide from him. He lived here. I lived here. Joe would know. Fuck. Would Joe know? Had Joe seen him put me to bed? *Damn you, fucking alcohol.*

Man. And I was already late. The sun was up and I wasn't, which on the farm meant I was really late. Pulling the covers back, I opened my eyes wide, determined to torture myself with the sunlight. I deserved it. *Open your eyes, Everly, and take a big hit of that sunlight because you are an asshole and you suck.* I sat up, still feeling not very steady, and noticed a tall glass of water and two small pills on the bedside table.

I threw the pills into my mouth and downed the entire glass of water, cursing Cole for being so nice and caring and giving. And oh, he was giving, all right. Because that orgasm—even drunk as hell, I wouldn't forget it any time soon. He had to have put those pills here. Damn do-gooder Cole and all of his good deeds. Ya know, taking a drunk girl home. Putting said drunk girl to bed. Making sure dumb drunk girl had water and medicine to nurse her hangover. Giving drunk girl an orgasm she'd never forget.

After a quick shower, in which I didn't sing a single bar because of my pounding head, some fast dressing, and I was downstairs in a flash. I was hoping everyone would be gone already, but it was just my luck that it was Saturday. I'd forgotten. At that moment, I hated Saturdays almost as much as I hated whiskey. Saturdays were slower on the farm. Most everyone slept in a bit, so when I walked in and saw everyone at the table, I mumbled, "Good morning," and headed to the stove to scoop some eggs and grits onto my plate. I ignored that Cole was sitting in his usual spot. I ignored the inquisitive look on his face. And I damn sure ignored the way my girly parts clenched at seeing him. Shit. If I thought for one minute that being around Cole had been hard before, it was going to be awful now.

Now that I knew what it felt like to ride him. Now that I knew the filth that came out of his mouth when he was underneath me. And, God, it was good. That mouth of his had sent my already sprinting libido racing towards an epic orgasm.

Yep, that was Cole Briggs. The giver of epic orgasms.

Although, I didn't know if he'd really given it, per se. I mean, I'd kind of taken it. I rolled my eyes at myself as I walked over to the table.

I sat next to Joe and kept my eyes on my food, not on the sexy cowboy across from me.

"Sleep well?" Cole asked, and I looked up at him.

That was a mistake, because fire and heat blazed in his eyes, and all of a sudden, I was back in the front seat of Cole's truck, my ass grinding against him. And I was way too sober to be there. Eep!

I dropped my fork onto my plate. "I gotta go." I bolted from my chair and out the front door. I left my plate there and everything. Apparently, alcohol didn't just make me horny as fuck. Evidently, I could add rude to that list as well.

"Everly!" Joe called, but I just kept right on trucking.

I thought about going to the stables, but that would be the first place Joe and Cole would try to find me, and I wasn't ready to talk about last night. I was embarrassed and some would say that was karma for having given Cody a hard time about being embarrassed last night, but I said it was all just bullshit.

I jogged over to the bed and breakfast to help Ms. Jane. She was always in need of someone to cook or clean or do paperwork. I spent the next hour organizing paperwork and cleaning the kitchen.

I also used the time away to think hard about last night. And me and Cole in general. I needed to get a grip on my feelings for him. Clearly, he didn't feel the same way. He hadn't touched or kissed me. I'd used him, and that wasn't right. I needed to get myself in check, and when I saw Cole, I'd just apologize. He was a good man and, above all else, understanding. I knew that. I was just going to explain to him that I had been drunk and out of my ever-loving mind.

I was on all fours, scrubbing the kitchen floor, when a pair of scuffed-up cowboy boots appeared in front of me and effectively blocked me in. He'd found me.

"Hey, Cole," I said, crawling around him, continuing to clean the floor, and pretending like hell I hadn't run out on breakfast like a crazy person.

"Get up, Everly," Cole ordered. He sounded mad.

Knowing he meant business, I got up, let out a sigh, and walked over to the sink to wash my hands.

I guessed that it was time to suck it up and get this uncomfortable conversation over with.

"I—" I started.

"Sit down. Now."

I looked up at him, surprised at how angry he was.

Geez. He really was pissed. I sat at the small kitchenette table and huffed.

Handing me a paper towel with something rolled up on the inside, he ordered, "Eat."

I opened the paper towel and found two biscuits already filled with butter and grape jelly—just how I liked them.

"We talked about you not eating and drinking enough on the farm, Everly. You promised," he reprimanded.

My heart beat double time. I didn't deserve this man's friendship, but I couldn't help but take it. Even if I hadn't planned it all, I was still a damn thief.

"Thank you." I smiled up at him and took a bite of biscuit, avoiding his eyes. Jeez. This was awkward to say the least.

He crouched in front of me and rubbed a bit of grape jelly from the side of my mouth. "I'll never let you go hungry." He looked at me intensely. "You know that though. Right?" He smiled a sad smile.

"I do," I whispered. I was so overcome with emotion that I could barely speak.

This man had me so twisted up that I didn't know up from down—left from right. Bringing me breakfast was his way of letting me know that everything was okay between us, but I still owed him an apology.

I studied my lap, avoiding his eyes. "I'm sorry about last night, Cole. I had way too much to drink. I don't usually drink, ya know..." I cleared my throat and put the biscuit on the table. "Anyhow, it was a mistake and I had no business straddling you and riding you like a prize bull." I twisted the paper towel between my fingers and then reached to my back pocket, making sure my picture was still there. My anxiety eased when I felt the frayed edges graze my fingertips.

Cole laughed. "And here I thought you were going to apologize for the passing-out part."

I rolled my eyes. Of course he'd bring that up. As if I hadn't already been mortified. "Well, I'm sorry for that part, too. And, of course, using you to get off." I blushed and giggled awkwardly. Jesus. *Somebody find some tape and slap that shit over my mouth pronto.* I couldn't stop.

He averted his eyes to the side. "No worries there, Eve, because I got off, too." Cole's cheeks were red. I didn't think I'd ever seen him blush.

"For real?" I breathed. *Curse you, whiskey. Curse you.* I hadn't been paying attention, and I'd missed all the good stuff.

He nodded. "Like a Goddamn thirteen-year-old." He shook his head, grinning, that blush still staining his cheeks.

We both laughed uncomfortably.

Still, I couldn't believe he'd come too. Did he want me the way I wanted him? Or had it been just the product of some chick grinding on his cock?

I swallowed hard. I stuck my hand out between us. "So… friends?" I asked, making sure we were good.

His eyes were soft when he said, "The best." He laid his hand over mine and squeezed. "Always."

I turned my hand over and squeezed his back, my heart flip-flopping in my chest like the pancakes Missy tossed around every Thursday morning.

He looked at me seriously and pursed his lips. "So, a prize bull, huh?" His mouth broke into a smile, and his eyes did that twinkling thing they did when he demanded, "Tell me more."

Chapter 20

Cole

"Marla called," Joe said, zooming after me.

Christ. She'd been trying to call me, and I'd been avoiding her calls like the fucking plague. I didn't want to hear about how she needed money or whatever stunt my brother had pulled lately. Their lives were like a fucking soap opera, and I didn't want any part of it.

I couldn't believe this woman's audacity. I couldn't even fathom what the hell she was thinking, calling Joe.

I walked towards the stables, determined to take Beast for a ride today. I needed some fresh air, and I'd been so busy lately with the peaches that I'd been lax in taking him out. In fact, I'd been so busy that I'd hardly even seen Eve since our talk at the bed and breakfast a little over a week ago except at meals at the big house, and I missed her like hell. The summer was a little over halfway done and I was starting to panic a little at the possibility of Eve leaving.

"What'd she want?" I asked, walking into the barn and straight to Beast. I didn't really give a fuck what Marla wanted, but I felt like I had to ask out of respect for Joe. He wanted to talk, so I'd listen.

I rubbed Beast down and started saddling him up, while Joe parked his wheelchair in the stall's doorway.

"She just wants to talk to you about seeing Grey, Cole. She seemed really upset." He cleared his throat. "She's sorry. Maybe you should call her?"

I wanted to tell Joe to mind his own damn business, to leave me the fuck alone and stop talking to fucking Marla, but I could see the reluctance to have this conversation written all over his face. This was Marla's fault for putting him in the middle. My fault for falling for her bullshit. Joe wasn't responsible for the shitstorm that was currently my life. No, Marla and I had cornered the market on that.

A thumping sound from Beauty's stall made me stop in my tracks. I looked over at Joe, who was staring towards the sound. Fuck. I was willing to bet my left nut Eve was in Beauty's stall, listening to this whole conversation.

Shaking my head, I said, "I'll talk to her," with a finality that let Joe know this conversation was over. I wasn't talking about this anymore in front of Eve. She'd try to fix it because that's what her good-hearted-self did.

"Sounds good," Joe said, nodding. He spun around and sprinted out of the barn at warp speed. He was probably as thankful as I was that the conversation was over.

I finished saddling up Beast like I hadn't heard Eve in the stall next to me. I'd been dying to take a ride with her, but now, I just wanted to be alone. I wasn't in the mood for one of her pep talks. I didn't want her assurance that everything would be okay. Not today. Today, I wanted to ride and think about what I needed to do to get Marla off my back. I wanted time to decide what I should do about Grey.

After an hour of hard riding, Beast was running out of steam. We came to a stop on a huge hill at the front of Preston's property.

The peach orchard was below us, the big house sprawled out behind it. The pink sun dipped behind the house as it set. I loved this farm like it was mine. Moving back here hadn't been a hardship after Marla and I had split. I'd never felt at home with her. This place was home. Joe was home.

I heard the familiar sound of hooves pounding the ground behind me, but I didn't turn around. I had known she'd eventually find me. She always did.

Eve and I had continued our easy friendship, and easy is exactly what I would call us. We just clicked. I still wanted her like my next breath, and I'd spent more than one night stroking my cock to the memories of what had happened in my truck. But our friendship was one that I valued above all else. Over the course of the summer, she had become my very best friend, my confidant, and the person I counted on more than anyone else. She'd come to mean something very special to me.

I continued to stare out over the property while Eve pulled Beauty to a stop beside me and Beast. I watched her admire the property, her eyes wide with wonder.

"Looks like a painting or a movie," she said quietly, admiring the view. "Sometimes, I feel like this place is all a dream. Like I'm going to wake up any minute and be back at Momma Lou's, in my tiny bed."

"Do you miss her?" I asked.

"Every day." She answered.

I nodded slowly. I knew a thing or two about missing people.

"But I can always just go see her, right? She's only a couple of hours away." She cleared her throat and looked over at me. "How far away is Grey, Cole?" she asked solemnly.

Nope. I wasn't doing this.

"No, Everly. I don't want to have this conversation, and you should stop your damn spying." I pulled my hat off and scrubbed a hand through my hair. "I heard you in Beauty's stall."

She huffed. "I was hardly spying. I was already in the barn when you and Joe came in."

"You need to mind your own damn business sometimes. You're always meddling and putting your nose where it don't belong." I was on a roll now, so I just kept going, getting it all off my chest. "I know what you've been trying to do since you got here, Everly," I accused. "And I know what you're doing now. So just cut it the fuck out. I'm not in the mood." I put my hat back on a little harder than necessary.

She pursed her lips. "Oh? Well, then please enlighten me. What *am* I doing, Cowboy?" She put a hand on her hip, tilting her head to the side in that "go on, tell me" kind of way.

So I did. "You've been trying to make me happy, always trying to cheer me up and make me smile." It came out like an accusation because it was. And I sounded like a child, but I didn't want to be fucking happy. I wanted to be mad as hell, and I wanted to stew in it. "For fuck's sake, woman, let a man brood sometimes!" I yelled.

I expected her to get offended—maybe lash out at me. And I was spoiling for a fight. Everly seemed like the perfect target.

I didn't get that though. She only sat astride Beauty looking like a Southern goddess. She took her hand off her hip and grinned—all damn smiles and rainbows and unicorns and shit—the hat I'd given her perched on her head like she'd been born with it there.

She was growing into this place like it was a second skin. And it was too damn gorgeous on her. She wore this farm like a beauty queen wore a tiara—she fucking owned it.

She leaned closer like she was going to tell me a secret. "Oh, see, that's where you're wrong, Cole. I stopped *trying* to make you happy a while ago." She beamed at me. "Now, I just *am*. I *am* making you happy. I *am* making you smile. And it's the most beautiful, wonderful thing I've ever done in my life. So, no, I'll never stop," she said with conviction. She backed away from me and leaned close to Beauty's ear. Then she gave the horse's torso a squeeze with her legs and a few clicks of the tongue before ordering, "Let's go, Beauty!" And they were off, leaving me and Beast in the dust.

I was stunned. Everly still never ceased to surprise me, even after we'd spent practically every day together for over a month. But she wasn't wrong. I smiled at her and Beauty as they galloped through the field. Everly's head was low, her brown tresses blowing in the wind. The sun was kissing her now-brown skin. She made me feel a lightness in my chest, and I wondered how Joe and I had ever survived without her. It seemed like the sun rose and set with her.

Damn her. She was right. She *was* making me happy.

I was like the darkest, coldest night and Everly was the sun.

Her light shining on me.

Her heat searing through me.

Forcing me to wake the fuck up.

To live again.

And, God, I wanted her sun. It felt so good to stand in it.

I couldn't resist her. I never stood a chance. And I didn't want to anymore.

"Yaw," I commanded, giving Beast a nudge with my heels, and he darted forward, trailing Beauty and Everly.

I was chasing the sun. Even if it killed me, I'd run it down.

Chapter 21

Everly

I skipped down the steps and ran into the kitchen, hoping to grab a drink and a fast lunch before I went to the stables.

"Oomph," I grunted as I slammed into a wall of a solid muscle.

"Where you headed to so fast, sugar?" Cody asked, his hands on my shoulders.

I smiled. "Cole and I are taking the horses swimming this afternoon." I rocked up onto my toes in excitement.

"Better make sure you eat and drink enough before you head out there. It's a hot one today," he said as he removed his hat. His hair was soaking wet.

"Whatchu been doing today?" I asked, looking at his belt.

"Working." He raised his eyebrows.

It had become this thing with me and Cody. Me and his belt buckles. He loved to see my reaction to them. Everyone else around here was used to his craziness.

I read it out loud, squinting. "Place forehead here." There was a picture of two hands pointing to the center of his belt buckle. I finished reading. "And blow. Sobriety Test." I chuckled. "Classy, Cody." I pursed my lips.

"Thought you'd like this one." He laughed.

We made our way into the kitchen and started making sandwiches.

He placed some bread in the toaster. "Fuck, I'll be happy when the season is over. I'm exhausted."

"How're things with you and Beau?" I asked before popping a chip into my mouth and taking a seat at the table.

"About the same, I guess." He sat across from me and frowned at his food.

I hadn't had a chance to ask Cody about what happened at the bar when we'd gone out, but I had a feeling that, whatever it was, it wasn't good.

"I noticed that you guys disappeared at the bar." I took a bite of my sandwich.

Cody finally looked up at me.

"Did y'all talk?" I asked.

"We didn't really talk, per se." He seemed thoughtful.

I grinned. "Well, what happened?" He was making me work for it.

He smiled back at me. "Wouldn't you like to know?"

"Yes, the hell I would, which is exactly why I asked," I sassed.

Cody raised his eyebrows. "Speaking of disappearing at the bar."

I shook my head. "Uh uh. No way. We aren't talking about me. We're talking about you and Beau. Quit trying to deflect."

"Deflect from what?" someone said behind me.

I turned around and found Cole standing in the kitchen looking at us.

"Nothing," I said, feigning nonchalance. I did not want to talk about that night again. It'd been embarrassing enough the first time.

"Everly was just explaining where she went to the night we were at Jack's." Cody batted his eyelashes at me and smirked.

Rat bastard.

"Oh," Cole said, opening the fridge and removing a bottle of water. "I heard it had something to do with a prize bull." He smiled behind the bottle of water.

I felt myself turn twenty different shades of red. "Okay!" I said a little loudly, jumping up from the table and then chucking my plate in the sink. I put my arm through Cole's and proceeded to drag him to the front door. "I think it's time for us to go. Bye, Cody." I waved on my way out of room.

"We'll talk about this later, Everly!" Cody called.

I pinched Cole's arm when we made it to the front porch. "That was dirty, Cole. How could you do that? I thought we agreed to never bring that up again!" I fanned my hot, red face with my hand.

Rubbing his arm where I'd pinched him, he smirked down at me. "We never agreed to that."

I gaped at him pointedly. "I did."

He laughed. "Are you excited to swim the horses today?"

I was more than excited. After our spat yesterday about me meddling, the last thing I'd expected was for Cole to chase me down and ask me to take a ride with him today. The way he'd asked had been surprisingly sweet, almost like he had been asking me on a date. Hey, a girl could dream, anyway.

"So excited. But I thought we were meeting at the stables?" I asked.

Cole grabbed my hand and pulled me through the small shed that held the four-wheeler. "I couldn't wait. I was excited too."

He hopped onto the ATV, and I climbed on behind him. There was a big difference between the first time I'd been on the four-wheeler with Cole and now. I hadn't really known my cowboy back then. He'd only been a fantasy—and memory. Now, I felt as though I knew him like the back of my hand. He was achingly familiar. Pressed as close to him as I could get, I laid my head on his back and wrapped my arms tight around his waist. His rigid body relaxed, and he patted my hand with his before taking off.

We hardly spoke as we saddled up the horses and made our way to the shallow creek that ran around the backside of the property. That was the thing with me and Cole. We joked, we fought, we talked, and sometimes, we didn't, but there was always an ease between us, a comfort that came naturally.

Cole was ahead of me as we approached the creek, and excitement thrummed in my veins.

"Wait," I called. I stopped Beauty, giving her a pat. "Good girl," I cooed.

Cole stopped right at the edge of the creek and turned Beast around to me, confusion on his face.

I shook my boots off into the grass on either side of Beauty. I unbuttoned my flannel and threw it next to my boots. Then I checked the ties at the back of my bikini top to make sure they were firmly in place. I'd embarrassed myself in front of Cole enough to last a damn lifetime; I didn't need to add flashing him to the long list.

The wrinkle between Cole's eyebrows deepened. "What in God's name are you doing, woman?" he demanded.

I shrugged. "Getting ready to swim with the horses?" I looked at my cut-off jean shorts and my pink bikini top. What was his problem?

Big guffaws of his laugher echoed out into the open air, and I jumped a little in surprise. What in the hell was he laughing at? Cole clutched his stomach and gasped for air before his ridiculous laughter started up again.

"What in the hell is so funny, Cowboy?" I gritted out, glaring at him.

"Oh, Eve," he chuckled out, wiping tears of laughter from the corners of his eyes. He and Beast trotted towards me and Beauty.

"Sometimes, I don't know what I would do without you." He smiled genuinely.

Even though I was spitting mad, butterflies swarmed my belly.

"You, Everly Woods, just like the small town, just like the train station I met you in four years ago. You. You're the only reason I get out of bed every day." His warm eyes were on mine. "You *do* make me happy, and I hope you never stop."

My throat was tight. My eyes burned with unshed tears. And those butterflies in my belly swarmed out of my stomach and into my heart. I clenched the reins to keep from trying to catch them before they flew right out of my chest. I did my best to contain the wobble in my chin, the tremble in my lips.

Cole had said a lot of wonderful things to me four years ago and this summer, but never had anyone, even Cole, said something so beautiful to me in all my life. And, for once, I was rendered completely speechless.

He cleared his throat in that way he did sometimes when he was uncomfortable and had said too much. He grinned. "Baby, we ain't taking *you* swimming." He laughed again. "We're taking the *horses* swimming, which is really just a fancy way of saying that we're gonna let them walk around a bit in that creek water that's so shallow it won't even touch our feet, so they can cool off." He ran his gaze the length of my neck to my breasts, where he kept it for just a second too long.

He looked back to my eyes and winked. "But I ain't mad about that swimsuit, so don't go getting dressed again on my account." His eyes burned a hot trail down to my breasts again.

My nipples hardened beneath the thin material. I wanted to cover them in embarrassment, but instead, I straightened my back, pushing my chest out farther, and moved Beauty towards the creek so she could cool off. I wouldn't give him the satisfaction of putting my shirt back on after the way he'd picked on me. Besides, I wanted to torture the hell out of him. He wanted me, I could tell, and it made me high. The realization settled on me hot and heavy, and I was intoxicated with the knowledge.

Cole and Beast joined us in the creek, but hardly a word was said while the horses walked through the water. The air around us was thick with sexual tension—or, better yet, frustration. Because, yeah, I was frustrated as hell. The only consolation was that Cole was a hell of a lot more frustrated than I was. He couldn't keep his eyes off my body. Every move I made, he watched, his eyes like fire on me. They traced the outline of my bikini top time and time again only to dip lower to the smooth expanse of skin above my low-riding jean shorts.

It didn't help that Cole looked gorgeous in the sun, sitting astride that big, black horse like he'd been born a damn cowboy. He walked Beast through the water with a practiced ease that said he'd done it a thousand times over. The black hat on his head shadowed his face, making him seem mysterious and dark in a dangerous way that only made me want him more. With every pull at the reins, his biceps flexed and bunched, which pulled his black T-shirt tight across his arms and his huge chest. I didn't know how he'd finagled himself into those jeans this morning, because good Lord, they were tight, but I thanked the sweet heavens he had. And those black cowboy boots he had on sealed the deal—Cole looked like a bad-boy cowboy today, and I couldn't help but think of all the bad things I wanted him to do to me.

Cole and Beast made it out of the creek first and over to my pile of clothes in the grassy field. Beauty and I were right behind them. He climbed off the black horse and reached for my boots and my shirt.

Handing them up to me, he said, "Wanna put your clothes back on?"

I smirked. He wanted me to end this torture. I never wanted it to end.

I took the clothes from him. "No, I'm good. Thinking I could use a little sun on my shoulders," I said.

His nostrils flared. His jaw ticked. Yes, my cowboy wanted me.

I slipped my boots on but laid the shirt over my lap.

We slowly made our way back to the stables. My breasts were heavy and achy, and with every step the horse took, they swayed and rubbed against the fabric of my bathing suit, which created the most delicious and punishing friction. But nothing compared to the sweet ache between my legs.

I was practically panting by the time we made it back. Cole and I quietly rubbed, fed, and watered the horses, the air still electric between us. Cole put out hay while I went to the four-wheeler to get the water cooler.

I perched myself against the wall, watching him work, and taking a sip of water. He finished up and joined me, leaning right next to me.

"Can I have some of that?" he asked.

I didn't know if he wanted the water or me, but I passed him the cooler.

"Thanks," he said, trying to keep his gaze off my body.

He took a few quick gulps of water and handed the water back to me. Cole stared as I lifted the cooler to my mouth once more and took long pulls. A little dribbled down my chin and my neck, falling onto the skin between my breasts. Cole watched that drop like it was the last bit of water on the entire planet.

"Fuck," he said, closing his eyes and pressing his head back on the wall behind us.

His chest rose and fell quickly. Air whooshed past his lips as he seemed to come to some sort of decision. He opened his eyes and stood at his full height before removing his hat from his head and setting it on the ground. He placed himself right in front of me.

"You enjoying this game, Eve?" he asked, his eyes hot on mine—his face fierce. He was at his snapping point, and my dangerous cowboy was hot as fuck.

I arched an eyebrow. "What game?" But I was a liar. Hell yes, I was enjoying this game. *Touch me, kiss me, take me,* I wanted to beg. Instead, I stood there, a dare in my eyes. *Do it,* they said. *Take what you want.*

He placed his hands on the wall on either side of my head, effectively blocking me in, but he didn't have to worry. I wasn't going anywhere.

He brought his face to mine like he might kiss me, but he only ran his nose down the side of mine before breathing across my lips, "Take it off."

I snapped my gaze to his, a little of the lust clearing my head. I looked around the barn. "But someone might—"

"Take it off. Now, Eve," he demanded, his lips practically touching mine.

I loosened the strings that held my top up. The cups of my bikini fell forward, and I stifled a groan as the air kissed my nipples. I arched forward, offering them to Cole.

He hissed before running his pointer finger down the center of my chest, careful to not touch my breasts—careful to not give me what I needed. I arched more towards him as his finger trailed over my stomach and the length of my jean shorts before he grabbed my hand. He cradled it in his, just as he had the day he'd shown me how to pick peaches, and brought it to my breast, pressing my palm into the soft flesh.

"That's it, baby. Show me those pretty tits. Let me see you play with them," his gravelly voice commanded as he watched me bring my other hand to my breast too. His gaze never wavered from my hands as I cradled and massaged myself. And, when I pinched my nipples between my fingers and my thumbs, he let out a raspy, "Fuck."

He placed his hands over mine, stopping me, and I let out a frustrated whine.

He stared me in the eye. "Ask me."

My forehead crinkled. Ask him what?

He smirked at me. "Be a good girl and ask me, and I'll give you what you want."

What was he doing? Shocked, I said, "What?"

"I thought you liked playing games, Eve," he said, his face smug.

I wanted to strangle him, but he ran his nose against mine again and his lips were only an inch from my own.

"Come on, baby. Just ask me," he whispered.

"Please," I whimpered. "Please, just kiss me." I was past the point of return. There was no way I *couldn't* ask even if I didn't like his damn game. I'd dreamt of kissing this man since I was sixteen years old. I brought my arms around his neck and pulled him to me.

He smiled and gently placed his mouth on mine, and I was lost. So gone. His lips feathered against mine so gently, so softly, before he ran the tip of his tongue along my bottom lip. And the flood gates burst open. His heartbeat thundered close to mine. His hands clutched me like he thought I might disappear. His breath fed me, making me feel like I'd die if I didn't get this feeling every day for the rest of my life.

My lips were hot and wet against his.

His tongue tentatively slid out yet demanded to taste mine.

It was more.

Everything.

More than the fireworks I'd felt at sixteen.

It was explosive.

Intoxicating.

Debilitating.

It was fire and ice.

Sunshine and rain.

It was better than any sunrise I'd witnessed from my rocker on the front porch. It was more encompassing than any pang of hunger I'd ever experienced.

It was heaven and hell all rolled into one, and I never wanted it to end.

But, most of all, it wasn't some teenage infatuation.

It was real.

It was magic.

It was Cole and Eve.

Chapter 22

Cole

Fuck.

She tasted like Goddamn candy, and I wanted to eat and eat and eat. I bit her plump bottom lip and growled before sweeping my tongue inside her mouth. God, I didn't think I'd ever get enough of this mouth. I'd waited so long to taste Eve, and it was better than I had ever imagined—and I'd imagined it plenty. But nothing had prepared me for the soft mewls she made when our tongues met, for the way she clung to me like I was her lifeline, for the way she kissed me back with such abandon.

We were desperate for each other. With a simple press of my lips against hers, a match was struck. Fire—we were burning the world down.

I slid my hands up and into her hair like I'd longed to do so many times before. "You're gorgeous," I whispered against her lips before taking a long, slow lick of the inside of her mouth again. Jesus.

I wanted to devour her.

I pulled her hair, angling her head back further so that I could kiss the delicate lines of her jaw, the fragrant spot where her neck met her shoulder. I pressed openmouthed kisses on every inch of skin I could. I was crazed with wanting her.

Eve and her games had driven me here. She'd teased me beyond the point of distraction all day. That damn bathing suit had nearly killed me—all of her smooth, tan skin on display for me. I'd been hard as a rock, and when I'd handed her her clothes and her boots, part of me had prayed that she'd put them the fuck on so I'd get some fucking relief. The other part of me had hoped that she'd never get dressed again because she was fuck hot.

Since our night in the truck, my obsession with her had reached all new levels. I thought about her while I harvested peaches, mended fences, ate dinner. Hell, I even dreamt about my tiny pixie of a girl. She was almost always in the forefront of my mind.

I wanted her, and I was tired of waiting. At some point in the last few weeks, I'd stopped thinking of Everly as Peaches, the broken young girl from the train. She was Eve now. A woman.

She was strong, fierce—a Goddamn force to be reckoned with. She was mine.

I breathed her in, pulling her scent into me. Honeysuckle. That's what she smelled like. I wrapped my arms around her ass, hoisting her up. Her legs wrapped around me and tightened, which brought her pussy into direct contact with my cock.

"Yes," Eve groaned as I walked us to the pile of hay in the corner and laid her down.

I cradled her ample breasts in my hands and rubbed my thumbs over her hard, dusky-pink nipples. My mouth watered at the thought of tasting them.

Arching her back, she offered them to me, and I knew she wanted my mouth. I wanted to taste her just as much, but I wanted her to ask me. It had all started as a game to tease her the way she'd teased me, but once she'd begged me to kiss her, I'd quickly realized I liked when she asked and begged. In fact, I loved it.

I leaned close to her chest, gently blowing across the sensitive peaks of her gorgeous tits. "Ask me," I ordered quietly, running my nose down the middle of her chest and taking in her sweet honey-suckle scent, which I'd never get enough of.

"Please," she breathed. "Fuck, please. Kiss them." She moaned. "Suck them. Do something, Cole," she gritted out.

There was my bossy woman. I chuckled and lowered my mouth, giving one nipple a long lick.

"Yesss," she hissed out when I blew on her now-wet nipple.

Placing my hands under her, I cradled her body. I looked at her glossy, brown hair fanned out in the hay, her pink bathing suit top around her waist, her cut-off jean shorts and her brown boots. She was a cowboy's wet dream, and she was mine. I was a lucky bastard.

With my hands on her back, I pressed her breasts up and took one of her delicious nipples into my mouth. I pulled hard on the peak before running the edge of my teeth across it.

Everly gasped at the contact, and I looked up, taking in her pink cheeks and parted, kiss-bruised mouth.

That gasp went straight to my dick and I snapped, feasting on her breasts, gorging myself on the globes, and tasting her candy-like nipples over and over again. She moaned and her body trembled beneath mine, and still, I couldn't get enough. I pulled hard with my mouth at one pretty, pink tip while pinching the other between my fingers to only switch and do it all over again. I could have gone all day.

"Cole!"

I froze. Then I gaped at Everly, seeing the panic on her face. I pulled my hand from beneath her and laid my finger across my lips. "Shh."

"Everly!"

Fuck, it was Joe, and he was coming our way and getting closer by the second. I covered Eve's body with my own in case he came back our way.

"Out!" I yelled from my spot over Eve.

"What?" Joe yelled back in a confused voice.

Eve's eyes were wide and scared.

I placed a soft kiss on her lips to soothe her before yelling, "For fuck's sake, Joe, get out!"

It was quiet for a moment before we heard a mumbled, "And here I thought I owned this joint." After another bit of silence, Joe said loudly, "Fine, I'm leaving, but I better see the two of you for dinner in fifteen minutes. Do not be late." Then Joe's wheelchair crunched over the dirt and gravel as he left.

"Fuck, that was close," she whispered.

I smiled at her. She was the most beautiful woman I'd ever seen. I looked at her kind, giving, selfless eyes and thought maybe Eve had been sent to me right when I'd needed her. She was there to save me from myself. And she had.

"Go out with me," I said.

She seemed confused. "What do you mean?"

"Go out with me," I said more slowly this time. "This Friday night."

Her eyes widened. "Like a date?"

"Yes, Eve. Would you please go out on a date with me this Friday night?" I spoke slowly again because she clearly wasn't catching on.

"I've never been on a date," she blurted out, obviously stressed at the prospect of it.

Laughing a little, I pushed some hair off her forehead, back behind her ear, "Stop panicking and say yes, Eve." I laid my forehead against hers. "Put me outta my misery already."

She leaned back, giving me her eyes. They got soft in that way that was only mine. She didn't share that arms-wide-open look with just anyone, and it made me feel special in a way I'd never be able to explain. That look said way more than she meant it to. It said, *I see you. I see the good. I see the bad. And I want it all.* And damn if that didn't feel like love.

"I'll go out with you, Cowboy."

"Yeah?" I smiled and planted gentle, slow kisses all over her face.

She giggled, "I've always been pure shit at saying no to you."

"Hey," I said, laughing. "That's always been one of my favorite things about you."

Her face got serious. "You have favorite things about me?" she asked, her eyes hopeful.

I cradled her jaw in my hand and rubbed my thumb across her bottom lip, thinking it was one of my favorites too. "Too many to count, baby," I said before laying my lips on hers once more.

Chapter 23

Everly

Oh. My. Hell. Glancing around my room, I drummed my fingertips on the tops of my thighs and tried to calm myself. Because I had a problem. I was in a predicament. I had a freaking dilemma. I was in a Goddamn bad situation, if you will. Because I had absolutely not a fucking thing to wear tonight and it was Friday. Friday. My first date ever, with the man of my dreams. And I didn't say *dreams* lightly. I had literally dreamt of Cole for years. This was some serious shit. I glanced around the room again at my very small collection of clothes tossed all over the place and my anxiety went through the roof.

Where in the hell was Cody? I'd only called him approximately five thousand times. He wasn't answering. I was going to kill him dead. DEAD.

I picked up the white sundress I'd worn to Jack's and tossed it aside. I couldn't wear it again, and I didn't even own another dress.

Full-on panic took hold as I glanced around the room.

I thought about calling Cole and canceling our date, but my cowboy never kept his phone on him, so it would have been useless. He usually left it back at his little house while he worked and hardly ever checked it.

"No, no, no," I mumbled over and over, taking in all of my worn jeans and T-shirts.

Okay. This was more than a bad situation. It was a huge disaster. I could have easily taken the money I'd made so far this summer and gone shopping, but I didn't have a few important things needed to leave Preston's like, ya know, a license or a car. And I had to be ready in one hour.

I picked up an old jean skirt and a white tank, thinking I could dress it up with a nice necklace. "Okay. You got this. It's no big deal. It's just clothes," I whispered, giving myself the pep talk of the Goddamn century.

A firm knock sounded on my door before Cody came swaggering in like everything was a-okay, like I wasn't in the throes of a freaking emergency. His bright silver buckle read *Rock out with your cock out.* I'd have laughed if I hadn't been so mad.

"Oh my God!" I said as Cody reclined on my bed. "Where in the hell have you been? I've been calling you all damn day."

Cody fluffed the pillow behind his head. "I know." His mouth tipped up into a half grin. "Nobody's blown up my phone like that since high school, when all the girls still thought I was straight." He crossed his dirty boots at the ankles.

I threw a pillow at him. "Now is not the time to be cute, Cody. Can't you tell I'm having an emergency? And get your dirty boots off my bed!" I took another look around at the mess that was my room.

Holding his hands up in a gesture of surrender and sitting up to remove his boots, Cody said, "Sorry. You know it's peach season, which means I've been in the orchards all day." He nodded at me. "All right, sugar. Tell me what the emergency is, and I'll see what I can do." He seemed sincere.

I sighed and flopped onto the mattress. "I'm going on a date with Cole and I have nothing to wear." I'd thought it would sound less drastic after I'd said it, but I was wrong, because admitting it out loud had only sent my already fast pulse skyrocketing.

Cody raised his eyebrows. "You called me a million times today because you don't know what to wear?"

I sat up and gave him big eyes. "Yes!" *I know, I know.* I was being shallow, and I hated myself for it, but I'd never been on a date. I'd never even had a man ask me on one. And it was Cole. God, I wanted it to be special.

Rolling his eyes, he said, "Baby, I may be gay, but I'm still a man. A man who doesn't know a fucking thing about women's clothes. You gotta find someone else to help you with your problem." He closed his eyes and crossed his legs at the ankle again, getting comfortable.

I slapped my forehead. "Oh my God, but you're all I have, Cody. You're it. Get your sexy ass up and pretend you're the kind of a gay man who knows something about women's clothing." I glared over at him. "Right the fuck now."

He gave me a lazy look. "We can pretend till the cows come home, sugar, and I'm still not gonna be any help. Why don't you ask Missy?" he asked, casually closing his eyes again.

My eyes bulged out of my head. Crap. I wasn't going to ask Missy. She was older. We didn't have similar taste. She'd put me in mom jeans and an apron for my date.

I shook my head. "No, I'm not asking Missy." I groaned and covered my eyes with my palms. I was screwed.

"Come here, Everly," Cody said, patting the spot next to him on the bed and then holding his arms open.

I rolled my eyes and huffed. Nope. I wasn't falling for his cuddle tricks. They'd make me feel all warm and fuzzy and loved and I'd forget that I was having a situation. A situation I needed to focus on.

"Come on now, sugar. Don't be like that," Cody said, giving me puppy-dog eyes and pushing his bottom lip out in a pout.

Arching an eyebrow, I asked, "That look work on Beau?"

He smiled so big that I could hardly see his eyes and said, "Every time." He winked and patted the spot next to him again before opening his arms wide.

Apparently, that look worked on me, too, because I crawled up the bed and laid my head on his chest, sighing. I already felt better. Damn him.

He wrapped his arms around me and then ran a hand through my hair. "Sweet Everly, I'm pretty sure you could answer the door wearing a paper sack and that man would still swoon at the sight of you."

I giggled against his chest. "You're so wrong. Cole Briggs has never swooned in his life." The preposterous thought sent me into another bout of laughter.

Cradling my chin with his fingers, Cody angled my face up towards his, his face serious. "He may not swoon, but I see the way he looks at you. We all do."

My laughter died on a gasp. "How does he look at me?" I breathed, my stomach somersaulting.

He smiled kindly at me. "Like you hung the moon, baby girl." He trailed a finger down the slope of my nose before lightly tapping the tip. He brought me closer, laying his head on the top of mine. "And I'm not convinced you didn't," he said so softly that I barely heard him.

My nose burned with emotion as I wrapped my arms encircling his torso and gave it a hard squeeze. I closed my eyes tightly to trap the tears behind my lids, because Cody, Joe, and Cole had managed to rip down every emotional wall I'd ever constructed around my heart and all that was left was, well, me. And she wasn't so bad.

I pressed my face harder into Cody's chest, thinking he had no idea what he meant to me. How special he was. That, if I had hung the moon, he'd been the one to hold me up so I could do it. That's what these people were to me. They held me up. They anchored me down. They made me a better version of myself. And, for the very first time in my entire life, I loved myself, and that feeling was priceless. How could I ever pay them back?

Lifting my head, I gazed at Cody, tears shimmering in the corners of my eyes, my heart on my sleeve. "Cody," I whispered, wanting to tell him everything. I wanted to tell him about the girl who'd stolen from the people who rode the line. I wanted to tell him about the almost-woman Momma Lou had taken in. And about me now. I wanted to tell him about Eve. How free she was. How at peace she was for the first time in her life.

"No," Cody grumbled out, uncomfortable. "Don't look at me like that."

"Like what?" I asked, grinning because I knew how I was looking at him: like he was everything.

"Like I'm some kind of knight in shining armor or some shit. Cut it out." He pulled on a few strands of my hair. "You're the only hero in this story," he finished.

I grimaced. "If you only knew." I blew out a breath. "Cody, I wasn't always a good person. I made—"

"Everly, I know who you are now. I know that you're the most caring, giving, loving person I've ever met, and that's all I need to know. Now, get your cute ass up and get dressed. Your cowboy will be here soon." Cody's eyes said this conversation was over. He sent me off with a hard slap to my ass.

I walked to the bathroom in sort of a daze, my emotions all over the place. I'd never had anyone be so accepting of me. Is this what happened when people loved you? They just accepted you the way you were? Flaws and all?

I smiled, my heart light and airy in my chest, as I dressed in my jean skirt and my white tank in the bathroom, while Cody continued to recline on my bed. I threw on a long necklace, my boots, and my hat before applying minimal makeup. Admiring myself in the mirror,

I was reminded of what Cody had said about Cole. About how he'd look at me like I'd hung the moon even if I wore a paper sack. And that offered me a little comfort.

"Let's see you," Cody said, twirling his finger in the air so I'd spin for him.

So I did.

He let out a long whistle before saying, "Beautiful—on the inside and out."

I blushed at his compliment. "Does Beau know how lucky he is to have your affections?" I asked.

He let out a dark chuckle. "I'm gonna go with a big, fat hell no." He pulled his cell phone from his pocket. "Looks like Cole is late," he said, effectively changing the subject.

With wide eyes, I said, "For real?" And, just like that, my anxiety was back in full swing. "What if he doesn't come?" I paced around the room, pushing my hat off my sweaty forehead. "What if he's changed his mind?" I bit my lip.

Cody snorted. "Stop talking crazy. Cole would never stand you up. Ever."

Literally two seconds later, I heard a light knock on my bedroom door.

My eyes shot to the door and back to Cody, and then I did it again. And then once more because I was a freaking lunatic. My eyes bugged out of my head at Cody, and he shooed me towards the door with a swing of his hand.

"Go," he mouthed to me, giving me a hard stare from my bed.

There was another knock, a little harder this time. I fidgeted like hell, checking every facet of my outfit again and then pushing my hat back down over my forehead before finally opening the door.

Cole looked gorgeous. Devastatingly handsome, even. And my skin prickled with the awareness that this sexy, ruggedly beautiful man was there for me. Despite trying to hold it back, a low moan grumbled out of me at the sight of him freshly showered and clean shaven. His hair was perfectly styled and a little damp. He was wearing a black, long-sleeved button-down shirt over dark-washed jeans. He rocked back a little on his black boots as he took me in.

I studied the bottom of my skirt, pulling at it a little, feeling like maybe I wasn't dressed up enough or my skirt was a smidgen too short.

"You look beautiful," Cole said.

I snapped my gaze up to him. He smiled at me with sweet eyes, and my panic immediately eased.

"You're late," I teased.

He raised his arm, showing me a white picnic basket. "Had to pick up food and take a shower."

"We're not going out, then?" I asked, reaching for my purse. I was curious what his plans were.

Coming into the room, Cole gave Cody a hello in the form of a nod. Boy speak.

"Nah," he said. "I thought we'd stay around here and have a bit of a picnic."

I wasn't underdressed, thank God, and a picnic was just my speed. I wasn't the type of girl who needed frills and fancy. "Sounds good." Then I waved at Cody. "Bye, Cody."

Yes, I left him in my bed. You don't kick hot men out of your bed. Ever. Even if he's your gay best friend.

"See ya later, man," Cole said, grabbing my hand with his free one as we turned to leave the room.

"You kids behave. Don't do anything I wouldn't do," Cody said, smirking.

"Is that even possible?" I threw over my shoulder while laughing.

"Hey, Cole," Cody called as we exited the room.

Cole turned back to Cody, raising his eyebrows.

"Wrap that pickle then slip her a tickle," Cody said, stone-faced.

It took me five solid seconds before I caught on. Oh Lord. My face flushed with embarrassment, and a nervous giggle bubbled out of me.

"Don't be a fool. Cover your tool," Cody laughed.

My mouth fell open. "Oh my God. Make it stop!" I yelled while Cole dragged me from the room, shaking his head and grinning.

We were almost down the stairs when Cody yelled, "Wrap it in foil before you check her oil!"

I stopped on the last step and gawked at Cole. "Why? Why is that happening?" I rubbed my forehead.

Cole only continued to laugh at Cody's antics and my embarrassment while pulling me towards the front door. I looked for Joe so I could say goodbye but didn't see him on my way out.

We hopped onto the four-wheeler, which happened to be parked at the front of the big house, and zoomed away, Cole's picnic basket strapped to the back. We sped through the orchard until we reached the center of it. I slipped off the seat and glanced up while Cole reached into the basket and pulled a blanket out. Then he laid it on the dirt floor beneath the trees.

"Our date is in the orchard?" I asked, smiling because it was breathtakingly gorgeous.

Cole sat on the blanket and patted the spot beside him. "I've always thought this was one of the most beautiful places at night on the farm. But here, lately, it's come to mean something more to me."

Reclining back on my elbows, next to Cole, I looked up at the trees over us, their limbs heavy with fruit, the stars twinkling between branches. He was right; it was beautiful there.

"Why's it come to mean something more to you?" I asked.

"Because here," he said, glancing around, "in almost this exact spot, is when I knew."

I looked at Cole, confused. "Knew what?"

He pointed to a tree about four feet to our left. "See that tree? You passed out right there. Scared me to damn death, and in more ways than one. I was scared you were hurt, but when you opened those eyes and looked at me so tenderly, I was terrified. Because I knew. I knew in that moment it was more than my body just wanting your body. It was just plain old me wanting you." He let out a sarcastic chuckle. "Still, I tried to fight it. I was an ass." He shook his head.

My mind flashed back to the day in the orchard. Him standing over me. I loved that he remembered that moment as I did, that it was just as special to him.

"No, you weren't." I placed my hand on his on the blanket, and his eyes met mine, smiling. "Okay, maybe you were a little bit of an ass." I chuckled, and he did too.

He reached for the picnic basket and placed it in front of us.

"I hope there's something good in there. I'm starving," I said, sitting up.

Cole seemed nervous as he opened the basket and produced two greasy cheeseburgers still in their wrappers from the fast food joint he'd picked them up from. "I'm praying you still like these as much as I remember." Then he pulled out two milkshakes.

Our meal in the diner flashed in my mind. He'd remembered. A slow warmth started in my chest and moved through my torso and out into my limbs, making me feel hot and lazy all over. This man. My heart almost couldn't take him. It was too much.

"You remembered." I smiled, took a sip of my shake, and made a low humming noise.

Cole leered at me like that noise made him want to kiss me senseless, so I did it again.

"You're playing with fire, Eve." He smirked.

"I like it hot," I said, my eyes daring him..

He laughed.

I asked between sips of my shake, "So, what's in this for you, Cowboy?" I was replaying our conversation at the diner from years ago and having way too much fun doing it.

Cole chewed on his bottom lip and nodded side to side in thought. But all I could focus on was that mouth, because damn. I wiped some sweat from my forehead and took a long pull of my cold milkshake.

"Kisses," he said out of the blue.

"Kisses?" I asked, confused.

He grinned. "All. The. Kisses. That's what I want." He took a bite of his burger.

My eyes widened. "Like, forever?"

His gaze seared me through. "And ever," he answered.

This was the conversation and date that dreams were made of. There wasn't a Southern little girl in the world who didn't dream about a handsome cowboy feeding her junk food in the country and asking her for all the kisses.

"I'm good with that," I murmured before taking a bite of burger.

We ate quietly underneath the gorgeous copse of fruit trees, the stars shining on us, the warm wind rustling our hair, tiny stars dancing in the sky above us. When our meals were done, Cole placed everything back into the basket and settled on the blanket, pulling me down with him. I laid on his chest, his heartbeat and the rustling of leaves the sweetest song I'd ever heard. He told me about what he had done on the farm that day. I told him about Cody's not answering my calls and how he was the most useless gay best friend I'd ever had. We talked and talked and talked until my eyes started to close. It felt so good to be that close to him. I recalled our day in the barn and wiggled against Cole's side. He'd been over the top, so in charge, so demanding. I'd been incredibly worked up, so in the moment, that I'd have done anything he'd asked of me, and I pretty much had.

And, even though I wanted more of those moments, I could tell what Cole was doing. This wasn't about sex. This was about more. Don't get me wrong. I wanted the sex—like *really* wanted the sex—I wanted the more, too. I wanted it all. So I didn't press for kisses or touches or any more than what we were already doing. And it was still perfect.

He walked me to the front door, and I wanted to invite him in.

Hell, I wanted him to invite me over to his place, where'd we have real privacy, but he just pressed me to the door and kissed me so slow, so sweet, so damn hot, the base of my spine tingled and my toes curled achingly in my boots.

"Goodnight, Eve," he whispered against my lips.

And it had been—the very best.

Chapter 24

Cole

"He's wooing her. It's the sweetest damn thing I've ever seen," Jane said, her voice dripping with the intonations of love in the air.

I rolled my eyes.

Cody grumbled before commenting, "Sweet isn't gonna cut it. He needs to tell her how he feels or at least invite her over to his place for the night. Everly is getting impatient, and that snake Leo is gonna try to make a move any day now."

"No. My boy knows what he's doing. Taking his time with Everly is smart and responsible. She deserves dates and wooing. Jane's right," Joe chimed in.

I gritted my teeth while I was beneath Joe's van. "You crazy people do realize I'm in the room, right?"

I'd come in here thinking I'd change the oil in the vehicles and have a little peace and damn quiet like I usually did every couple of months when I worked on the cars and the four-wheeler, but no. This nosy, meddling group had decided to interrogate me the entire time I had been working on the cars.

"What are your plans for you and Everly?"

"Are you guys serious?"

"Do you think she'll stay longer than the summer?"

"When are you going to make it official?"

These were just a few of the million questions they had thrown my way. Summer was wrapping up. And I needed to make things more permanent with Eve, but Joe and Jane were right. I'd spent the last few weeks wooing my girl. I had been taking her on long dates at all of my favorite spots. Last week, I'd even taken her back to Jack's. I hadn't let her drink an ounce of alcohol, but I had taught her to two-step. I'd brought her flowers, and we'd parked at a spot on the lake and talked and listened to slow songs on the radio. I was the wooingest damn cowboy around. Everly wanted more than dates and kisses. And trust me. I did, too, but I was on a mission.

Everly had spent the beginning of the summer earning my trust, giving me her friendship, and making me care for her, and most of that time, I'd been either a raving asshole or holding back from her. So, now, I was demanding she give me everything back in return ten-fold. Only I didn't want her to just care for me. I didn't want just her friendship. I wanted everything. I wanted her to love me. It may have taken me a while to warm up to the idea of Everly and me as an us, but now, I was all in.

"Oh, we're completely aware you're in here, Cole. Why the hell else would we all be in the damn garage in the heat of the day?" Missy snarked, clearly a little annoyed she had to be out in the hot garage but too nosy to stay away.

I twisted the oil cap back in place on the van and scooted out from beneath it. I sat up and wiped my hands off on a nearby rag. Everyone crowded around. I gave them all an annoyed look.

"If all of you are in here, who the hell is running this place?" I asked grouchily.

They all just looked at each other.

I got up and walked over to the sink to wash my hands. "What happens between me and Everly is our business and you guys need to stay out of it," I said, examining my oil-stained hands, but I knew they were all listening because I could have heard a damn pin drop in that garage.

A firm hand landed on my shoulder, and I turned my head and found Cody standing behind me, his face earnest.

"We care about her."

"We love her," Jane threw in.

I looked behind Cody to my family. They were clearly more worried about Everly than they were about me. And it didn't bother me a bit. It made me proud that they loved her like I did.

I dried my hands on my pants and said, "Okay, y'all, I get it. You're worried I'm gonna fuck this all up."

"Watch your mouth, Cole." Missy pointed at me, Jane nodding in agreement.

I smiled. "I'm not gonna mess this up. I want Eve to stay, and I've made plans with Marla to have her come over at the beginning of next week so we can move past all of this sh—"

Missy and Jane stared me down, daring me to curse again.

"Stuff. All of this stuff. After that, I'm gonna talk to Eve, make all this more official. She's not going nowhere, okay? So everyone take a damn chill pill and get back to work." I glowered at Cody and huffed. "I dare Leo to make a move on my girl."

The women looked over at me, their faces all full of mushy emotion, and I ran for my truck and dove under it to change the oil before they attacked me and we ended up hugging or singing "Kumbaya" or some bullshit.

"Cole's right. Time for everyone to go and get back to work," Joe said, herding everyone out with his wheelchair.

The crowd all headed out quietly, murmuring and giggling.

Just when I thought I was finally alone, I heard Joe's wheelchair pull up beside the truck. I looked over to the right and could see his wheels stopped there. It was on the tip of my tongue to ask him what he needed when he spoke.

"Real proud of you, Cole." And he was gone in a flash.

I smiled beneath the truck in the hot-ass garage. Joe was proud of me, and it was Saturday night. We were having a big bonfire on the property, and everyone was coming. I couldn't wait to sit around the fire with my girl.

Because of the mob of busybodies in my garage, I finished the cars a little later than I'd thought I would. By the time I'd washed up and gotten dressed, the fire was already going and the beer and barbecue were already being served. I grabbed a beer and walked around, trying to find Eve.

It figures I found her seated on a log near the fire, Joe at her side. Because, if I wasn't with her, chances were he was. He was beyond protective of her, and I loved him for it. I never had to worry about her because Joe or Cody or I almost always had eyes on her. Which was good because Eve was a bit of a wildcard.

"What did she look like?" Eve asked as I walked up.

I took a spot next to her on the log, moving in closer until my leg was pressed to hers. She gave me a soft look and then turned back to Joe, giving him her full attention.

Joe laughed, and his eyes got dreamy. "My momma was beautiful. She had blue eyes like the sky." He studied Eve. "A lot like yours. And she had thick, long, dark hair. I remember my daddy couldn't hardly be in her presence without touching her in some way."

Eve's eyes got all dreamy, too, and I smiled at the two of them, such hopeless romantics.

Joe went on. "When I was younger, it grossed me out how they kissed and held hands or even how he would sit next to her but always have his hand on her leg or back. But, when I got older, I realized what they had was something special. And, when I think of them, it's always both of them together, never separate. Theirs was a unique kind of love and so very rare."

Eve pressed her leg closer to mine as she gave Joe her attention. "I wish I could have met them, Joe."

"Me too." He sounded a bit choked up. "They would have loved you."

Joe's parents had passed in a car accident when he was only nineteen. He talked about them often and always with a fondness that made everyone aware of how much he loved them.

He let out a sigh. "Well, I'll let you two spend some time alone together. Don't need me cramping your style."

"Thanks for keeping me company, Joe," Everly said a bit shyly.

In the moment, a thousand emotions crossed Joe's face, and every one of them said that Everly had come to mean a lot to him. He looked like he was going to say something important, so I leaned forward, waiting for it, but his face cleared of emotion and he bit his bottom lip, seeming to change his mind.

"Anytime, sweetheart," he finished before riding off.

Eve fidgeted with her back pocket like she did sometimes when she was nervous and said, "What about your momma, Cowboy? Where is she at now? I think the last I heard you talk about her was four years ago on the train." Her voice was a bit strained with emotion.

I looked away from Eve and instead focused on the fire. "She passed away two years ago. It was sudden, heart attack while she was baking a cake in her kitchen."

Eve looked heartbroken. "I'm so sorry, Cole." She leaned closer to me, laying her head on my shoulder.

I smiled softly at her. "I miss her every day, but I'm not sorry. My momma and me were close, and I have no regrets when it comes to her. She knew how much I loved her, and I knew how she felt about me." I wrapped my arm around Eve, cradling her to me. "I take solace in that and the fact that she died quickly and it wasn't some long, drawn-out thing."

"Oh, Cole." Everly sighed and backed out of my arms, her face grief-stricken. "I stole something from you."

I quirked an eyebrow at her, not sure what was happening.

"On the train, four years ago," she whispered.

I laughed. "I know. I was there, remember?" I leaned forward, rubbing my nose against hers.

She pulled back again, shaking her head.

"Eve, we've been through this already," I said, trying to console her.

She was determined as she reached around to her back pocket and pulled out what looked to be an old piece of paper.

Eve longingly gazed at this paper for a minute, like she was saying goodbye to an old friend before holding it out to me. I tried to grab it, but she brought the paper back to her and lovingly ran her finger over it one last time. Then she finally handed it over with more yearning in her eyes than an old piece of paper warranted.

Concerned with the look on her face, I took it from her and quickly studied it. And my breath stopped. In fact, it seemed like time had stopped.

My mother peered back at me, her face soft and sincere, her eyes bright and sweet like I remembered. I ran my fingers over the yellow, slightly burned, worn edges while studying the photo in shock.

"She was in your wallet, stuffed behind your driver's license," Eve breathed, staring at the ground, lost somewhere in the past. "I took the money and went to toss the rest in the big dumpster behind the train station you left me at. Only I couldn't throw her away."

A tear slipped down her cheek, and her bottom lip trembled. I wanted to hug her, tell her that it was okay, and comfort her, but I also wanted to hear what she had to say. I thought of all the times I had seen her reach for her back pocket when she was stressed, and I couldn't help but wonder if she'd been reaching for my momma. And, if she had been, for how long had she been doing it? So, instead of comforting her, I waited and implored her with my eyes to continue.

Finally making eye contact with me, she swallowed hard. "I couldn't put her in the trash. She looked too much like my cowboy from the train. Too much like the only person who'd ever taken the time to know me, to take care of me." She smiled sadly at me. "She had your smile. Your eyes. So I kept her in my back pocket, and when I became too scared, too sad, too hungry, I'd pull her out." She nodded solemnly towards the picture. "She was the only thing that kept me going in those days."

I stared at the picture, letting her words sink in. Really letting the whole situation settle on me. She'd kept a picture of my mother in her back pocket for four Goddamn years because it had brought her comfort. Because *I* had brought her comfort. My heart was half aching for her. The other half was so full of love, of pure, raw, unadulterated, naked emotion, that I thought it would burst right out of my chest. Because that small girl on the train from four years ago? I'd felt sorry for her and wanted to help her, but the woman in front of me—God, I fucking loved her.

"What's her name?" Eve's voice snapped me out of my thoughts.

I wondered if she saw it in my eyes. How Goddamn much I loved her. I felt like I was wearing a blinking neon sign on my forehead that said it all.

I clutched the photo too hard in my big hands. "Margaret," I choked out, so overcome with emotion that it itched and burned behind my eyes.

"Margaret," Eve repeated, smiling and nodding like it made perfect sense to her. Like she was thrilled at the prospect of knowing the woman in the photo's name.

And then it hit me. She was. She was thrilled to know my momma's name. She loved this woman almost as much as I did. She'd obviously cherished this photo. And, even though I didn't have very many pictures of my mother because the fire had taken most of them, I couldn't imagine keeping this one. Besides, I didn't need it like my girl did. I had my memories I could play whenever I wanted.

I turned Eve's hand over and placed the photo in her palm, our warm hands making contact around the picture. "You should keep her."

"No. I couldn't." She shook her head, her eyes wide. "I can't, Cole. I shouldn't have taken it in the first place."

I pressed the photo into her hand harder. "She'd want you to have it. *I* want you to."

Relief passed over her face before she reluctantly took the photo, but I could tell she was happy to have it back. And I knew then that I'd do pretty much anything to make this woman happy.

Eve took one last long look at the photo before placing it back into her pocket, where it belonged. "Thank you." Her gaze pierced me. "For everything."

I grinned. "It's been my pleasure, Eve. Everything I've ever done for you has been my pleasure."

Her velvety eyes studied me, and I felt naked, totally exposed to her as she took me in. I wondered if maybe she finally knew how I loved her. How I adored everything about her.

I brought her body back to mine, and this time, she let me hold her. Eve stared into the fire while I took in the people milling about. I'd completely forgotten about them; I'd been so wrapped up in us. Her presence always seemed to blot out the rest of the world, and I didn't mind at all.

"I love the smell of campfire," she mumbled into my chest.

"Yeah?" I asked, smiling because I was deliriously fucking happy. Because Eve had made me this way.

"Mmm hmm," she hummed. "Smells like you."

"Me?" I asked, tilting her face towards mine with my hand.

She nervously cleared her throat and drummed her fingers on her lap. "I noticed the day on the train that you smelled like smoke. Like a campfire, sweet and earthy. You still smell that way." She ran her nose along the side of my neck, breathing me in.

I closed my eyes, enjoying the way her skin felt against mine. She stopped her exploration of my neck at my collarbone and placed a small kiss there. My cock went rock-hard at that kiss.

It was too much. So overwhelming. The combination of so much love and lust swirling around inside me made me dizzy to the point that I thought my cock would explode with it.

"Fuck," I moaned low and long, running my hand up the inside of her thigh just under her cut-off shorts.

And, when she whimpered and ran her hand over my hardness through my jeans, I was ready to erupt with this lust-love feeling I was trying to my damnedest to contain. I needed her. Now.

"Let's go," I demanded, dragging her hand away from my cock and clutching it in my own.

Chapter 25

Everly

I was pulsating with warmth, and my legs were like jelly, so I let Cole drag me the few yards to his place. I knew we were going there. His determined, sex-filled eyes said it all.

We climbed the porch steps to his cottage, me behind him, my hand in his, my heart feeling ready to erupt. I slowed my pace as we approached the front door, but he surprised me by pulling me around him and placing me in the small space between the door and him. He leaned forward, closing that space. I expected him to kiss me senseless against that door like he'd done almost every night the past couple of weeks at the big house, but he only delicately laid his forehead to mine.

He closed his eyes, his sweet breath fanning fast over my face, and then I felt his hand slide up the inside of my thigh and under my shorts.

He couldn't even wait to get us inside, and my head spun with the knowledge of how bad he wanted me.

I spread my legs, offering myself to him the only way I knew how, my thighs trembling at the prospect of what was to come. And, oh, I wanted to come. His fingers played at the edge of my panties for a second, teasing me, taunting me, before he moved them aside and ran one long finger along my slit.

Like he was in pain, he groaned lowly. "You're wet," he softly puffed across my lips, his face ruddy and sweaty with need. "And hot. So hot," he growled out, running that thick, rough finger back and forth over and over, driving me mad.

"Please," I begged, needing more. Needing him.

He pressed the pad of his finger to my clit, and we both gasped at the contact. I rolled my head back against the door and closed my eyes. But he was having none of that.

"Look at me," he demanded quietly, rubbing a slow circle around the tight nub.

And I did. His savage eyes stared back at me, so full of power and strength and love that they nearly destroyed me. The intimacy of that moment was almost too much to bear but too damn good to let go of.

"You're so beautiful," he rumbled. "Pressed up against my door, your face flushed with sex, my fingers exploring your pussy."

I moaned low and long. He knew what his words did to me. We both did. I was so caught up that I barely noticed the door give behind me as Cole ushered me through, his lips brushing the slope of my neck, his finger still firmly pressed to my clit.

The cold kissed my skin as he stepped back before swooping me up in his arms. I placed my hands around his neck, holding tight as he carried me through the house like some kind of damn western Prince Charming. I giggled, and Cole laid me down and stood beside the bed, gazing at me, hunger ablaze in his eyes.

Sitting up, I grabbed the buckle of his belt, determined to get this show on the road. Ready for him to finally be mine.

"No," he growled out, placing his hand over mine. "Let me." He grabbed the bottom of my T-shirt.

I lifted my arms as he slowly pulled it over my head. I shivered though the room wasn't the least bit cold. He tugged my shorts off my body, running the tips of his fingers all the way down my legs as he did. He removed my bra and my panties like he was unwrapping a special gift: slowly, carefully, dotting my body with hot, wet, open-mouthed kisses I felt right at my center. And, when I was completely naked, he laid me back on the bed and hovered over me, his eyes eating me up like I was his favorite meal, like he was in awe of me. Like he was the lucky one.

My body arched beneath his stare, craving more than just the touch of his gaze along my skin.

Running one finger from the dip in my neck all the way down to my naval, Cole praised, "You're so fucking gorgeous."

"Please," I whispered into the quiet room, arching further into his touch, needing him like I needed my next breath.

"Fuck, I love when you beg me." He palmed the thick length of his cock through the denim of his jeans and squeezed hard, grunting.

My pussy clenched and pulsated at the sight, and I wanted more than anything to see all of my cowboy.

I ran my hand over his, helping him squeeze and stroke himself. "Take it off."

The pupils of his brown eyes dilated until I saw nothing but black.

He moaned low like it pained him to separate from me as he stood next to the bed. Eyeing me like he wouldn't ever see enough of my skin, he started working his big belt buckle and toeing his boots off.

I hardly heard the clang of his belt as it hit the floor for the blood pounding in my ears. With every article of clothing that fell, my pulse raced, my pussy wept, and my blood heated in my veins. This gorgeous, muscular, kind man was mine, and I was never giving him up. It was a powerful feeling, knowing he was mine. I'd never owned anything so precious in my life, and I felt heady and drunk with the knowledge that I finally did.

Those broad shoulders. Those thick arms. The muscles tightly packed at his stomach. The hard lines of his hips. That small smattering of hair that led to his glorious cock. They all belonged to me.

And his good heart—that was mine too.

Lying on top of me, he pressed his body along the length of mine, and it somehow felt like I'd been waiting my entire life for this moment. His skin to mine. His hard muscles intertwined with my soft ones, and it was like coming home, a place I'd never been before. A place I only had with Cole.

The urge to touch him was impossible to resist, so I ran my hands through his thick, soft hair, down his broad back, and across his ribs before gripping his muscular ass and pulling him closer to me, until his cock was snug against my wet heat.

"Yes," he hissed before slipping his tongue into my mouth.

I expected his mouth to be rough and demanding, only he surprised me with the gentleness, with the deliberateness with which his mouth kissed mine, like he'd planned this kiss his whole life. He dined on me slowly, sweetly, like I was delicate and breakable beneath him. And maybe I was. But just for him, because only this man had the ability to completely undo me.

"I need you," I breathed while Cole slid the length of his cock along my slit, the head of it catching my clit over and over.

His hands cradled my breast. His fingers pinched the pink tips of my nipples. His mouth touched every available surface of skin it could reach.

And I was gone. So far gone that I was nothing but a panting, sweaty, wanting ball of need beneath him. *Nows* and *pleases* and *mores* poured from my mouth in garbled sentences he somehow seemed to always understand. And, when he reached into the bedside table, pulled that foil packet out, opened it with his teeth, and rolled that sucker on, I nearly wept with relief.

His cock poised at the entrance to my sex, Cole paused, peering down at me. "Okay?" His brow creased with concern, his gaze sincere.

I smiled, a tear slipping down my cheek and into the crease of my smile line. Because I was more than okay. I was amazing, but I knew what he was asking, so I nodded once, giving him permission to take what I'd been trying to give him since I could remember.

In one smooth stroke, he filled me up and I felt him everywhere, big and hard and smooth. He was in me, on me, all around me. I felt him from the tips of my fingers to the bottoms of my feet.

"So tight. So perfect," he gritted out before plundering my mouth, stealing my air, breaking off a part of my soul, and keeping it for his own.

I tightly wrapped my legs around him, the heels of my feet pulling him closer to me. I met his every thrust with one of my own. His pelvis hit my clit in the most devastatingly delicious way.

"Ask me," he demanded into my mouth, his breath shuddering, his voice husky and rich.

Even with my sex-addled brain, I knew what my cowboy wanted. And I gave it all too willingly.

"Make me come, Cole."

Reaching between us, he pinched my clit and hammered into me, pushing me farther into and up the mattress until my hands left the softness of his hair and clutched the wooden headboard.

"Yes, yes, yes!" I chanted again and again, my orgasm starting at my core and rolling through me like a huge tidal wave, taking me under, crashing into me, and stealing my air.

Hot and tingly and barely able to gasp the words, I exhaled, "Come. Come for me, Cowboy."

His brown eyes blazed down at me as he planted his big hands on either side of my body and surged up into me again and again, pummeling my body, using it for his pleasure.

"Take me."

"I'm yours."

"Fuck me."

"Harder."

"Come in me."

I whispered filthy words, my lips pressed to the lobe of his ear. Every whisper, every encouragement, they only spurred him on, making him surge into me harder and harder until he froze over me. He threw his head back and roared into the room, his body jerking, his face red and wet from sweat as he emptied into me on a long grunt that sent another tiny orgasm radiating from my core.

We lay together, sweaty skin to sweaty skin, beating heart to beating heart, exposed soul to exposed soul, Cole's crushing weight pressing me exquisitely into the soft mattress below us. And I never wanted to move.

I was finally home.

Chapter 26
Cole

I stretched and rolled to my stomach, reaching for the satin skin and honeysuckle smell I'd been surrounded by all night, but my hand only hit slightly warm bedsheets. A moment of ridiculous panic swept over me until I smelled it. Bacon.

My girl was making me breakfast, and I almost felt bad about the poor state of my refrigerator and my cabinets, but it seemed she was making do. I rolled out of bed and looked at the clock. It was eight in the morning. Christ, she was up early, and we'd had a very, very long night.

I'd taken her in every possible way I'd imagined over the past couple of months. And I'd imagined a hell of a lot of ways, but I wasn't done with her by a long shot, and I found myself exasperated that she'd woken before me and I hadn't had a chance to bury myself inside her again.

I'd wanted to wait until everything was sorted with Marla, until

I'd asked her to stay with me here at Prestons, to make love to her, but I hadn't been able to wait any longer. Our dates, our intimate moments, our undeniable love for one another—those had finally outweighed my need to wait. But I didn't have any regrets. I'd wanted her more than I'd wanted anything in my entire life, and I'd finally had her. And it had most definitely been worth the wait.

I grabbed my faded jeans from a pile on the floor and slipped them on. I tucked my cock in and zipped up, not bothering with the button. I started walking towards the small kitchen in my little house.

Eve stood at the stove, a fork in her hand, a dish towel over her shoulder. She was in front of a pan of frying bacon. Her hair was damp, and she was wearing my black T-shirt from last night and a pair of my socks she had pulled all the way up to her knees. Her hips swayed back and forth as she sang an old country song about a momma who turns her daughter into a prostitute and moves her up town. I contained my laugh as she flipped bacon with flare, and I couldn't help but hope and pray that I got to see this sight every morning for the rest of my life.

I leaned against the entrance to the kitchen, watching her putter around resembling every fantasy I'd ever had. I was one lucky motherfucker.

"Mornin'," I spoke from my spot.

A sound like, "Eep!" shrieked out of her. "How long have you been standing there?" She pointed the fork at me. Her eyes were accusatory.

I chuckled. "Long enough, Fancy." I winked at her.

She chucked the dish towel at me, blushing. "It's not nice to spy on people, Cole."

I sauntered towards her as she took me in, her gaze blazing across my naked chest and then pausing at the waist of my undone jeans. Then her eyes widened.

"I wasn't spying. I was enjoying the view." I grinned.

She raised an eyebrow, her eyes playful, lustful. "You see any-thing you like?"

"Plenty," I answered quickly, coming up behind her, placing my hands on her hips, and pressing my rock-hard cock into the crevice of her ass.

Fuck, she was the sexiest woman I'd ever seen in my life. I ran my nose over her damp hair and smelled my shampoo and soap.

"Mmm, you showered," I hummed. She smelled like me, and de-spite how many times I'd had her last night, I wanted her again. I wanted her now.

"Yep," she popped out. "I made breakfast, too," she said proudly, holding her hand out to the almost-done bacon in the pan and the toast she'd buttered. "You didn't have much, but I did what I could."

"Looks delicious," I mumbled distractedly, dragging my mouth down her neck, but I wasn't talking about the food.

She tilted her head back to give me her eyes. "You hungry?"

Using my hands at her hips, I spun her body towards me. My gaze traveled from the toes of those ridiculous but too-sexy-for-their-own-good socks up her body, all the way to the damp hair fall-ing over her forehead. "Starving."

A shudder ran through her as I reached behind her and turned the stove off. Then I lifted her and set her on the counter beside the stove. A breath whooshed out of her as I pushed her legs apart and ran my hands up the outside of her thighs.

I grinned when my fingertips hit her bare hips. "You don't have on any panties, Eve."

"I don't," she confirmed on an exhale, pride in her voice.

I laughed. "You're a bad, bad girl, baby," I accused playfully, plac-ing my palm at the center of her chest and pushing her back to lie down across the counter like my own personal buffet. I moved her feet up and out, placing her heels at the edge of the counter and far apart so that she was spread out for me.

I stood back, looking her over, counting all of my damn blessings.

"Now, be a good girl and let me have my breakfast." I leaned over and lightly raked my nose over her pussy, breathing her in. "You smell delicious."

And she did. My body wash and a sweet scent that was uniquely her filled the air.

She whimpered and brought her knees together a bit.

I tapped her leg with my finger and mumbled across her pussy, making her spread herself again, "Uh uh, baby. I told you I was starving. Now, let your man eat." Then I took a long lick from the bottom of her pussy up to her clit before running my tongue around it a few times.

Arching off the counter, she gritted out a, "Fuck!" that had me pushing the zipper of my jeans down so that I could reach in and grip the length of my cock.

I rubbed my fingers over the wetness clinging to the tip. God, I couldn't believe how ready I was for her all the time.

I brought her legs over my shoulders and pulled her pussy even closer to me, until my face was buried in it. She tasted like all of my favorite things.

I stroked myself hard with one hand and pushed her shirt up with other, past her quivering belly to her round, full breasts. Rolling her nipples, I devoured her, licking and sucking at her like she was my favorite damn meal. Every groan, every whimper, every sound that came from Eve's lips struck me like lightening, driving me mad.

After letting my cock go, I slipped one finger deep and hard into her, and that was all it took. Her hands pushed my head close to her heat, pulling the strands of my hair, creating the most magnificent fucking sting in my scalp. Her thighs closed around my head, squeezing. Her body arched off the counter and trembled as she came on my tongue, in my mouth, down my chin.

I slowly ate at her until she came down and relaxed. Sitting up, I drank up the length of her body draped over my kitchen counter. Her pussy bare and open, her dark-pink nipples peeking out from beneath the hem of my black shirt, all of that tan, creamy skin on display for me. It was too much. I placed my hand to my cock, giving it a long stroke and groaning. I could come just like this—watching her, smelling her, her taste still in my mouth.

It appeared that Eve had other plans though. She watched me too, my hand moving up and down my length seeming to captivate her. Sitting up, she slid off the counter and hit her knees in front of me.

I warned, "I won't last long." I was beyond worked up. I had a feeling that, with one touch of those kiss-bruised lips, I'd explode.

She slipped her fingers into the sides of my jeans and pushed them down to my knees before running one finger from the base of my cock to the head. It jerked at the attention. She smiled up from her spot on the floor, and, God, I wanted to tell her that I loved her. That I wanted her for forever. That, if she ever left me, I'd waste away on this farm until there was nothing left of me. But she leaned forward, taking my entire cock in her mouth, and all of my words of love evaporated into the air around us.

"Yes." I threw my head back and swallowed hard to keep from instantly coming down her throat. Fuck. I was overwhelmed.

I could still smell her, taste her, feel her all around me. I braced my hands on the counter on either side of her head to keep from fucking her beautiful face. Because, God, I wanted to. I wanted to grab her head and surge into that gorgeous mouth over and over. I wanted to feel the head of my dick at the back of her throat. I breathed through my nose, trying to calm myself, gripping the damn counter for dear life.

"That's it. Just like that," I gritted out between clenched teeth.

Fuck, she was beautiful on her knees, my cock between those fucking lips I adored. Her gaze fixed on my face, daring me to come.

It was her eyes that did it. I lost all control, grabbed the back of her head, and pumped harshly into her mouth. She moaned around my dick, it jerked against the top of her mouth. Christ.

"I'm gonna come, baby." I stepped back and released her head, but Eve wasn't having that.

She grabbed my ass in both hands and pulled me forward and into the back of her throat again.

"Fuck," I grunted. "I'm coming. That's it. Take it all, baby," I whispered, watching her swallow me. My knees trembled. My hands shook against her head as I emptied myself into her throat on a long groan.

She sucked down every bit of me.

"Jesus Christ," I breathed out as she licked me clean. Fuck, this woman. So unexpected and everything I hadn't known I'd wanted.

I didn't know where I found the energy, but I picked my beautiful girl up and hoisted her up and over my shoulder before giving her ass a firm slap. I ran down the hallway, my jeans still around my knees.

"Wait!" she yelled. "We didn't eat breakfast." She slapped my ass back, giggling.

"I'm not hungry for food," I said, throwing her in the middle of the bed and crawling over her, thinking I'd never get enough of her.

"Oh," she said softly, smiling and blushing.

"Yeah. Oh." I grinned, pulling her bottom lip into my mouth and running my tongue across it. "Unless you're hungry?" I raised my eyebrows at her.

She laughed. "No, I think I'm good." She wrapped her arms around my neck.

I didn't go to work. I didn't leave the house. I didn't eat. I made love to Eve in the soft sheets of my bed, her smell surrounding us. I fucked her bent over the bathroom counter, watching her reflection in the mirror as she came over the sink. I took her up against the tiles in my bathroom shower, the steam so thick around us that I could barely breathe. And then I laid her on the kitchen table and ate her for dinner too.

Chapter 27

Everly

In the orchard beneath the trees. On the haystack in the stables. Along the side of the creek bed. On top of the four-wheeler in the little shed out back. And in the small cottage Cole called home. He took me everywhere and in every way imaginable. My cowboy was insatiable. And I couldn't say I was much better, because if I wasn't with Cole, I was thinking about him.

I ran down the steps and into the kitchen, grabbing an apple off the counter. I'd helped pick peaches in the fields, and Cole had been busy doing other things, so I'd hardly seen him at all, except for at dinner. After that, I'd showered and dressed at warp speed, eager to spend the night at Cole's like I did most nights now.

It had only been days since our first night together and we hadn't spent a night apart since. Cole and I had settled into our new relationship just like we had our friendship: easily.

I turned around, headed for the back door, but Joe appeared in front of me, cutting me off.

"You headed to Cole's?" he asked, his brow furrowed.

"Yeah, what's up?" I sat at the kitchen table. I didn't like that look on Joe's face. He had seemed happy about me and Cole taking things to the next level, and I was worried he wasn't so happy about it anymore.

"Nothing, really," he said, joining me at the table. "I just wanted to have a talk with you and you haven't been around much lately."

"We can talk now," I said, and I meant it. I'd always make time for Joe. He and I had forged an incredible bond this summer, one I'd thought impossible to have with any man.

"Nah, you go on to Cole's and we'll talk later. Missy and I are headed into town tonight, so I won't be home for a couple of days." He swallowed uncomfortably.

"Something wrong?" I asked, curious why he was leaving town for a couple of days.

His soft smile eased me somewhat. "No, sweetheart. Just typical doctors' appointments and such. The appointments are super early both tomorrow and Thursday, so we're gonna stay over." His face fell a bit. "Being like this requires a ridiculous amount of appointments."

Nodding, I got up from the table. "Are you sure you don't want to talk now, Joe? It's okay, ya know? I don't have plans with Cole. I was just going over there to hang out."

He pursed his lips for a moment before answering. "No, we'll talk when I get back. You go have fun with our boy."

"Okay. If you're sure?" I made my way towards the front door, looking over my shoulder at him for confirmation and grinning.

He smiled back at me. I was hoping Joe wanted to talk to me about staying on longer or permanently. The summer was almost over. My time was almost up.

"Y'all drive safe now," I threw over my shoulder on the way out the door.

"Keep our boy in line while I'm gone," Joe called out as I ran down the steps of the big house.

I laughed because there was no way I was keeping him in line. That man had a mind of his own, and more times than not, I followed his lead. In fact, I'd follow him pretty much anywhere.

I was so eager to see Cole that I practically skipped across the field. I'd seen him at dinner, but I wanted to be alone with him. I wanted to see him without the prying eyes of others.

When I approached the small cottage, I noticed an unfamiliar blue car out front. My stomach dropped at the sight of it. I wasn't the type of girl who believed in premonitions, but I did have intuitions, and right there, while standing in front of Cole's house, staring at that old, dirty, blue car, I knew. Something wasn't right, and when I grew closer to the house, I walked right past the car. The car seat in the back sent my already dropping heart plummeting.

Part of me wanted to turn around and skip my ass right back to the big house, but my pride wouldn't let me. Cole was mine.

I usually didn't knock on the door, but the car in the driveway possessed me to do it before turning the doorknob and yelling, "Hey, hey!"

After pushing open the door the rest of the way, I entered the house feeling like my heart was in my throat. I hadn't felt this way in Cole's house since the first time I'd been there, when I'd been snooping and shouldn't have been there in the first place. Before I could think about that too much more, a woman appeared in the small foyer, a big smile on her face.

"Hey there," she said, seemingly at home in Cole's space.

I clenched my teeth and grinned back.

Her hand shot out to take mine, and I obliged because, even though I didn't have a momma, I still knew my manners.

"You must be Everly," she gushed. "I've heard so much about you."

I knew who she was. It didn't take a rocket scientist to figure out that the owner of that old, blue car and baby seat was none other than Marla. And the first thing I noticed about her was the set of white pearls draped on her lovely neck. Because those pearls sat delicately on her neck, just like they had on Cole's momma in the photo I carried around in my back pocket. But it wasn't just the pearls that made my stomach feel sour. No. It was her gorgeous, blue eyes. Her silky, perfectly styled, blond hair. Her impeccable makeup. Her pretty yellow sundress that complemented her hair to a T. She was stunning, this woman, and nothing like I'd expected.

In my head, Marla was the bad guy in our story, and bad guys didn't look like Southern beauty pageant queens. But she did. And, to make matters worse, she seemed genuinely nice. Not the kind of nice that was forced. No, this girl was happy to meet me. And me? I was thrown for a damn loop.

She pulled her hand back, and I realized mine was still hanging out there, so I snatched it back as well.

"I'm Marla." She smiled again, and I wanted to throw up. How could she be so perfect?

I nodded. I forced a weak smile back, which I knew looked that way. "Nice to meet you," I mumbled, but it wasn't. It was terrifying. She wasn't supposed to be so beautiful. So damn perfect. So fucking nice.

"Eve," Cole said behind Marla.

I stepped around her and found my cowboy standing there, his eyes unbelievably soft on mine. A baby sat perched on his hip, Cole's arm wrapped protectively around his tiny body.

Lord have mercy, but the sight of my cowboy holding a sweet baby made my ovaries ache. It made me think of our babies, Cole's and mine. It made me think of making a family with him. Only this wasn't my baby.

I stared at Grey, thinking how much he looked like Cole. And I thought that Austin must resemble Cole pretty darn closely for his child to look so much like him.

"This is Greyson," Cole explained, walking over to me.

No explanation was needed. I was all caught up on what was happening here, but what I didn't understand was why. Why were Marla and Grey there?

One chubby, tiny hand pressed against Cole's cheek, and he grinned at the baby before turning his face towards Grey's palm and buzzing his lips on it. Grey gave a hiccupping giggle, and Cole laughed right along with him.

My heart lurched in my chest, their connection playing on all of my insecurities.

"Hey, Grey," I said, taking his small fist in my hand and giving it a squeeze. I felt awkward, like maybe Marla wouldn't like me touching her baby, but she only grinned over at me, which only made me want to scowl at her.

She had the decorum of the Queen of fucking England, and I wanted to launch myself across the room and tear her hair out in jealousy. I took a deep, calming breath, reining my crazy in.

Not today, Satan, I coached myself.

Grey gripped my finger in his hand, garbled some words, and smiled at me, and I couldn't help but grin back at him. He was gorgeous and sweet and so innocent.

"Marla brought Grey over for a visit," Cole explained, his eyes imploring me to understand.

And I did understand, but that didn't mean I had to like it. Because I didn't. Not one fucking bit.

I wanted Cole to see Greyson; I just didn't want him to see beauty pageant Marla. I felt an odd ache I'd never experienced before in my life behind my ribs. I could feel that ache coiling inside me like some kind of vicious snake ready to strike. Envy. Jealousy. I hated myself for feeling that way, but I couldn't help it. I couldn't stop it.

"I didn't realize they were coming by," I said, my forced smile still on my face.

I was blindsided. Maybe if he had warned me, then I wouldn't have this hot emotion pulsing through me, trying to get out.

Cole's understanding eyes fixed on mine. "I know. I was going to tell you earlier today, but I was so busy I didn't have a chance to."

I nodded back, trying not to be the crazy lady I was.

"Do you mind if I come by the big house to get you after they leave?" he questioned, and I felt my stomach plummet to my feet.

God, I was intruding. There they were, doing family stuff, and I was an outsider.

I swallowed hard. "Yeah, of course." I barely got those words out.

I rushed to the door on swift feet, eager to get the hell out of there.

"Nice to meet you," Marla called out.

I gave a quick wave without turning around and choked out a, "Yep."

But I didn't stop. I couldn't, because if I did, that perfect woman with her gorgeous, sweet baby would see me break, and for the first time all summer, I didn't want to be Eve. I wanted to be Everly Woods. Tough as nails. Non-crier. No-bullshit Everly. Because Eve cared too much.

"Eve," Cole called out.

I stopped in the middle of Cole's yard, my back to him, my mouth thick and dry. Bitterness. That's how it tasted. I couldn't look at him, either, so I didn't turn around.

"I'll be over in a little while, okay?" He sounded resigned.

My throat ached. I nodded, but still, I didn't dare turn around.

And then I ran. I ran as fast as I could through the space that separated the homes, straight into the house, and up the stairs to my room, thankful Joe and Missy were gone for the night, relieved I wouldn't have to answer their questions.

I paced around the room. Why had Cole sounded like that? What were they talking about? Why had he asked me to leave?

I wanted to pick the phone up and call Momma Lou. I wanted to ask her what I should do. If I should do anything. I wanted to cry and tell her how much I loved Cole. How devastated I'd be if he went back to Marla. Only I couldn't make myself pick the phone up. I couldn't bring myself to be so emotionally vulnerable. I'd already put myself out there over the summer with Cole and look at me. I was about to have my heart smashed to smithereens. So I did what I'd done time and time again in my life. I rummaged through my duffel bag in the bottom of my closet until I found the shirt that always brought me comfort when nothing else could, not even Cole's momma's photo.

I slipped the old, patched-up shirt over my tank top, buttoning it up and rolling the sleeves almost to my elbows. I peered down at it, studying the patches and running my hands over the seams, praying that this worn piece of cloth that was older than me comforted me in the same small way it had my entire life.

I crawled under the bedsheets and pulled them over my head, lying in the dark, too many questions in my head. Too many hurts in my heart.

Chapter 28
Cole

It had only been an hour since I'd asked Eve to go home, but it had felt like an eternity. I'd seen her face. I knew she was worried about us, but there was absolutely nothing to worry about, and I needed to set her straight. So I hurried over to Joe's, let myself into the house, and went up to her room. I quietly knocked on the door but didn't get an answer, so I opened the door, careful not to scare her.

The room was pitch-black, but I did manage to make out the silhouette of a big lump in the middle of the bed. I walked to her side and sat, but I couldn't see her face. She'd managed to cover herself all the way up past her head.

I turned her small bedside lamp on and murmured softly, "Baby."

I pulled the covers back, exposing her messy hair and her rosy cheeks. I wanted to kiss the red on her cheeks. I wanted to run my hands through that mess of hair. And I wanted to do those things for the rest of my Goddamn life. No one twisted me up the way she did. No woman had ever had me so inside out and upside down.

"Wake up, baby," I tried again. I ran my finger over her eyebrow and down the side of her face before placing a kiss on her forehead.

She slowly opened her eyes, squinting at the light from the lamp. "Cole?" she croaked out sleepily.

Looking at her, I asked, "Why'd you go to sleep? I told you I'd be over soon."

She bit her lip and glanced away. "I wasn't sure if you were really coming."

"Baby—" I started.

But she sat up in the bed and scooted close to the headboard and away from me, the blanket falling from her body but all of her defenses coming up around her. I didn't like that at all, so I leaned forward, prepared to pull her back to me.

"Wait," she demanded, holding her hands out in front of her.

I sat back, prepared for her to unload on me for having sent her away. I'd let her, and then I'd explain that Marla and I were through. That she loved Austin, and I loved her. That I would see Grey as his uncle. And that hopefully I could persuade Austin to get his ass home to take care of his responsibilities.

I hadn't wanted to send Eve away, but it hadn't been fair to Marla to have the conversation we'd needed to have in front of Eve.

I grabbed one of her hands and brought it to my lips. I wanted to reassure her. Only halfway there, I noticed the shirt she was wearing. It was old. So worn that it was faded to practically white in some places, but where it wasn't faded, it was a blue-and-white plaid. But it wasn't the color or the age of the shirt that stopped me in my tracks. No, it was the patches at the elbows. Fucking jean patches.

Blood roared in my ears like a siren wailing. I was sure Everly was talking because I could see her mouth moving, but I couldn't hear a thing. I could only focus on those patches.

And then memories assaulted me like a machine gun, pouring

into me fast and furious like tiny bullets. Each one paining me with realization.

"We took care of what we had. We knew that nothing was really broken or irreparable. Not really. Anything could be fixed, even with something as small as a hug or friendship. Or a simple jean patch."

Fuck. How many times had Joe told me that story about the patches? No. No. No. This wasn't happening. It just couldn't be happening. This had to be some kind of fucking coincidence.

My conversation in the barn with Joe, when I'd been so hurt about Grey, bombarded my mind.

"I had a child once, ya know? She passed, Cole. I didn't get the option to have her in my life."

Had he been talking about Eve? Why would he have told me she'd died? Maybe Joe didn't realize Eve was his?

I thought of Joe and Eve together, their brown heads thrown back in laughter, their smiles so similar. Their fucking dancing, blue eyes so much alike.

I thought of how quickly they'd grown to love each other. How he fawned over Eve. How protective he was. How he told her stories of his momma and his daddy. How he treated her like his Goddamn daughter.

Oh, no. He had to know. He'd lied to us all, and it was going to ruin everything.

I took a deep, calming breath. Maybe I was jumping the gun. Maybe Joe had given her his shirt, but my gut said otherwise.

I grabbed Eve by the arms, jerking her close to me. She startled, shrinking back, so I grabbed her arms harder.

"Where did you get that shirt?" I demanded.

"Cole, what's wrong?" She seemed terrified, but I was too. I was shaken to my damn core.

I shook her a little, my temper flaring, so scared of losing her that I was sick with it. "Where did you get the fucking shirt, Eve?" I yelled.

She flinched. "Please, you're hurting me." She looked at my hands, which were wrapped around her upper arms, and I immediately loosened them.

Her frightened face fucking shredded me, so I let her go, moving back on the bed and clutching my hands in my lap so I wasn't compelled to put my hands on her again. Even though blood was still pounding in my ears like a drum beat and I wanted to scream with it, I softened my tone.

"Please, Eve," I hissed out on a whisper. "Tell me where that shirt came from."

I must have sounded like a deranged person to her ears.

She pressed herself against the headboard, getting as far away from my crazy ass as possible. Who could blame her? I was acting like a lunatic.

She clutched the front of the shirt like she was afraid maybe I'd rip it off her in my rage. "I don't know where it came from. I've had it always. I'm guessing it belonged to whoever left me at the train station when I was a baby. I was told I was wrapped in it when the authorities found me," she said so softly that I barely heard her.

But I had heard her. And, God, I wished I hadn't. She didn't know. But it all made sense now. Me not knowing who Momma Lou was. Joe hiring Everly for the summer out of the Goddamn blue. My whole body hurt. Because, when my sweet, loving, caring, giving girl found out that she'd been lied to all summer, she'd feel betrayed. Hurt beyond words. And fuck, I knew one thing for sure. She'd leave.

Trust didn't come easy to Eve. I'd learned that on the train four years ago. And, now, Joe was going to blow it out of the fucking water. He'd been lying to her all summer. Dread rolled over me like a semi-truck.

"Cole, what's going on?" Everly questioned from across the bed. She was curled up against the headboard still and looked more frightened than the girl I'd left standing on the platform at the train station long ago.

My heart fucking broke for her. She didn't even see it coming. Everything was getting ready to change. Our little bubble of perfect we'd had here the past couple of weeks was about to explode.

"I'm sorry," I mumbled, covering my face with my hands. And I wasn't just sorry for what had already transpired. I was sorry for what was to come too, because it was so much worse.

She'd never trust us again. She'd leave and never come back. Bile rose in my throat at the thought.

This was Joe's fault. He should have told her. How could he have let her go all summer without knowing? I stood up and headed for the door, ready to confront him.

"Wait, Cole." Her eyes pleaded from the bed, but I could barely see her through all the shit swirling in my head. "Did something happen with Marla? Is everything okay?" She looked so confused.

I couldn't bring myself to tell her right then. I couldn't bear to see the heartbreak on her face if I told her of Joe's betrayal.

"I'm sorry, baby. I have to go. I'll be back, okay?" I said as tenderly as I could, but my voice sounded gruff and distant. I needed to get to Joe.

I took the stairs two by two, eager to get to his room. Entering the small hallway off his room, I called out for him.

"Joe."

Nothing. I walked into his room and immediately noticed the made-up bed and empty room. Fuck. He was gone. Out of town. I'd forgotten. I looked up at the ceiling and closed my eyes. I wasn't a religious man by any means, but I felt myself asking God for a little guidance. I didn't have a fucking clue what to do.

Unfortunately, God didn't answer when you rung him up on the fly, so I jogged across the yard, back to my house, my chest and my eyes burning with emotion. Eve was Joe's daughter. Why hadn't he told her? Why hadn't he told me? What would she do when she found out?

I poured myself a tall glass of whiskey and paced my house for hours. I thought of calling Joe, but this wasn't the type of thing someone accused another person of over the phone. And I thought of Eve, all alone at the big house, probably terrified out of her mind at my outburst. So I drank until I was numb, something I hadn't done since Eve had come back into my life and made me happy.

Fuck, she'd made us *all* so fucking happy, and we were going to destroy her.

Four years later and she was finally there, with me and Joe. Where she was supposed to be, and, God, she'd found her stride there. She'd grown by leaps and bounds over the summer, and while I knew she'd changed our lives with her mere presence, I also knew we'd changed hers, too.

The more I drank, the more desolate and desperate my thoughts became. She was going to leave me. I could bear anything. I'd learned that when Marla had taken Grey and left, but I didn't think I could bear this. I couldn't live on this farm knowing I'd never see her in the barn, brushing Beauty. I couldn't eat in that kitchen knowing I'd never see her sleepy face in the morning over coffee.

I couldn't stand it anymore, so I texted Joe a 911 message telling him we needed him home as soon as possible.

Around three a.m., I staggered back to the big house on drunk feet, the half-empty bottle of whiskey dangling from my fist. I'd given up drinking out of a glass hours ago. I knew she'd be sleeping, but I needed to see her. I couldn't stay away. I didn't know how long I had left with her.

I trudged up the stairs, my legs heavy under me, my brain swimming around in my skull. I reached the open door to Eve's room and leaned on the doorjamb for support.

I'd expected her to be asleep, but there she sat in almost the exact same spot I'd left her, the light from the lamp casting a shadow across her beautiful face.

"Cole?" she asked, seemingly surprised to see me there.

Chapter 29

Everly

My cowboy stood in the doorway, watching me, a brown bottle hanging from his hand. The night I'd taken him the roll of quarters flashed in my mind. That was the last time I'd seen him this way. I wanted to lift my comforter and beckon him under my covers so that I could hold him. But I didn't know what he was going through. Since his visit with Marla, his behavior had been erratic at best. I didn't know where we stood, but I had an inkling it wasn't in a good place. I was just waiting for the ball to drop. For him to tell me we were over and he was going back to Marla and Grey.

And the shirt. I had no idea what the hell that had been about. He'd been so completely crazy. Studying the bottle of liquor in his hand, I wondered if he had been drinking all day. That would explain the insanity that had been tonight.

"Are you okay?" I questioned, studying his desperate eyes. And they scared me. Those eyes said everything I didn't want to hear. They said that we were over.

"No," he answered, shaking his head, and my heart hurt for him almost as much as it hurt for me.

Was he there to say goodbye?

If he was, there was no way I could stay at Preston's, no matter if Joe wanted me to or not. This farm didn't exist for me unless there was an Eve and Cole on it—together.

Cole's shoulders sagged, and he dropped his head to his chest. He looked like he might fall over, and my stupid, kind heart did the talking before my head could stop it.

"Come here," my heart said from my mouth, and my dumb hands followed suit by lifting the covers and patting the spot next to me.

His eyes blazed over my face, desperation and heat mingling in the air between us. It felt hot and thick and dangerous, and still, I reached my hand out to him, urging him closer.

Slow, meaningful strides brought Cole to me, his intense stare never wavering. And I got lost in that gaze. I forgot that Marla had come back. I wasn't thinking about how he'd scared me earlier that night with his crazy behavior. I didn't care that he'd been drinking.

It was just us, and this passionate connection—this undeniable love that extended between us like a piece of string—holding us together even when we were falling part.

"You're mine," Cole said, his voice gravelly above me, his face fierce. His jaw set and determined.

Oh, Cowboy. Was there ever a question? I wanted to ask. I'd been his since he'd offered me a seat on a train I hadn't even paid for. Didn't he know that? How could he not? For heaven's sake, I carried my love for him around in my back pocket everywhere I went. How could he ever question it?

I wanted to scream and shout the house down with my love. I wanted to pound my fist on his chest and demand that he tell me that he loved me too. But he seemed as fragile as the glass bottle in his hand. Like, with one hard blast from me, he'd smash to the floor, scattering his tiny pieces all around my room. I couldn't bear to break him, so I only nodded, still holding the covers back for him. *Let me hold you.*

Ignoring the pulled-back covers, Cole crawled over my body, settling his weight on top of me, before taking my mouth in a punishing kiss that bruised my lips and hurt in a way that made me ache between my legs. He slipped his tongue past mine over and over, tasting every corner of my mouth until I was breathless and boneless beneath him.

"You're mine," he groaned out again as he trailed hot whiskey kisses from my mouth, down my neck, and across my chest, his day-old stubble burning me and then setting my skin aflame. His open-mouthed kisses were biting, hard, and relentless, branding me with their ferocity on the outside and in.

He didn't take his time undressing me. He didn't savor me like I was a gift this time. No, he feasted on me. He took me. He consumed me. He fucked me like he owned me.

We were all lips, tongues, hands, passion, and fever. No one could touch our love.

"You'll never leave me," he demanded.

"I'm yours," I whispered over and over.

He took me again and again until the sun peeked in through the windows. Until my body felt sore and used. Until we finally wore ourselves out. Until we succumbed to the exhaustion, clutched around each other, desperate for one another even in our sleep.

For the first time in days, I woke up without Cole wrapped around me. Panic fluttered in my belly as I searched the room for him. My entire body hurt with the events of yesterday. It seemed I'd slept most of the day away. My head pounded, and my eyes were sore and puffy. Even the sweet ache in my body from Cole's lovemaking couldn't stave off the rawness I felt. And I did feel gritty and weak, nearly to the point of breaking emotionally.

Where had Cole gone? Had last night been goodbye?

It had certainly felt like goodbye. I wondered if I'd get the answers I so desperately needed. I slowly got out of bed, feeling tired and too weak to deal with the day's bullshit. I didn't bother showering before I pulled my clothes on. I threw my hair up into a messy bun and headed downstairs, hoping coffee would somehow make me feel more human.

Strained voices drifted up the stairs, and I paused, wondering who was home. Joe was supposed to be out of town until tomorrow. In fact, I was counting on that. I couldn't deal with his prying questions today, and once he saw the state I was in, he would definitely pry. He'd worry and fuss over me, and I couldn't deal with that.

A loud bang sounded, and I flinched, paying extra-close attention.

"You didn't see her, Joe!" Cole yelled.

I stood on the stairs as still as a statue. I'd never heard Cole raise his voice to Joe like that.

"Keep it down, Cole," Joe hissed. "I know you're upset, but—"

"No," Cole interrupted. "You don't get to tell me to keep it down. You didn't see her." He sounded pained. "You didn't see how starved she was. How distrusting. How fragile. You don't understand." He was talking through clenched teeth. "You've ruined everything. She'll never trust us again."

My skin prickled with an unwelcome awareness as I stood stock-still, one foot perched just above the last step of the staircase. That step seemed almost ominous. Just two more steps and my life was going to change forever.

Still, I walked down them, knowing I would probably regret it but too damn stubborn to walk back upstairs and bury my head beneath the covers in my too-nice-for-an-employee bedroom.

"I was going to tell her. But the time has never been right," Joe said. He sounded exhausted.

"You'll tell Eve now! Today, Joe!" Cole snapped out, and that was all the permission I needed to come around the corner and enter the room.

My heart had been stupidly holding out hope that Joe and Cole weren't fighting about me, but my body had known. It had known it down to its bones.

They didn't even notice me enter the room. Cole was standing next to the kitchen table, his body over it, his hands pressed into the hard, wood top. His face was red with emotion as he leaned forward, his jaw ticking, his lips pressed together, like he was trying to hold himself in check.

I looked over at Joe, who was sitting across the table from him in his chair, his face equally fierce.

"Tell me what?" I said slowly, hoping to hide the fear in my voice.

I was terrified of the answer to that question. I clutched my shaking hands together and looked at my guys, afraid it would be the last time they were mine.

Cole leaned away from the table, his chest heaving like he'd run a marathon.

Joe turned his chair towards me. "Why don't you sit down, sweetheart?" Sad eyes bracketed an even sadder smile, and I knew I needed to stay standing in case I needed to get the hell out of there.

"I'm good," I said, glancing at Cole for some hint of what was going to happen. I could usually read him like an open book.

Not this time though. He just looked angry and desperate and ready to explode wide open all over this kitchen.

"God, Everly," Joe blew out on a breath. "I don't even know where to start."

He looked so heartbroken and forlorn.

"How about the damn beginning?" Cole spat out, and my gaze

flashed to him.

When he slammed his fist on the table again, a loud bang sounded in the room and I jumped. I stared at him, shocked at his outburst, but he averted his gaze from me and shook his head before breathing heavily through his nostrils and turning completely away from me. He gazed towards the ceiling and placed his hands on his hips with his back to me, so I looked back to Joe, imploring him to go on.

Upon letting out a sigh, Joe started. "I told you about my wife Anna."

He smiled sadly and swallowed hard, like talking about Anna pained him. It probably did, but I couldn't help but wonder what this had to do with me. Praying that it didn't have to do with me.

"I told you she left because she was mentally ill and couldn't handle the pressure after I lost my ability to walk. But what I didn't tell you was that, when she left, she took my newborn baby with her." He stared at me.

My air caught in my throat, and I was momentarily overcome with the feeling like I was suffocating. As if all the air in the room was so thick that I couldn't draw any in.

I shook my head back and forth slowly, my breath a hard lump, still stuck in my throat.

"A baby girl," he whispered, closing his eyes.

"A girl," I repeated back on a breath, desperate to believe that what I thought he was telling me was wrong. Because that would mean he hadn't come for me all these years. That would mean Joe had lied to me all fucking summer, even after I'd confessed everything to him. Even after I'd told him that I'd been homeless, that I'd become a thief to survive. I'd cried against his chest. I'd opened my heart to him and let him in, and he'd lied. It couldn't be true. My Joe wouldn't do that to me—he loved me too much.

"I couldn't go after her right away. I was still recovering from the accident. So, I hired a private investigator to hunt her down. He found her months later, living in a homeless shelter by herself. Shelby was nowhere in sight."

"Shelby," I said, letting the name roll over my tongue, tasting it.

Joe smiled sadly, looking up at me, "Yes, Shelby." Tears shone in his eyes, and I wondered if he thought I resembled the tiny baby he'd lost so long ago. "Anna told the PI that Shelby had died. Starved to death in the cold."

The tears from Joe's eyes slid down his cheeks, and I wanted to reach out and wipe them for him because I knew he couldn't. But I couldn't touch him. Not now. Not when I knew what he was going to tell me. What he *was* telling me.

"And, for almost twenty years, I thought she was dead. I thought I'd lost the only chance I'd ever have to be a father," he choked out, his tears a constant stream down his face now.

I rubbed my hand across my face, surprised to find tears falling from my own as well.

"I thought I'd lost my baby girl," he sobbed out, but then he smiled. He grinned through his tears. "Until four months ago. A nice woman named Louise called me. Said she'd been digging around. Said she thought she'd found my baby."

God, I hadn't thought about Momma Lou. She'd lied to me, too. Why? Why hadn't she just told me the truth? Why did the people I loved most in my life desert me, lie to me, betray me? I couldn't do this. Not even tough-as-nails Everly could do this. It was too fucking much.

I backed away from Joe and Cole, feeling like the room was closing in on me.

Joe rolled forward to me. "My girl finally came home this summer."

"No." I shook my head, terrified. "No, Joe, I'm not Shelby. I'm just Everly."

I couldn't be his sweet baby girl. I was not her. I was a thief. I was trash who had grown up on the streets. Nobody had wanted me.

I hiccupped on a sob when I thought of Shelby. Of what she

would have been like had she grown up on this magical farm, with this man's love. I instantly wished that had been true. How different our lives would have been, me and Shelby. I mourned for her as much as I did for myself in that moment. We'd almost had it all.

I stood there, shocked, betrayed, and hurt beyond words. I wiped the tears from my face with the long sleeves of my shirt. Cole looked at me like he wanted to come hug me, fix this. But this wasn't something that could be fixed. This was a fucking mess, and I didn't know if it would ever be better.

He made to come for me, but I threw my hands up. I didn't even really know where I stood with Cole. Had he and Marla reconciled? How long had he known about Joe being my father? Fuck, my life had never been this messy, not even when I had been living on the streets.

I was learning a hard lesson. Having people in your life and loving them gave them the ability to hurt you, and it seemed that almost everyone I loved felt like destroying me today.

"How long?" I whispered at Cole.

"What?" he asked.

"How long have you known?" I cried out, my voice betraying every emotion I was feeling. It sounded raw and split open to my ears.

"No, baby," he crooned, his face so sincere, so full of love, that I almost wept for it. "I'd never lie to you. I just found out, same as you. I—"

"No," I said, backing out of the room. "No," I cried. "I can't do this now."

"Please, Eve." Cole came forward, his hands out in front of him like he meant no harm. And I knew he wanted to hold me, but there weren't enough arms in the world to hold all of my pieces.

"I can't," I croaked out. "Not now." I brought my eyes to Joe. "How could you? I told you everything. Everything!" I screamed, and the shrill sound of my voice scared the hell out of me. It sounded broken and hysterical. "How could you continue to lie to me after that? How?" I wailed.

I ran upstairs, my vision blurry with tears, my legs shaking in shock. Joe. My father.

I remembered how he'd instantly accepted me. How we'd laughed together until our bellies hurt. How he'd told me about his momma and his daddy. How understanding he'd been when I'd told him about my childhood.

I'd been so blind. This fucking place had put some kind of spell on me. I'd only seen what I'd wanted to see. I hadn't seen the truth. How Joe and I looked so much alike, with our identical brown hair and blue eyes. How our connection had been almost instantaneous.

I looked around my room. No, Shelby's room. I felt sick. Like the last two months had been nothing but a lie. Why hadn't he just told me from the beginning? Was this some kind of sick test to see if I was good enough? Would he have even told me if it hadn't been for Cole's threats?

I wanted to throw up. What if he was never going to tell me because I wasn't good enough? Because I was never good enough. My own mother hadn't wanted me, and now, my father didn't, either. God, and was Cole going back to Marla? Would I ever be enough for anyone?

My door opened, and I found a worried Cody standing in my doorway. I was more than relieved that Joe or Cole hadn't come for me. I wasn't ready to talk to them. I wasn't sure if I'd ever be.

I launched myself at Cody, and he grabbed me up, hugging me tight to his strong body. My torso shook against his. I wet the entire front of his shirt in tears.

"Shh," he soothed me, rubbing my hair, my back.

"Promise me you didn't know," I mumbled into the front of his shirt, gripping big fistfuls of the material.

"I had no idea, baby girl. None." He consoled me. "Please stop crying, sweet girl. You're breaking my heart."

"I don't know what to do," I sobbed. And I didn't. I couldn't trust anyone aside from Cody.

Rubbing his palm over my back, he said, "There's nothing to do, baby girl. You're just gonna take some time and think about things. Everything will work out. I promise."

I didn't think anything was going to work out. But I did need time to think things over, and I couldn't do that in this house with Joe around. In Shelby's room. I needed to get the hell out of there, and Cody was my only chance.

"How much do you love me, Cody?" I asked.

He used his thumbs to wipe the tears under my eyes. "Girl, you know I'm ride or die for you," he said, smiling.

"Then you'll take me to the bus station?" I questioned, hope in my voice.

He frowned, and I thought he'd say no. But then he said, "I'll take you anywhere if you really want to go."

"I want to," I whispered.

His forehead wrinkled, and he pursed his lips. "Are you sure?" he asked, tucking a piece of hair behind my ear.

"I'm sure, Cody." I laid my head over his heart and squeezed him to me.

But the words sounded mucky and grimy in my mouth. I was a dirty liar. I'd never been more unsure about anything in my entire life.

Chapter 30

Cole

One week. Apparently, that's how long it takes for a man to reach his fucking wit's end. It was also how long Eve had been gone. I had known she would leave, but there were a few things I hadn't anticipated. Like how quick it would be. Or that she wouldn't say goodbye. That was the one that really chapped my ass. Christ, it hurt.

Fuck, I missed her.

I'd gone up to Eve's room that night determined to calm her down but found all of her belongings gone, the room as clean as it'd been when she'd arrived. It was like she hadn't even been there at all. Like maybe I'd dreamt her up for the summer, and the thought of that made me sick, because if she wasn't real, then that meant she wasn't coming back. And I just couldn't have that.

I'd grilled Cody nonstop since then, but he said that he didn't know where she'd gone, only that he'd dropped her at the bus station.

And the thought of that, well, it made me want to fucking kill someone. My girl. Out there all alone again. Pain gripped my gut in its tight fist. This was fucking torture.

Fucking Cody, taking my Eve away.

At least she had the money Joe had paid her for the summer, I told myself. But still, every time I thought of her out there without me, I felt panicked—wrecked.

And, just like every night since she'd been gone, I sat across from Joe, barely saying a word. I was livid with him, and he fucking knew it. Every bit of this was his fault. The only reason I even showed up at dinner was to find out if he knew anything about where she had gone, if he'd heard from her.

So, tonight, one week later, I sat across from him and asked him the same question I'd been asking for seven days.

"Have you heard anything?" I scooped some food into my mouth. It tasted like sawdust, but I chewed and choked it down.

"Nothing," he said quietly, just like he had every night before.

Missy tried to spoon some food in his mouth, but he refused to open.

I knew he was hurting, but I was too.

Usually, we quietly finished our meal, sometimes with Cody and Missy looking at us like we were never gonna be the same. Maybe they were right, because I didn't know how I was ever going to forgive him for having chased off the best thing that had ever happened to me.

Tonight, Joe switched it up by saying, "I don't know how to fix this situation or make things better with Everly, Cole. Even when I do find her, I don't know how to fix her. She's suffered years of abandonment."

I listened to Joe, and every word out of his mouth only made me angrier and angrier. How dare he? Eve was fucking perfect. Even with all of her imperfections, she was still a million times better than anyone at this table.

I slammed my fork down on my plate. "She doesn't need to be fixed, Joe. She just needs to be found." Emotion clogged my throat, so I paused, trying to contain it because it felt like it was going to spill all over this damn room. I stared Joe in the eye. "She just needs to be found and loved for the person she is, flaws and all. Just like she's done for us all summer."

I got up and threw my napkin onto my plate before storming out of the kitchen with the biggest fucking chip on my shoulder I'd ever had. Turned out my love for Eve weighed a hell of a lot.

"Cole!" Joe shouted.

I paused, turning around. "Yeah?"

He seemed as shaken up as I was. Like neither of us was going to make it without her. "Then find her and bring her home."

"I'm working on it," I said gruffly, walking out the back door and letting it slam behind me with a bang.

And I was working damn hard on it. I'd been calling Louise every day. And, every day, she'd tell me that she hadn't heard from Eve but she'd call as soon as she did. She'd also told me how stubborn Eve was, and I'd smiled like a loon because it wasn't like I didn't know that already. And I told her how much I loved Eve, how she'd made me happy when I'd been so sad. How amazing she was. How I needed her to come home like I needed my next breath. Sometimes, our talks would last seconds, and other times, we'd talk for hours about her Little Bird. After only one week, I could completely see why Eve loved Momma Lou like she did. In fact, I was banking on the fact that she'd go to her.

But it had been a week, and I was becoming desperate. There was some consolation in all of this. And that was the phone calls. Eve had been calling my phone late at night when I was asleep or during the day when she knew I was working and didn't carry my phone. I was hoping it was because she was missing me like crazy, like I was missing her. I couldn't be sure because she never left a message, but I thought maybe she was just calling to hear my voice.

So I'd started carrying my phone with me at all times, terrified I'd miss a call, but if I answered, she only hung up or said nothing at all. Fuck, it killed.

The fact that she was calling gave me some small comfort though. My girl was okay. She was probably still devastated, but she was still alive and well enough to pick the phone up. I had tried to call her back more times than I could count, but her phone was always off. I had a feeling she only turned it on when she made an outgoing call. I wanted to hear her voice too, only her voicemail had that stupid computer automated message that made me want to throw my phone across the room every time I heard it.

I lay in my bed, cradling my phone in my hand like the damn thing was going to ring any moment even though I knew that it wouldn't. I'd been doing this all week. She only called when she knew I was busy or asleep, she never left a message, and the few times I'd answered? Nothing. I rolled the metal around and gave it a hard stare, an idea coming to me. She didn't want to talk to me. She just wanted to hear me. Well, I'd make sure she heard me loud and clear.

Chapter 31

Everly

The message started off the same, the same way it did every time I called.

"Hey, this is Cole. I'm not around, so leave a message at the beep."

Closing my eyes, I basked in the only luxury I had right now: the deep timbre of Cole's husky voice.

I pressed the warm phone hard against my ear, waiting for the beep. Only it didn't come this time.

"Eve," Cole said through the phone, and I gripped it harder against my ear on a gasp, thinking I'd heard wrong.

There was a long pause, and I held my breath, afraid I wouldn't hear his next words with my own air whooshing in my ears. I wished I could see his face. I could picture it in my mind at this time of night—sweet, chocolate eyes peering at me from all the hard, manly angles of his face. The day-old stubble running along his jaw and his chin. His perfect mouth always begging to be kissed. My body ached as I thought of that face.

"Baby, I miss you. Beauty misses you, too. I went out to brush her today, but she didn't want anything to do with me." He chuckled and blew out a long sigh.

Wetness slid down my cheek and dampened the pillow beneath my head.

"We all miss you."

A sob bubbled up out of me and sounded too loud in the quiet, empty hotel room. I bit my lip to stifle it. I wouldn't hear him over my cries.

"I just wanted you to know I'm thinking of you. I'm always thinking of you, Eve."

His voice sounded like he smelled, all thick and rich, gravelly and smoky. I wished I could press my nose into his shirt like I'd done so many times before. He'd never know how much his smell, his voice, his kindness—just *him*—comforted me. It wasn't his fault all this had happened. He was just a victim of circumstance, much like myself. It didn't matter though. I couldn't go back there.

"I hope you're taking care of yourself."

The beep sounded and the tears came like waterfalls then. Through blurry eyes, I dialed Cole again and again and listened, intent on absorbing every word into my skin so I'd remember it. I memorized the hitch in his voice when he said Eve. The slow breath before he called me baby. The quietness when he said he missed me. The firm way he said he was always thinking of me. I couldn't forget a single inflection in his voice. I wanted this memory to play whenever I needed it, and I knew I'd be needing it plenty.

Chapter 32

Everly

"**W**hy?"

It was the very first word that passed my lips when Momma Lou opened the door. I'd given myself two weeks to calm down. To have this conversation rationally. But I'd knocked on that door, stood on that porch, and waited, and for the first time ever, I'd felt like this cute, little, humble house in the country wasn't my home. It made me furious. And, once again, her betrayal suffocated me. Tears burned my eyes. My face was hot with rage. Clearly, two weeks hadn't been enough time, but at this point, I didn't think two years would have, either.

"Little Bird," Momma Lou breathed, her voice part relief at seeing me okay and part remorse over how she'd lied to me.

I knew her face better than I knew anyone's, and I didn't want her damn remorse or relief. I wanted answers.

"Why?" I demanded again, my fists clenched, my heart pounding in my ears. I thought of my time at the hotel on the outskirts of town the past two weeks and only grew angrier. I thought of the tears I'd shed for virtually everyone I'd loved—everyone who had lied to me. How everything had changed in the blink of an eye. How I'd gone from being blissfully happy to so very alone. How I'd curled up on that old mattress and longed for my bed at the big house. How I'd longed for Joe's smile even though I hated him. How badly I'd needed Cody to make me laugh. How I'd wished Cole had been lying next to me because I missed him so much that my bones ached with it. Instead, I'd clung to all I had left of Preston's—the hat Cole had given me, the picture of Margaret, and Cole's voice messages.

I'd pressed the hat and the picture close to my chest and cried my eyes out. I'd been sick with grief. I still was.

Momma Lou's forehead wrinkled in concern, and she sighed. "Why don't you come inside, baby? So we can talk."

I bit my quivering lip to still it before saying, "No. There's nothing to talk about. You lied to me." A lone tear slipped down my cheek, and I used the sleeve of my flannel shirt to angrily wipe it away. I hadn't wanted to cry in front of her. "You *all* lied to me," I accused.

She tilted her head to the ceiling and closed her eyes. I'd seen her do this too many times to count. It was her way of gathering every bit of patience she could.

She finally looked back at me before saying with too much patience, "Everly, I'd like to answer all of your questions, but I wish we didn't have to do it in the front yard. Come inside."

"No," I said again. Yes, I was acting like a child, but I thought I was doing pretty well at keeping my shit together. I hadn't once stomped my foot or raised my voice.

Momma Lou rolled her eyes and placed her hand on her hip, and I knew I was in for it. "Girl, get your skinny ass in this house right now."

"Fine!" I yelled, stomping past her, my attempt at keeping my shit together gone in the wind, damn her.

She closed the door behind her and demanded, "Sit."

A few of the children greeted me with hugs as I made my way over to the worn, blue couch that had been there longer than I had.

"Everyone out for a bit," Momma Lou said to the children. "Y'all can say hi to Everly in a little while. We need to have a private chat right now."

Everyone left and we were finally alone, the room too quiet, the mood beyond tense.

Momma Lou sat in the arm chair across from me, her back straight, her hands folded in her lap. "Ask your questions, Little Bird."

I huffed at her practicality. How unflustered she was. How could she be so calm in the face of my turmoil? Didn't she know my pain?

Rubbing my back pocket, I checked for my picture before asking, "Why'd you send me there without telling me?"

My heart thundered in my ears as I awaited her answer. Maybe Momma Lou didn't love me like I'd thought she did. Maybe she didn't care for me at all. Maybe she just wanted to be rid of me just like everyone else.

"Because you never would have gone, Little Bird," she said so bluntly, so unemotionally, that I wanted to scream at her. "And then you never would have met Joe and loved him so much. And you sure as hell wouldn't have your Cole."

She was right. I probably wouldn't have gone. I would have been too scared. Too insecure. And let's face it. Even now, after having known Joe and caring for him, I was still so damn angry that he hadn't found me sooner. That he'd stopped looking in the first place.

But all of that still didn't change the fact that she had taken that choice away from me. I should have been the one to decide if I wanted to see Joe. Not her.

"That wasn't your call to make!" I shouted, throwing my hands up in the air.

She nodded. "You're right. It wasn't."

She just sat there all composed, her hands still folded in her lap, and here I was, screaming and throwing my hands in the air like a maniac.

"You don't even care!" I cried, fresh tears running down my cheeks. "You don't care how this has hurt me." I buried my face in my hands, angry with myself for letting her see me cry. And hating this new me. The me Joe and Cole had brought about. I hated how vulnerable I was. Jesus, I was so hopeless—powerless. It was terrifying. I rocked back and forth on the old couch I'd sat on a million times, sobbing.

"I care," Momma Lou said.

I looked up and found her on her knees, in front of me. She grabbed my hand, folded it between hers, and laid them in my lap.

"I care so much, Little Bird." Her eyes glistened with unshed tears. "Which is why I'd do the same thing all over again."

Her eyes pleaded with me to understand, but I just couldn't. Why would she put me through this again if given the choice? Couldn't she see how raw I was? How emotionally beat down I felt?

I averted my gaze, but she squeezed my hand, so I brought it back to hers.

"I love you, Everly. I wanted more than anything to find your people. You deserve a family. I have a friend at the state. I had her dig around in the state's hospital medical records. I didn't actually think she'd find anything, but she did. And I wanted you to meet Joe without the anger, the reservations. Without the solid walls you throw up at anybody who wants into your heart. Joe and I both wanted your relationship to have a fighting chance. We felt it was the only way. And I'd do it again because it worked, baby. I heard the light in your voice when you called. You love it there. You love him."

The truth shone in her eyes, and I hurt with it. She was right. My walls had crumbled, and I hated it.

"It doesn't matter," I sobbed, my shoulders shaking. "It's over. Done. I can't go back there." I shook my head.

I'd told Joe my darkest secrets and he hadn't even blinked because he'd already known. He'd had the perfect opportunity that night to tell me everything, yet he hadn't. How would I ever trust him?

"Oh, baby." Momma Lou wrapped me in her arms, and I breathed in her coconut scent. "What oftentimes feels like the end is just the beginning. Some of those times, it's the beginning of something really great." She squeezed me hard. "Sometimes, all it takes to keep from breaking, Everly, is just bending a little."

I snuggled into her, gripping my hands together behind her back. "I don't think this is one of those times, Momma Lou," I whispered into her coarse hair, defeat evident in my voice. But I needed this hug like I needed air.

She leaned out of my embrace and looked me in the eye. "That's not what Cole tells me."

"You've talked to Cole?" I asked, shocked to my core. My cowboy had called my Momma Lou. I felt all wiggly on the inside at the knowledge.

She smiled. "Every day for two weeks, that boy has called me trying to find you. I think he wants you to come home, Everly."

"I don't have a home," I snapped. And that had been true most of my life, but saying it now felt all wrong.

Momma Lou smacked her teeth and grabbed my face in her hands. "Look at me when I say this, girl."

I did because she didn't give me a damn choice. She held my face firmly in her grip, with absolutely no give.

"Home isn't a place. It isn't a thing. It's the feeling people give you when you're with them. That's home, Little Bird. Now, look at me and tell me that Cole isn't your home," she demanded.

Cole, Joe, Cody—they all gave me that feeling. And I wanted them. I wanted to go home. I just didn't know how.

Chapter 33

Everly

I did what I had done every night since I'd left Preston's. Three weeks now since I'd seen my cowboy. I lay in my twin bed at Momma Lou's and pressed the green button on my phone, the green glow from the screen lighting the dark bedroom.

His voice came over the phone like warm honey, sweet and rich, and I immediately melted into the stiff sheets beneath me. There might have been three other kids sleeping in the room with me, but each night, when I pressed the call button, it was just me and my cowboy.

He didn't even bother with the traditional "not available" messages anymore. He just dove right in.

"I've been thinking about you a lot today, Eve. I consider myself a patient man, but I feel like you might be pushing it a little."

Patient, my ass. I smiled into the phone.

"You sure are missing a lot around here. Something big is going on with Beau and Cody." He sighed. "If you come home, I might tell you." He stopped talking for a moment.

He was resorting to gay-cowboy bribery. I hissed a quiet laugh and closed my eyes, pretending I was there with him.

"Jane is holding my quarters hostage again. Seems her good mood disappeared with you."

He did this almost every night, catching me up on everything at Preston's, but he never mentioned Joe, and I wondered if maybe he knew I wasn't ready to hear about him yet.

"I wish I could hear you throw me some snark. I miss it." He gave a dry laugh. "Well, really, I just miss your voice. I reckon I'd settle for anything at this point. Won't you leave me a message just this once?" He sounded sad, and my smile fell.

He did this every night too. He wanted me to say something, but I didn't know what to say. I wasn't ready to go back to Preston's, and I knew that was the only thing he wanted to hear from my lips.

"I know. Play me a memory. Anything." He paused. "I'll play you one, okay? An eye for an eye. That way, when the phone beeps, you can play me one." The desperation in his voice almost made me want to cave.

Almost.

"You, Eve. Just you. You're my favorite memory. You in your rocker on the front porch every morning, waiting on me to walk up those steps. You and those ridiculously adorable songs you sing in the shower. You cooking me bacon in my kitchen, with my socks pulled to your knees. You smiling at me. Not just any smile though. The ones you give only me, the smiles that cover your entire face all the way from your chin to your hairline. Those are my favorite. Just you."

I buried my face in my pillow to keep my cries from waking everyone. As far as I knew, Cole still called Momma Lou every day. He knew where I was. Momma Lou had said that he was giving me the time I needed, but I still had my doubts about Marla.

"But I don't want to play you anymore, baby. I don't want you to be some memory I carry around in my heart. I want the real you. Here. Now." Despair dripped from his words.

I loved how much he wanted to see me as much as I hated it.

He cleared his throat, but his voice still sounded strained. "Marla is dropping Grey off to see me today. And then she's leaving. You hear what I'm saying, baby? She's not staying. Not ever again." A frustrated sigh hit my ears. "Fuck, I just wish you were here."

He wanted me to come home. He wanted *me*. And it scared me to death.

Chapter 34

Everly

Two weeks later, I'd eased back into my life at Momma Lou's like I'd never left. My life fit here like an old glove. It wasn't extraordinary like my life at Preston's, but it was safe—predictable.

I finished my shift at the shelter and took the bus home, so tired that I almost fell asleep before my stop. I walked to the house from the stop with my back aching, wishing I had my giant bathtub at the big house to soak in. Wishing I had a lot of things from a month ago that I didn't anymore.

I stepped up onto the stoop, grabbing my keys from my bag. Then I stopped short. There sat Joe and Missy on the front walkway of Momma Lou's little rundown house, and they'd never seemed so out of place in their lives.

Joe looked me over from head to toe. "Everly," he said as hello, but I couldn't manage one for him.

I was too shocked to see him. Joe didn't travel too much and not very far at all. His condition made it hard for him to do long road trips.

"Hey, Everly." Missy waved awkwardly.

I snapped out of it. "Hi, Missy." I smiled awkwardly, well, because this whole thing was awkward as hell. What were they doing here?

She reached over for a hug, and I couldn't help but hug her back. I'd missed her nosy, meddling ass.

"Missy, can Everly and I have a moment alone?" Joe spoke as Missy pulled out of our embrace.

She gazed tenderly at him and patted him on the shoulder. "Sure thing, honey. I'll go wait in the van." She squeezed my hand as she walked by.

But I was hyper-focused on the man sitting in his wheelchair on the front sidewalk. My father. He looked different now that I knew that. I could see all of our similarities laid out before me like a map, and I wondered how I'd never pieced it together before.

I searched around, hoping like a teenage girl with a crush that Cole had come with him.

"He's not here," Joe said. "He doesn't know we're here. We thought we'd make a quick day trip out of it." His words sounded grand and brave, but he just looked sad and withdrawn. Joe's big personality and body seemed so small and fragile right then.

"Why are you here, Joe?" I questioned. I didn't want to prolong this whole uncomfortable, painful conversation anymore.

He studied me for a beat before answering bluntly, "Because I miss you, Everly. Because I'm sorry for so, so many things."

A tear tracked down his cheek, and I turned away. I couldn't bear to see him cry. It broke my heart all over again.

He didn't care that I wouldn't give him my eyes. He just kept going, and every word pierced my heart.

"I'm sorry that I didn't keep looking for you. I'm sorry that, when I finally found you, I didn't tell you the truth. But I knew you wouldn't want to see me. I wanted to give us a fighting chance, you and me. I'm sorry I didn't tell you the truth, but I don't regret it because this summer has been the best in my entire life, and it's all because of you.

"I love you, and you'll always have a home at Preston's if you choose to. And, even if you don't, I'll still love you. Nothing will change that, sweetheart. Not ever," he finished, and I panicked.

No. He'd hurt me again. I couldn't be with these people I loved so intensely. They had the power to destroy me. I'd spent my life so isolated, so unloved, that I was like thin glass: One tiny pebble could shatter me beyond repair. I couldn't let them break me.

"You need to go," I said though my tears, rubbing my sweaty hands on my pants. I couldn't do this. I looked around in panic, my whole body strung tight.

He would hurt me again. He'd decide I wasn't good enough and he'd leave me. I couldn't believe him. He was a liar.

"Please, Everly. Just—"

"No, Joe. Leave!" I screeched. I pushed past him and unlocked the door, my hands shaking around the keys. I closed it behind me and ran upstairs to my room, thankful none of the children were in here. I closed myself behind the door and locked it before sliding down and sitting on the floor.

I had myself a good ol' pity party, my hand pressed to my aching chest for about an hour before I heard a soft knock. I stood up and wiped the damn tears off my face. I was so over this crying thing.

Momma Lou was on the other side of the door when I opened it.

"You wanna talk about it?" she asked, but it wasn't really a question. She wanted to talk about it, so we would.

"Talk about what?" I played dumb because I was sick to death of talking about it. It, as in everything. I was talked to damn death. Old Everly never would have stood for this nonsense. All this talking and crying. It was ridiculous.

She pushed her way past me into the room and sat on my bed. "I saw what happened, Little Bird. I saw it all."

"And?" I asked, looking past her. I couldn't stand all of the emotion in her eyes.

"You love him," she stated.

I didn't say anything. I only stared at the crack in the wall behind her head.

"If you love him, why can't you forgive him?" she asked.

That question just pissed me off. How dare she decide what I should forgive?

"Forgive what?" I yelled. "Forgive him for letting my mother run off and take me with her? Forgive him for not finding me? Forgive him for lying to me?" With every word, my voice got louder.

"You know what I think, Everly?" She stood up and got in my face. "I think you've already forgiven that sweet man who has been dealt a raw hand in this life."

I flinched, the reality and truth of her words slapping me in the face. God, it stung.

"I think you forgave him the minute you knew." She pointed her finger close to my face.

I backed up and closed my eyes. I didn't want to hear this. I couldn't stand it.

"I think you're running scared. You love him and Cole and that special farm you talk about so much that you're terrified. You're so terrified you're gonna lose them that you've already thrown them away. And that's no way to live, Little Bird. You can't be running scared of everything you love, or you're gonna miss out on all the best things in life."

I wanted to deny everything. I wanted to scream at her and tell how wrong she was, but I didn't because it was all true. I was so scared. I'd never loved anyone like I loved Joe and Cole. I'd never had the love of someone like that, either. I didn't know how to love and be loved. It was a frightening concept, how these people held my heart in their hands. I couldn't handle it if they threw my love away.

"Snap out of it, baby girl. You've never been a victim. Stop acting like one now."

I spent the afternoon and night hiding in my room, but I didn't feel hidden. I felt exposed and bare, like Momma Lou had somehow ripped me wide open and, now, my insides were hanging out for everyone to see. And I didn't want them to, so I stayed in my bed, wallowing and absolutely hating myself for it. I didn't even turn on my phone that night and call Cole's voicemail.

Chapter 35

Everly

"You haven't called in two days." He sounded irate. "Is this what you're doing now? Pretending the summer didn't happen? Hoping I'll just go away? Don't do this to us."

Guilt washed over me like a tidal wave, and it threatened to submerge my already sinking ship.

"I know you're scared, Eve. I'm scared too," he whispered. "I'm scared of how I feel about you. Sometimes, it's overwhelming, so encompassing, this feeling, but there's no one in the world I want to be scared with but you."

I clutched the phone in my hand, Cole's words washing over me, bathing me in sweet, sweet tenderness.

His frustration was palpable. His words were grave and final, and I immediately knew that this message was different from the others. He was done waiting.

"I need to see you. Please," he begged, his husky voice punching me right in the feels. "Meet me, baby. You know where."

The familiar beep played in my ear and I hung up, a ringing in my ears. I knew exactly where he wanted to meet; I just didn't know if I could.

I lay in bed until morning but didn't sleep a wink.

My brain whispered, *It's impossible. It'll never work out.*

My experience said, *He'll hurt you. He'll abandon you, just like the others.*

But my wildly beating, hopeful, love-filled heart screamed and wailed against my rib cage. *Go to him. Try. At least try.*

And, sometimes, the heart just can't be ignored.

Chapter 36

Everly

Momma Lou dropped me at the Everly Woods Train Station at eight on the dot the next night, and for the first time, I walked up to the ticket counter and bought an actual train ticket. Canton, Georgia, was the destination. With shaking hands and weak knees, I boarded the train, feeling like I had tiny ants crawling around in my stomach. I didn't let those stop me from walking up the aisle, perusing the open seats, and searching for him.

The train looked exactly as it always had. Brown, worn-looking seats flanked the dirty, blue carpet of the aisles. The familiar stale smell made my gut churn, but I reminded myself that, yes, everything there was the same. But me—I was different. My low ponytail swung as I looked from seat to seat. I pushed my hat low on my head. I tugged my navy T-shirt down to smooth the wrinkles. My sandals flopped down the aisle with every step. My stomach didn't growl in hunger. I was clean. I was happy. I was scared to damn death, but I was in love.

I smelled him before I saw him. His earthy smell set me equal parts at ease and on fire before I could even put my eyes on him. My stomach calmed, and I forged ahead until I saw a white Stetson seven rows up and on the left—the exact seat he had been sitting in four years ago.

I picked my pace eager up to get to him, but still, my mind played the short seconds I raced to him in what felt like slow motion, like I was wading through quicksand. I couldn't get to him fast enough.

The moment I pushed in beside his seat, his eyes met mine, all hot and warm like melted milk chocolate, and, God, I wanted to eat him up.

"Do you need a seat, miss?" he asked, grinning, his eyes gleaming.

I bit my lip, trying not to smile at his game.

I put my hand on my hip. "See something you like, Cowboy?" I asked, replaying the night we'd met right there in that same spot.

He slowly shook his head, his grin fading. Tenderness smoothed the fine lines of his facial features. "No," he said with finality. "I see someone I love."

I took the seat next to him and told myself to be brave, fearless, daring. "I love you, too," I whispered on a quivered breath, tears shimmering in my eyes. Upon removing my hat, I set it in my lap and nervously fiddled with the brim.

He beamed at me, every shiny tooth in his mouth showing. He grabbed my fidgety hands in one of his and brought them to his mouth to kiss them. "What took you so long?" he mumbled against them.

I shrugged playfully even though my words felt heavy with importance. "It took Everly Woods a long time to figure out who she is," I said lightly, jokingly, but it was one of the most serious statements of my life. "It's a girl's prerogative to be late, Cowboy," I said, trying to lighten my previous words. With ants back in my belly, I looked away, my emotions too high.

Holding my jaw in his hand, he maneuvered my head back to his, our faces mere inches apart. "And who is she?" he asked, his face serious, his eyes demanding all the answers.

He wasn't going to let me cover my feelings with jokes and sass, and I thought of the night on Cole's front porch at Preston's when he'd accused me of playing him and Joe. When he'd asked me the very same question. I hadn't known the answer then, but I thought I did now.

I breathed deep, garnering every bit of courage I carried in my minuscule body, which wasn't much, but it would have to do.

"She's Momma Lou's Little Bird." My voice trembled, and I cleared my throat so I could continue. "She's Joe Preston's daughter. She's Cole Briggs' Eve," I finished on a rush, relieved to have said it all but so afraid of what it all meant.

The train started to move, and Cole laid his forehead to mine on a deep exhale and closed his eyes. "Yeah." He smiled. "Yeah, I like that." His minty breath drifted across my lips, and I felt some of my fears being left behind on the platform we were rolling away from.

I leaned forward, wanting a taste of the mint and man.

He moved his lips back an inch but kept his forehead to mine. "Ask me," he ordered, and I giggled, pressing my nose to his.

"Are you gonna kiss me or what, Cowboy?" I sassed against his mouth.

And he did. He slammed his lips to mine, his hand at the back of my head pressing me closer, like he couldn't get enough of my mouth. He nipped at me, ate at my lips, whispered his love for me, told me that he missed me—all right on the very train line we'd met on years ago. It was like a dream.

I had a long road ahead of me. Joe and I had a lot to work through, and even though I was as scared as a person could possibly be, I knew what I wanted. And that was Preston's, my cowboy, Cody. I wanted them all.

The line had brought us together, irrevocably entwining our fates. Destiny had written our names in the stars, reuniting us in the strangest and most magnificent of ways. And love had steamrolled her way in, barreling over us and healing us in unspeakable ways.

Epilogue

Cole

Ten Years Later

"**M**argaret Louise Briggs, if you do not stop jumping on every bed in this house." Eve yelled upstairs, and I laughed to myself.

Maggie was six years old and the spitting image of her mother. She had come into the world kicking and screaming, demanding food and love, and hardly sleeping a damn wink, and most days, she was still much the same, but I wouldn't trade her for anything. She was her momma through and through, and I felt beyond blessed to have two gorgeous, strong-willed women to keep me in line.

I stepped back from the photo I'd just hung over what used to be the front counter of the bed and breakfast, only it was now the entrance to something Eve and I had been working on for almost two years—a horse riding camp free to children in the foster care system.

Eve had always been eager to give back, and today was finally the big day. When Jane had retired a few years ago, we couldn't decide what we wanted to do with the space. Joe, Eve, and I had put our heads together and come up with a plan that made us all feel good. We were all nervous, but Eve seemed to be the worst of us. I knew how important this day was to her, seeing all of our hard work and planning come to fruition.

I heard Maggie's boots thunder across the ceiling over us, and I shook my head.

"How's it look, Grey?" I asked, gazing down at my favorite guy. He was ten now, and the older he got, the more he looked like Austin.

He stared up at me. "It looks awesome, Uncle Cole. Aunt Eve looks so pretty," he said dreamily, and I thought sometimes he loved her more than he loved me.

I studied the photo again, nodding in agreement. She looked more than pretty. It was our engagement photo. We were on the railroad tracks outside the Everly Woods Train Station at sunset. Eve was leaned up against my side, wearing a pale-blue sundress and brown boots, her head tilted up towards me, her profile stunning against the backdrop of the pink sky.

Eve had been firm in her resolve to have our engagement photos there. Me? I hadn't been so sure. Yes, it was the place we'd met, but it was also the source of so much pain and suffering for her. When I'd told her that, Eve had only shaken her head and smiled before saying, "It's where I fell in love with you," like that somehow negated all the bad that had happened to her there. And the thought of that made me so proud of how far she'd come.

"What time are Mom and Dad coming?" Grey asked as we made our way off the front steps.

"Should be here in just a few minutes," I answered, happy they had let him stay last night with Maggie.

He'd kept her entertained with movies and popcorn so that I could calm Eve the hell down about today. Grey was a great kid, and a lot of that had to do with how amazing Austin was with him. Luckily, Austin had hightailed it home with his tail between his legs when Greyson had been just a year old. Marla had taken him back, because even though my brother was a selfish bastard at times, she still loved him. And they'd been good ever since. I was happy for them.

Maggie came thundering down the stairs with all the grace of a one-thousand-pound elephant. She ran to me, her pink boots on the wrong feet, which made her journey harder than it needed to be.

"Oomph." She slammed into my legs.

I picked her up so we were eye level.

"Hey, Daddy," she beamed up at me, and I chuckled at the sight of her toothless grin.

I raised my eyebrows. "You know your boots are on the wrong feet, right?"

We had this conversation at least once a day.

Her smile fell, and her eyes lit with snark. "It's how I like them, Daddy," she said with finality, and I shrugged before putting her down.

"I've been telling her all day to fix those boots, but all she's done around here is act like a damn monkey, jumping on all my clean beds," Eve said, coming down the steps.

And, just like every time my girl came into the room, my pulse kicked up a notch and I lost my breath. Ten years and a baby later, my woman was still fucking gorgeous. I was the luckiest man in the world.

Maggie made monkey noises and jumped around the room. Eve rolled her eyes, but I didn't miss the small smile playing at her lips. She adored our stubborn daughter as much as I did. Even when she was misbehaving.

I pulled her under my arm, and she studied the photo on the wall.

"It's perfect there. It will tie in with the whole train theme," she said.

I nodded. It would. Railroad signs, tracks, and big trains looking like they were coming out of the walls were the decor for the house. In fact, next to our photo, over the front desk was a large sign that said, *All aboard,* and every bedroom had a train set with a track set up on the floor for the children to play with. I had to admit that Eve had done a great job making it cool for the kids.

"The place looks amazing," I said into her hair, planting a kiss on the top of her head. "You're amazing."

She melted against me, and I knew I'd eased some of her tension, though it was short-lived because Joe's booming voice sounded from outside, which set her spine straight again.

"Where's my girl?" he shouted at the top of his lungs outside, and Eve and I both laughed.

"He acts like he doesn't see her every day," Eve pretended to complain, but she loved the attention he slathered on Maggie. She loved the way Joe Preston loved his granddaughter. It meant everything to her.

We'd been living together in the big house with Joe since we'd been married underneath the peach trees in the orchard seven years ago. There was plenty of room there, and Eve had wanted to stay with Joe in case he'd needed her. That was her excuse, anyway. I knew the truth. She *needed him* close, and that was fine by me.

"Better go see what your papa wants before he yells all my hard work to the ground," she said, looking at Maggie.

Maggie took off towards the front door, with Grey on her heels. "I bet Papa has cookies," she threw over her shoulder at Grey as they ran down the front steps.

I noticed cars pulling in around the old bed and breakfast. "You ready for this?" I asked.

Today was our official grand opening and ribbon-cutting ceremony. The children wouldn't be there until the beginning of summer, which was still a month away, but we expected the whole town of Canton to come out and support Eve's endeavor, even the mayor.

She looked nervous but beautiful as she fidgeted like she did. She touched her back pocket and said, "Ready as I'll ever be, I guess."

Eve didn't like crowds and big attention, but she knew that this place needed it to get the grants and funding required to run a place like this.

"Let's do this." I ushered her outside. I had a surprise for her, and I couldn't wait.

Beau and Cody were finishing up the final touches on the front porch when we passed by.

"Looking good, guys," Eve said giving them a wink.

I didn't know if she meant the painting or the guys themselves, but I gave her ass a little smack as punishment anyway. She shamelessly flirted with them every chance she got, which was plenty because they lived in my old cottage-style home behind the big house. She did it to get me worked up, but I knew that those two were harmless. They were too much in love to pay Eve any mind. Still, I pretended to get into a snit because my jealousy made Eve hot, and hot was my favorite way for Eve to be.

People were starting to fill the place in droves, so I steered Eve back towards the big house, where her surprise was waiting. Joe sped along behind us, Maggie on his lap and Grey hanging on to the back of his wheelchair for dear life.

We rounded the corner, and then Eve stopped dead in her tracks.

"Oh my God," she cried, placing her hand over her mouth. Then she was gone, sprinting across the yard, her arms flailing. "You came!" She threw her arms around Momma Lou.

Momma Lou cradled her face in her palms and wiped Eve's tears away with her thumbs. "No crying, Little Bird," she said, smiling, tears in her own eyes.

Eve stammered over her words, emotion making them clumsy and cluttered. "But how… I thought you couldn't come? Who has the kids? How did you get here?"

"You don't worry about me, baby girl," Momma Lou soothed.

"Today is about you and this special place."

"Lou, Lou!" Maggie yelled, running towards Eve and Momma Lou.

They all clutched each other close. I smiled smugly, feeling like the best husband and father ever.

The rest of the day went off without a hitch, and anyone and everyone we loved was there to witness Eve's big day. We cut ribbons. We ate too much food. We drank wine and celebrated a huge success for the small, cold, hungry girl from the train.

And, when we unveiled the large sign at the front of the new camp house, my eyes stung with too much emotion because it made my heart so full. It was like everyone we loved really was present, even my momma. I read over it again and again, with more pride in my heart than words could describe.

Welcome to The Line—where you'll make enough memories to play for a lifetime.

THE END

Acknowledgements

Momma: I thought a lot about you writing this book and how lucky I was to have you. So, thank you for always being there for me. I don't know what I would do if I couldn't call you up when I needed you.

Kelly Markham: It's been a rough year, but you did it. And you did it with a grace I greatly admire. It makes me so proud to be your friend. And you did it all, helping me and encouraging me and supporting me. Thank you. Your friendship is so incredibly special to me.

Miranda Arnold: You're my Cody. Making friends late in life is hard, and I feel so fortunate that fate was on our side. Who would I discuss makeup tips with? Who would share my love of food? Who would listen to me ramble on about the characters in my head? Big imaginary hugs. That's the best I got, sister.

Aly Martinez: I'll probably always have to put you in my acknowledgements since you're my author momma. I don't know what I would do without your advice. Thanks for answering all of my questions. Even the dumb ones. But, mostly, thanks for being hard on me when I need it. For not sugarcoating shit and telling me to quit whining and write. Sometimes, a girl needs someone to snap her out of it, and you're that person for me. Thank you.

Ashley Teague: I'm so glad we've become more than author friends through this whole writing thing. It's been so priceless to have someone to come up through the ranks with. Your advice and support mean so much.

Danielle Palumbo: Girl. What would I do without you? Your help is so invaluable to me in so many ways and in so many different facets of my life. You're priceless, and anyone who doesn't tell you that is a fool! I love you, and I cannot wait until our next trip together.

Jamie Schlosser: I can't believe how fast our friendship grew the past couple of months, but I am thankful for it. Thanks for showing me your crazy and beta reading this book even though beta reading is no fun. I'm counting down the days until we're actually together. Thank you for smelling plane farts for me.

Megan Cooke: Thank you for your amazing beta notes, and I'm so glad this crazy book world has made us friends. I cannot wait until June!

Amber Goodwin: Your help has been invaluable to me. Thanks for pimping me nonstop. Thanks for sharing and spreading the word every day! Thank you, thank you, thank you.

The most awesome beta readers ever, Nicole Sullivan, Nicole McCurdy, and Erin Fisher: I know how busy you all are with your own lives, so thank you for taking the time to read and support me. You guys are rock stars.

Amor Caro: Thanks so much for the pep talks and for offering to proofread *The Line!* You are awesome!

Aubrey Brenner: You are a missing word finding bad ass. I can't thank you enough.

Bloggers and Readers: I know I'm a newbie around here, and I'm so incredibly honored and amazed by the love that *See Through Heart* was given. I hope you guys love this one, too. Thanks for reading. Thanks for sharing. Thanks for being a part of this amazing community. Just…thank you.

About The Author

Amie Knight has been a reader for as long as she could remember and a romance lover since she could get her hands on her momma's books. A dedicated wife and mother with a love of music and makeup, she won't ever be seen leaving the house without her eyebrows and eyelashes done just right. When she isn't reading and writing, you can catch her jamming out in the car with her two kids to '90s R&B, country, and showtunes. Amie draws inspiration from her childhood in Columbia, South Carolina, and can't imagine living anywhere other than the South.

FACEBOOK: www.facebook.com/authoramieknight
TWITTER: www.twitter.com/AuthorAmieKnigh
GOODREADS: www.goodreads.com/AmieKnight
WEBSITE: www.authoramieknight.com

Other Books

See Through Heart

Made in the USA
Columbia, SC
24 July 2017